The Best of DAMON RUNYON

With an introduction by Damon Runyon, Jr.

HART PUBLISHING COMPANY, INC.

New York City

New York, N.Y. 10011

Manufactured in the United States of America
Library of Congress Catalog Card No. 66-22460

CONTENTS

The Best of
DAMON RUNYON

The World of Damon Runyon

BY DAMON RUNYON, JR.

Alfred Damon Runyon, newspaper reporter—some thought him "the best" when the best were not so rare—columnist, motion picture producer, boxing promoter (sideline) and general authority on sports (he could always pick a loser in a horse race of more than one), poet, Broadway swell whose clothes were not made but "constructed," veteran of several wars (depending on what you call war), Man about Manhattan (both his birthplace in Kansas and in New York), was the father of the fictional Broadway guys and dolls and of factual me.

Although he was a man of many worlds—Broadway was only a decade in his 66 years—I gloss over the others in this introduction to his guys and dolls. His own story has been fictionalized by several so-called biographers, complete with legends treated as fact. I once wrote a reportorial account from a family viewpoint.

My father was born in Manhattan, Kansas, in 1880, when the West was wild and woolly. He grew up like the country: the innocent died with their booties on. As a boy he was without shoes or mother, which marked him tender in foot and heart. His parents gave him the curiously poetic name, derived from the maiden name of his mother, Elizabeth Damon, and his father, Alfred Runyan. Somewhere along the years he dropped the Alfred, since it did not fit as a by-line in newspaper column measure; and he spelled it Runyon, since printers were forever misspelling it that way.

Damon Runyon (inexplicable combination of Greek and French!) knocked about the West, from newspaper to newspaper—as was the custom in days when such freedom was possible in Pueblo, San Francisco, and Denver. He interrupted these wanderings to join the Army at the age of 14, became the youngest soldier in the Spanish-American War and in the Philippine Insurrection. This was managed by bold-faced lying in Minnesota, where they were apparently having difficulty finding older targets. From then on, he was always four years younger than life.

The young West, much of it then untamed and given to six-gun law, shaped the iconoclastic views and deadpan humor of the developing writer. Hand-hacked out of wilderness, where death lived in myriad mysterious forms, the American frontier demanded wit, wisdom, and sheer nerve for survival.

The pioneers who found the way and the settlers who followed were sorely tested daily by life so harsh they had to laugh to keep from crying. Rugged individualism ruled. The newcomer was tried; no questions were asked about the past; he became accepted on his value to the community, whether in wagon train or in new-born city. A man's word was his bond—and one who broke his bond was himself broken; he could face the wilderness alone or trigger tempers. To live took all that could be squeezed out of a man, and more. To go on, when going on seemed beyond wisdom, the America-makers turned to humor for quick relief. Western humor was based on evidence that destiny is a roll of the dice. The joke is on the player who is sure he is sure. Nothing is funnier than finding out the hard way that the dice are fixed.

Such was the education and background of Damon Runyon when he sought the East. Outwardly, he wore the straight face of the Indian contemplating the fact that even the sun seemed to go home at night, but that man has no home unless he creates a place for himself. Inwardly, he was the man who had acquired uncertainty by experience and feared the dark.

Before leaving Denver's newspaper heights, he turned in his stripes as a ripsnorter: he quit drinking and married society reporter Ellen Egan. The wandering boy of the West hoped to settle down in the East.

In 1910, Damon Runyon became a star in Hearst's heavens, where rewards were high. Until the late thirties, he was ostensibly a sports writer and columnist, riding America's fascination for monarchs of muscle. He was in the right place at the right time to apply the ability to write which he was forever painstakingly trying to improve.

The sports writer was not chained to the asininities that ruled other departments of a newspaper. He was free to experiment—even to be poetic if the event so moved him. He was a spectator at open displays of the emotions that govern men.

On stories requiring the services of someone more than a clerk, the editors turned to the only staff permitted the luxury of exercising talent—the sports reporters. Damon Runyon was frequently detached from the various playing fields and stadiums to inform the public on such enlightening subjects as murder by a housewife and the wholesale murder known as war. He covered the U. S. Army's vain galloping after a Mexican pilferer named Pancho Villa, and went on to World War I in France with the First Army.

In 1914, the Damon Runyons became parents of a daughter, Mary Elaine; a son (Damon, Jr.) was born in 1918. These events spurred him in work, for inside him, he would forever be the worried barefoot boy of the West, although he put up a front as a dapper cynic. He had the habit of silence, from the lonely early days when there was simply no one to listen to him, although with an audience of one he exercised the campfire habit of spinning yarns. In fact, he frequently mumbled his stories aloud when writing at home.

In the Roaring Twenties, America's Prohibition era (or error), my father struck it rich in the literary lodes, with the first of many short stories (5,000 words) that featured the guys and dolls of Broadway. He adopted the so-called O. Henry form—a trick or unexpected ending.

But the Runyon style stood apart from others because of (a) the "characters," (b) the use of a narrator, and (c) the usage of the present-tense. Indeed, as of this writing (1966), Damon Runyon characters and Runyonese are still abused in print and in radio-television references.

It was highly embarrassing when the description "Damon Runyon character" was applied to the defendant in the Dallas trial of Jack L. Ruby, who with a record number of eyewitnesses looking on by television, shot and killed Lee Harvey Oswald, accused assassin of President John F. Kennedy. In questioning one witness, a legal eagle asked a television news staffer if he would type Ruby as a "Damon Runyon character," and the answer was yes. In the first place, the witness was not established as an authority on Damon Runyon characters and secondly, it is highly unlikely that any Runyon character would do such a thing before so many eyewitnesses. For it is well known in such a case the odds are all against a lam and furthermore, the chances are that such goings-on turn up the heat everywhere and annoy a lot of parties.

In fact, a certain strongarm who might be classed as a Damon Runyon character blows his cool and works out a plan to knock off Thomas E. Dewey when he is racket-buster around New York City. But the strongarm turns up at the morgue; for if there is anything the mob does not need at the time it is more heat. A Damon Runyon character would have been likely to regard Ruby as strictly no dice; there is no gain getting mixed up in a Presidential assassination. The Runyon characters, in fact, do not go out of their way to knock off any strangers.

My father himself once wrote in a column: "To me any 'character' used to be a distinctive, colorful and interesting person; a Broadway 'Character' is merely one of that description who happened to make the big street his habitat. But now the term is applied so generally it has me confused."

His guys and dolls are still around and about for, in a sense, they are timeless. A guy comes, a guy goes, which is the way life is, but the types live on. They live on mostly within a certain area bleeding off the most famous street in the world.

When he brought the guys and dolls to light, Damon

Runyon's working center was a small penthouse atop the Forrest Hotel on 49th Street, between Broadway and Eighth Avenue. In the world of his guys and dolls, Broadway included Sixth, Seventh, and Eighth Avenues, from 42nd Street to Columbus Circle.

The Forrest Hotel is very much alive in 1966; and I, myself, lived there a number of years. It's what is known as a theatrical hotel because the major showplaces are only footsteps away. Madison Square Garden is on its way out from 49th Street and Eighth Avenue, half a block away, but a Cinema Center is to take its place. Across the street, at 49th and Broadway, is the song-writing capitol, the Brill Building. Only a few night clubs remain; but in the gaps are the hip dancing joints, where the sports, dandies, high and low shots hang out come nightfall. The vast vice industry is in the area, too, if anyone cares to notice, but it shifts around like a go-go dancer's hips.

The underworld, which furnished the background for so many of my father's guys and dolls, was fermented by Prohibition from the old gangs of New York City. Americans voted themselves dry, then realized—too late, alas—that they were all wet. Millions promptly became conspirators in ways to break their self-inflicted law. Booze became big business.

The pious public pose of Prohibition was a reaction of an America rudely disenchanted by World War I. Americans were horrified by the new war machines that so efficiently cut down the best of a generation in numbers beyond common comprehension. Old traditions were trampled in the mud of tired and thankless far-away lands. Gone was the glory (if, indeed, there ever was any).

When the glitter flaked off, Americans found themselves burdened with the woes of a world. Public penance seemed appropriate. But soon Prohibition seemed like a bad dream. Jazz-age Americans sought escape—which wasn't hard to find if you knew the password, and who didn't?

The underworld went into the business of supplying the demand through speakeasies and night clubs that grew like crab grass. Like in all societies, the lawless found they needed laws as they spawned outlaws among their own. If the boys were hijacked by a turncoat, they could not very well holler copper. So they set up their own police force and judicial system. If anything, the law of the lawless was more efficient than John Law—in fact, some of the boys who tried to beat the system were known to have wound up thumping on jail doors, yelling to be let in. Violence became an accepted way of life in an era that grew out of wartime, when citizens were conditioned to mass mayhem. The stock view was: "So what?"

The stage was set.

In the hangover Twilight Twenties when Damon Runyon's guys and dolls first pranced in public, laughs were in demand and brought high prices. The literary lode he worked in the Broadway area made Runyon the highest paid short story writer—$1 for each word, 5,000 words to a story. At the same time, he continued newspaper work as a columnist and special reporter-writer for William Randolph Hearst, first on the old New York *American*, later called the *Journal-American* as the result of a wedding with the afternoon *Journal*. He also served Hearst's ill-fated New York *Mirror*. His columnist "beat" was switched from sports to the general editorial side. He was not allowed, even during World War II, to get serious: Hearst believed readers liked the light patter of the humorist as a relief from the woes of the world.

The newspaper work was important, because it gave my father the security of a paycheck which always was high in scale, and it kept him in the habit of daily writing. The easiest part of a writer's job is thinking up reasons why he shouldn't lay off at any given time of day or night; a daily column forced him out of seclusive moods and into the mainstream of strife on Broadway. The sports beat and the psychotic schedule of a morning newspaper led him to the night spots, where the guys and dolls are. Where else can you go after work at three o'clock in the morning?

My father always had chipped away at fiction. Already widely known as a newspaperman, he established his fame by hard, lonely, long hours working on the mold and the formula that finally hit the popular whim. The Runyon–O. Henry fiction form demands a continuing backdrop (such as the Broadway area), specific character types, and a string to hold everything together.

My father used the device of a narrator. The stories are all told from *his* viewpoint. His language has been a stumbling block to every writer who ever attempted to rewrite Runyon for stage, screen, radio, or television.

The narrator remains anonymous; what he tells about himself shows that he may be identified, if at all, with (not as) my father. It is he, not the characters in general, who uses the present tense.

The present tense is common in story-telling. It is the Now time sense of the insecure, the embattled, the lost, the doomed—all the people trapped on an island of Now by circumstances beyond themselves. The present tense may develop in a person who is trying to avoid drifting back to a Past, or who cannot face a Future which may be potentially good or bad, but can never be evaluated until it becomes the Past.

The present tense is found in tales told by many pioneers and early settlers of the American frontier, where life was a daily battle against man or nature. German war writers (if we assume correct translations) frequently lapse into the present tense, as in *All Quiet on the Western Front,* to convey the combat soldier's inner struggle to stay in contact with objective reality, the Now, and out of all contact with Past or Future.

In the Damon Runyon stories, which were painstakingly written, first by hand and then by typewriter, the narrator persists in pure Present.

Of course, the Damon Runyon characters are based, certainly each in part, on real people. Nick the Greek is one of the few whose real monicker was bestowed upon his fictional twin. Sam the Gonoph, in reality, was Joe the Gonoph. Johnny Brannigan was after John Broderick, a real-life plainclothesman with the so-called Strongarm Squad, a detail that rarely if ever used guns, but was free with muscle.

My father simply put some names together. Sky Masterson of *The Idyll of Miss Sarah Brown,* basic story for the later Broadway hit musical, *Guys and Dolls,* clearly would seem to follow from Bat Masterson, who came out of the Wild West to die as a newspaper rewriteman.

Mindy's, restaurant headquarters of the narrator, was

Lindy's when it was originally a relatively small place about the middle of the block, on the east side of Broadway between 49th and 50th Streets. The Brain was Arnold Rothstein, the Broadway financier suspected in some circles of being behind the fix of the Black Sox World Series scandal; my father nicknamed him The Brain in real life, too.

If I knew, I would not care to say who were the counterparts of such Runyon characters as the three parties from Brooklyn wearing caps as follows: Harry the Horse, Little Isadore, and Spanish John, who are always doing something that is considered a knock to Brooklyn, such as "robbing people, or maybe shooting or stabbing them, and throwing pineapples, and carrying on generally." Even in my time I hear of a party wishing to demolish another party by hand grenade in a midtown joint. The parties from Brooklyn sound very hard, indeed, and *real.*

For the record, I should point out that such parties in the Runyon stories, as in real life, confine their mayhem to their own circle; any citizen who gets knocked off is strictly through accident.

In my father's time the Broadway dolls had definite ambitions and goals which they usually did not make exactly clear to the guys. In some circles the doll was described as a "gold digger"—meaning that such a doll aimed to live beyond some chump's means. Not all the guys and dolls are underworld characters or Broadway types. *Little Miss Marker* was accurately portrayed in the motion picture of the same name by Miss Shirley Temple when she was only knee-high to a horse player.

The Lily of St. Pierre—the story that was my father's

own favorite—is the one tragedy he wrote.

A major difference between the Broadway dolls of my father's time and those of my day is in the way they dress in public. The dolls *Then* would sooner commit hara-kiri then step outdoors unless they were arrayed for a visit to Buckingham Palace; they might run into a producer or even a sucker, although the way show business goes today, they could be one and the same. The dolls *Now* think nothing of sashaying up and down Broadway dressed in pin curlers, sweatshirts, blue jeans, and sneakers, and not necessarily their best, either. This is a reflection of their lack of goals, and their failure to relate themselves to the world about them. They are, of course, not alone.

But, of course, Runyon's guys and dolls are still around and about. Their business is the kind you do not ask about, as it is none of your business. It took a Damon Runyon to reveal these characters in a unique style that has made literary history.

The Best of
DAMON RUNYON

Butch Minds the Baby

One evening along about seven o'clock I am sitting in Mindy's restaurant putting on the gefillte fish, which is a dish I am very fond of, when in comes three parties from Brooklyn wearing caps as follows: Harry the Horse, Little Isadore and Spanish John.

Now these parties are not such parties as I will care to have much truck with, because I often hear rumors about them that are very discreditable, even if the rumors are not true. In fact, I hear that many citizens of Brooklyn will be very glad indeed to see Harry the Horse, Little Isadore and Spanish John move away from there, as they are always doing something that is considered a knock to the community, such as robbing people, or maybe shooting or stabbing them, and throwing pineapples, and carrying on generally.

I am really much surprised to see these parties on Broadway, as it is well known that the Broadway coppers just naturally love to shove such parties around, but here they are in Mindy's, and there I am, so of course I give them a very large hello, as I never wish to seem inhospitable, even to Brooklyn parties. Right away they come over to my table and sit down, and Little Isadore reaches out and spears himself a big hunk of my gefillte fish with his fingers, but I overlook this, as I am using the only knife on the table.

Then they all sit there looking at me without saying anything, and the way they look at me makes me very nervous indeed. Finally I figure that maybe they are a little embarrassed being in a high-class spot such as Mindy's, with legitimate people around and about, so I say to them, very polite: "It is a nice night."

"What is nice about it?" asks Harry the Horse, who is a thin man with a sharp face and sharp eyes.

Well, now that it is put up to me in this way, I can see there is nothing so nice about the night, at that, so I try to think of something else jolly to say, while Little Isadore keeps spearing at my gefilte fish with his fingers, and Spanish John nabs one of my potatoes.

"Where does Big Butch live?" Harry the Horse asks.

"Big Butch?" I say, as if I never hear the name before in my life, because in this man's town it is never a good idea to answer any question without thinking it over, as some time you may give the right answer to the wrong guy, or the wrong answer to the right guy. "Where does Big Butch live?" I ask them again.

"Yes, where does he live?" Harry the Horse says, very impatient. "We wish you to take us to him."

"Now wait a minute, Harry," I say, and I am now more nervous than somewhat. "I am not sure I remember the exact house Big Butch lives in, and furthermore I am not sure Big Butch will care to have me bringing people to see him, especially three at a time, and especially from Brooklyn. You know Big Butch has a very bad disposition, and there is no telling what he may say to me if he does not like the idea of me taking you to him."

"Everything is very kosher," Harry the Horse says. "You need not be afraid of anything whatever. We have a business proposition for Big Butch. It means a nice score for him, so you take us to him at once, or the chances are I will have to put the arm on somebody around here."

Well, as the only one around there for him to put the arm on at this time seems to be me, I can see where it will be good policy for me to take these parties to Big Butch, especially as the last of my gefillte fish is just going down Little Isadore's gullet, and Spanish John is finishing up my potatoes, and is dunking a piece of rye bread in my coffee, so there is nothing more for me to eat.

So I lead them over into West Forty-ninth Street, near Tenth Avenue, where Big Butch lives on the ground floor of an old brownstone-front house, and who is sitting out on the stoop but Big Butch himself. In fact, everybody in the neighborhood is sitting out on the front stoops over there, including women and children, because sitting out on the front stoops is quite a custom in this section.

Big Butch is peeled down to his undershirt and pants, and he has no shoes on his feet, as Big Butch is a guy who likes his comfort. Furthermore, he is smoking a cigar, and laid out on the stoop beside him on a blanket is a little baby with not much clothes on. This baby seems to be asleep, and every now and then Big Butch fans it with a folded newspaper to shoo away the mosquitoes that wish to nibble on the baby. These mosquitoes come across the river from the Jersey side on hot nights and they seem to be very fond of babies.

"Hello, Butch," I say, as we stop in front of the stoop.

"Sh-h-h-h!" Butch says, pointing at the baby, and making more noise with his shush than an engine blowing off steam. Then he gets up and tiptoes down to the sidewalk where we are standing, and I am hoping that Butch feels all right, because when Butch does not feel so good he is apt to be very short with one and all. He is a guy of maybe six foot two and a couple of feet wide, and he has big hairy hands and a mean look.

In fact, Big Butch is known all over this man's town as a guy you must not monkey with in any respect, so it takes plenty of weight off of me when I see that he seems to know the parties from Brooklyn, and nods at them very friendly, especially at Harry the Horse. And right away Harry states a most surprising proposition to Big Butch.

It seems that there is a big coal company which has an office in an old building down in West Eighteenth Street, and in this office is a safe, and in this safe is the company pay roll of twenty thousand dollars cash money. Harry the Horse knows the money is there because a personal friend of his who is the paymaster for the company puts it there late this very afternoon.

It seems that the paymaster enters into a dicker with Harry the Horse and Little Isadore and Spanish John for them to slug him while he is carrying the pay roll from the bank to the office in the afternoon, but something happens that they miss connections on the exact spot, so the paymaster has to carry the sugar on to the office without being slugged, and there it is now in two fat bundles.

Personally it seems to me as I listen to Harry's story that the paymaster must be a very dishonest character to be making deals to hold still while he is being slugged and the company's sugar taken away from him, but of course it is none of my business, so I take no part in the conversation.

Well, it seems that Harry the Horse and Little Isadore and Spanish John wish to get the money out of the safe, but none of them knows anything about opening safes, and while they are standing around over in Brooklyn talking over what is to be done in this emergency Harry suddenly remembers that Big Butch is once in the business of opening safes for a living.

In fact, I hear afterwards that Big Butch is considered the best safe opener east of the Mississippi River in his day, but the law finally takes to sending him to Sing Sing for opening these safes, and after he is in and out of Sing Sing three different times for opening safes Butch gets sick and tired of the place, especially as they pass what is called the Baumes Law in New York, which is a law that says if a guy is sent to Sing Sing four times hand running, he must stay there the rest of his life, without any argument about it.

So Big Butch gives up opening safes for a living, and goes into business in a small way, such as running beer, and handling a little Scotch now and then, and becomes an honest citizen. Furthermore, he marries one of the neighbor's children over on the West Side by the name of Mary Murphy, and I judge the baby on this stoop comes of this marriage between Big Butch and Mary because I can see that it is a very homely baby, indeed. Still, I never see many babies that I consider rose geraniums for looks, anyway.

Well, it finally comes out that the idea of Harry the Horse and Little Isadore and Spanish John is to get Big Butch to open the coal company's safe and take the payroll money out, and they are willing to give him fifty per cent of the money for his bother, taking fifty per cent for themselves for finding the plant, and paying all the overhead, such as the paymaster, out of their bit, which strikes me as a pretty fair sort of deal for Big Butch. But Butch only shakes his head.

"It is old-fashioned stuff," Butch says. "Nobody opens pete boxes for a living any more. They make the boxes too good, and they are all wired up with alarms and are a lot of trouble generally. I am in a legitimate business now and going along. You boys know I cannot stand another fall, what with being away three times already, and in addition to this I must mind the baby. My old lady goes to Mrs. Clancy's wake tonight up in the Bronx, and the chances are she will be there all night, as she is very fond of wakes, so I must mind little John Ignatius Junior."

"Listen, Butch," Harry the Horse says, "this is a very soft pete. It is old-fashioned, and you can open it with a toothpick. There are no wires on it, because they never put more than a dime in it before in years. It just happens they have to put the twenty G's in it tonight because my pal the paymaster makes it a point not to get back from the jug with the scratch in time to pay off today, especially after he sees we miss out on him. It is the softest touch you will ever know, and where can a guy pick up ten G's like this?"

I can see that Big Butch is thinking the ten G's over very seriously, at that, because in these times nobody can afford to pass up ten G's, especially a guy in the beer business, which is very, very tough just now. But finally he shakes his head again and says like this:

"No," he says, "I must let it go, because I must mind the baby. My old lady is very, very particular about this, and I dast not leave little John Ignatius Junior for a minute. If Mary comes home and finds I am not minding the baby she will put the blast on me plenty. I like to turn a few honest bobs now and then as well as anybody, but," Butch says, "John Ignatius Junior comes first with me."

Then he turns away and goes back to the stoop as much as to say he is through arguing, and sits down beside John Ignatius Junior again just in time to keep a mosquito from carrying off one of John's legs. Anybody can see that Big Butch is very fond of this baby, though personally I will not give you a dime a dozen for babies, male and female.

Well, Harry the Horse and Little Isadore and Spanish John are very much disappointed, and stand around talking among themselves, and paying no attention to me, when all of a sudden Spanish John, who never has much to say up to this time, seems to have a bright idea. He talks to Harry and Isadore, and they get all pleasured up over what he has to say, and finally Harry goes to Big Butch.

"Sh-h-h-h!" Big Butch says, pointing to the baby as

Harry opens his mouth.

"Listen, Butch," Harry says in a whisper, "we can take the baby with us, and you can mind it and work, too."

"Why," Big Butch whispers back, "this is quite an idea indeed. Let us go into the house and talk things over."

So he picks up the baby and leads us into his joint, and gets out some pretty fair beer, though it is needled a little, at that, and we sit around the kitchen chewing the fat in whispers. There is a crib in the kitchen, and Butch puts the baby in his crib, and it keeps on snoozing away first rate while we are talking. In fact, it is sleeping so sound that I am commencing to figure that Butch must give it some of the needled beer he is feeding us, because I am feeling a little dopey myself.

Finally Butch says that as long as he can take John Ignatius Junior with him he sees no reason why he shall not go and open the safe for them, only he says he must have five per cent more to put in the baby's bank when he gets back, so as to round himself up with his ever-loving wife in case of a beef from her over keeping the baby out in the night air. Harry the Horse says he considers this extra five per cent a little strong, but Spanish John, who seems to be a very square guy, says that after all it is only fair to cut the baby in if it is to be with them when they are making the score, and Little Isadore seems to think this is all right, too. So Harry the Horse gives in, and says five per cent it is.

Well, as they do not wish to start out until after midnight, and as there is plenty of time, Big Butch gets out some more needled beer, and then he goes looking for the tools with which he opens safes, and which he says he does not see since the day John Ignatius Junior is born, and he gets them out to build the crib.

Now this is a good time for me to bid one and all farewell, and what keeps me there is something I cannot tell you to this day, because personally I never before have any idea of taking part in a safe opening, especially with a baby, as I consider such actions very dishonorable. When I come to think things over afterwards, the only thing I can figure is the needled beer, but I wish to say I am really very much surprised at myself when I find myself in a taxicab along about one o'clock in the morning with these Brooklyn parties and Big Butch and the baby.

Butch has John Ignatius Junior rolled up in a blanket, and John is still pounding his ear. Butch has a satchel of tools, and what looks to me like a big flat book, and just before we leave the house Butch hands me a package and tells me to be very careful with it. He gives Little Isadore a smaller package, which Isadore shoves into his pistol pocket, and when Isadore sits down in the taxi something goes wa-wa, like a sheep, and Big Butch becomes very indignant because it seems Isadore is sitting on John Ignatius Junior's doll, which says "Mamma" when you squeeze it.

It seems Big Butch figures that John Ignatius Junior may wish something to play with in case he wakes up, and it is a good thing for Little Isadore that the mamma doll is not squashed so it cannot say "Mamma" any more, or the chances are Little Isadore will get a good bust in the snoot.

We let the taxicab go a block away from the spot we are headed for in West Eighteenth Street, between Seventh and Eighth Avenues, and walk the rest of the way two by two. I walk with Big Butch, carrying my package, and Butch is lugging the baby and his satchel and the flat thing that looks like a book. It is so quiet down in West Eighteenth Street at such an hour that you can hear yourself think, and in fact I hear myself thinking very plain that I am a big sap to be on a job like this, especially with a baby, but I keep going just the same, which shows you what a very big sap I am, indeed.

There are very few people in West Eighteenth Street when we get there, and one of them is a fat guy who is leaning against a building almost in the center of the block, and who takes a walk for himself as soon as he sees us. It seems that this fat guy is the watchman at the coal company's office and is also a personal friend of Harry the Horse, which is why he takes the walk when he sees us coming.

It is agreed before we leave Big Butch's house that Harry the Horse and Spanish John are to stay outside the place as lookouts, while Big Butch is inside opening the safe, and that Little Isadore is to go with Butch. Nothing whatever is said by anybody about where I am to be at any time, and I can see that, no matter where I am, I will still be an outsider, but, as Butch gives me the package to carry, I figure he wishes me to remain with him.

It is no bother at all getting into the office of the coal company, which is on the ground floor, because it seems the watchman leaves the front door open, this watchman being a most obliging guy, indeed. In fact he is so obliging that by and by he comes back and lets Harry the Horse and Spanish John tie him up good and tight, and stick a handkerchief in his mouth and chuck him in an areaway next to the office, so nobody will think he has anything to do with opening the safe in case anybody comes around asking.

The office looks out on the street, and the safe that Harry the Horse and Little Isadore and Spanish John wish Big Butch to open is standing up against the rear wall of the office facing the street windows. There is one little electric light burning very dim over the safe so that when anybody walks past the place outside, such as a watchman, they can look in through the window and see the safe at all times, unless they are blind. It is not a tall safe, and it is not a big safe, and I can see Big Butch grin when he sees it, so I figure this safe is not much of a safe, just as Harry the Horse claims.

Well, as soon as Big Butch and the baby and Little Isadore and me get into the office, Big Butch steps over to the safe and unfolds what I think is the big flat book, and what is it but a sort of screen painted on one side to look exactly like the front of a safe. Big Butch stands this screen up on the floor in front of the real safe, leaving plenty of space in between, the idea being that the screen will keep anyone passing in the street outside from seeing Butch while he is opening the safe, because when a man is opening a safe he needs all the privacy he can get.

Big Butch lays John Ignatius Junior down on the floor on the blanket behind the phony safe front and takes his tools out of the satchel and starts to work opening the safe, while Little Isadore and me get back in a corner where it is dark, because there is not room for all of us back of the screen. However, we can see what Big Butch is doing, and I wish to say while I never before see a professional safe opener at work, and never wish to see another, this Butch handles himself like a real artist.

He starts drilling into the safe around the combination lock, working very fast and very quiet, when all of a sudden what happens but John Ignatius Junior sits up on the blanket and lets out a squall. Naturally this is most disquieting to me, and personally I am in favor of beaning John Ignatius Junior with something to make him keep still, because I am nervous enough as it is. But the squalling does not seem to bother Big Butch. He lays down his tools and picks up John Ignatius Junior and starts whispering, "There, there, there, my itty oddleums. Da-dad is here."

Well, this sounds very nonsensical to me in such a situation, and it makes no impression whatever on John Ignatius Junior. He keeps on squalling, and I judge he is squalling pretty loud because I see Harry the Horse and Spanish John both walk past the window and look in very anxious. Big Butch jiggles John Ignatius Junior up and down and keeps whispering baby talk to him, which sounds very undignified coming from a high-class safe opener, and finally Butch whispers to me to hand him the package I am carrying.

He opens the package, and what is in it but a baby's nursing bottle full of milk. Moreover, there is a little tin stew pan, and Butch hands the pan to me and whispers to me to find a water tap somewhere in the joint and fill the pan with water. So I go stumbling around in the dark in a room behind the office and bark my shins several times before I find a tap and fill the pan. I take it back to Big Butch, and he squats there with the baby on one arm, and gets a tin of what is called canned heat out of the package, and lights this canned heat with his cigar lighter, and starts heating the pan of water with the nursing bottle in it.

Big Butch keeps sticking his finger in the pan of water while it is heating, and by and by he puts the rubber nipple of the nursing bottle in his mouth and takes a pull at it to see if the milk is warm enough, just like I see dolls who have babies do. Apparently the milk is okay, as Butch hands the bottle to John Ignatius Junior, who grabs hold of it with both hands and starts sucking on the business end. Naturally he has to stop squalling, and Big Butch goes to work on the safe again, with John Ignatius Junior sitting on the blanket, pulling on the bottle and looking wiser than a treeful of owls.

It seems the safe is either a tougher job than anybody figures, or Big Butch's tools are not so good, what with being old and rusty and used for building baby cribs, because he breaks a couple of drills and works himself up into quite a sweat without getting anywhere. Butch afterwards explains to me that he is one of the first guys in this country to open safes without explosives, but he says to do this work properly you have to know the safes so as to drill to the tumblers of the lock just right, and it seems that this particular safe is a new type to him, even if it is old, and he is out of practice.

Well, in the meantime John Ignatius Junior finishes his bottle and starts mumbling again, and Big Butch gives him a tool to play with, and finally Butch needs this tool and tries to take it away from John Ignatius Junior, and the baby lets out such a squawk that Butch has to let him keep it until he can sneak it away from him, and this causes more delay.

Finally Big Butch gives up trying to drill the safe open, and he whispers to us that he will have to put a little shot in it to loosen up the lock, which is all right with us, because we are getting tired of hanging around and listening to John Ignatius Junior's glug-glugging. As far as I am personally concerned, I am wishing I am home in bed.

Well, Butch starts pawing through his satchel looking for something and it seems that what he is looking for is a little bottle of some kind of explosive with which to shake the lock on the safe up some, and at first he cannot find this bottle, but finally he discovers that John Ignatius Junior has it and is gnawing at the cork, and Butch has quite a battle making John Ignatius Junior give it up.

Anyway, he fixes the explosive in one of the holes he drills near the combination lock on the safe, and then he puts in a fuse, and just before he touches off the fuse Butch picks up John Ignatius Junior and hands him to Little Isadore, and tells us to go into the room behind the office. John Ignatius Junior does not seem to care for Little Isadore, and I do not blame him, at that, because he starts to squirm around quite some in Isadore's arms and lets out a squall, but all of a sudden he becomes very quiet indeed, and, while I am not able to prove it, something tells me that Little Isadore has his hand over John Ignatius Junior's mouth.

Well, Big Butch joins us right away in the back room, and sound comes out of John Ignatius Junior again as Butch takes him from Little Isadore, and I am thinking that it is a good thing for Isadore that the baby cannot tell Big Butch what Isadore does to him.

"I put in just a little bit of a shot," Big Butch says, "and it will not make any more noise than snapping your fingers."

But a second later there is a big whoom from the office, and the whole joint shakes, and John Ignatius Junior laughs right out loud. The chances are he thinks it is the Fourth of July.

"I guess maybe I put in too big a charge," Big Butch says, and then he rushes into the office with Little Isadore and me after him, and John Ignatius Junior still laughing very heartily for a small baby. The door of the safe is swinging loose, and the whole joint looks somewhat wrecked, but Big Butch loses no time in getting his dukes into the safe and grabbing out two big bundles of cash money, which he sticks inside his shirt.

As we go into the street Harry the Horse and Spanish John come running up much excited, and Harry says to Big Butch like this:

"What are you trying to do," he says, "wake up the whole town?"

"Well," Butch says, "I guess maybe the charge is too strong, at that, but nobody seems to be coming, so you and Spanish John walk over to Eighth Avenue, and the rest of us will walk to Seventh, and if you go along quiet, like people minding their own business, it will be all right."

But I judge Little Isadore is tired of John Ignatius Junior's company by this time, because he says he will go with Harry the Horse and Spanish John, and this leaves Big Butch and John Ignatius Junior and me to go the other way. So we start moving, and all of a sudden two cops come tearing around the corner toward which Harry and Isadore and Spanish John are going. The chances are the cops hear the earthquake Big Butch lets off and are coming to investigate.

But the chances are, too, that if Harry the Horse and the other two keep on walking along very quietly like Butch tells them to, the coppers will pass them up entirely, because it is not likely that coppers will figure anybody to be opening safes with explosives in this neighborhood. But the minute Harry the Horse sees the coppers he loses his nut, and he outs with the old equalizer and starts blasting away, and what does Spanish John do but get his out, too, and open up.

The next thing anybody knows, the two coppers are down on the ground with slugs in them, but other coppers are coming from every which direction, blowing whistles and doing a little blasting themselves, and there is plenty of excitement, especially when the coppers who are not chasing Harry the Horse and Little Isadore and Spanish John start poking around the neighborhood and find Harry's pal, the watchman, all tied up nice and tight where Harry leaves him, and the watchman explains that some scoundrels blow open the safe he is watching.

All this time Big Butch and me are walking in the other direction toward Seventh Avenue, and Big Butch has John Ignatius in his arms, and John Ignatius is now squalling very loud, indeed. The chances are he is still thinking of the big whoom back there which tickles him so and is wishing to hear some more whooms. Anyway, he is beating his own best record for squalling, and as we go walking along Big Butch says to me like this:

"I dast not run," he says, "because if any coppers see me running they will start popping at me and maybe hit John Ignatius Junior, and besides running will joggle the milk up in him and make him sick. My old lady always warns me never to joggle John Ignatius Junior when he is full of milk."

"Well, Butch," I say, "there is no milk in me, and I do not care if I am joggled up, so if you do not mind, I will start doing a piece of running at the next corner."

But just then around the corner of Seventh Avenue toward which we are headed comes two or three coppers with a big fat sergeant with them, and one of the coppers, who is half out of breath as if he has been doing plenty of sprinting, is explaining to the sergeant that somebody blows a safe down the street and shoots a couple of coppers in the getaway.

And there is Big Butch, with John Ignatius Junior in his arms and twenty G's in his shirt front and a tough record behind him, walking right up to them.

I am feeling very sorry, indeed, for Big Butch, and very sorry for myself, too, and I am saying to myself that if I get out of this I will never associate with anyone but ministers of the gospel as long as I live. I can remember thinking that I am getting a better break than Butch, at that, because I will not have to go to Sing Sing for the rest of my life, like him, and I also remember wondering what they will give John Ignatius Junior, who is still tearing off these squalls, with Big Butch saying: "There, there, there, Daddy's itty woogleums." Then I hear one of the coppers say to the fat sergeant: "We better nail these guys. They may be in on this."

Well, I can see it is good-by to Butch and John Ignatius Junior and me, as the fat sergeant steps up to Big Butch, but instead of putting the arm on Butch, the fat sergeant only points at John Ignatius Junior and asks very sympathetic: "Teeth?"

"No," Big Butch says. "Not teeth. Colic. I just get the doctor here out of bed to do something for him, and we are going to a drug store to get some medicine."

Well, naturally I am very much surprised at this statement, because of course I am not a doctor, and if John Ignatius Junior has colic it serves him right, but I am only hoping they do not ask for my degree, when the fat sergeant says: "Too bad. I know what it is. I got three of them at home. But," he says, "it acts more like it is teeth than colic."

Then as Big Butch and John Ignatius Junior and me go on about our business I hear the fat sergeant say to the copper, very sarcastic: "Yea, of course a guy is out blowing safes with a baby in his arms! You will make a great detective, you will!"

I do not see Big Butch for several days after I learn

that Harry the Horse and Little Isadore and Spanish John get back to Brooklyn all right, except they are a little icked up here and there from the slugs the coppers toss at them, while the coppers they clip are not damaged so very much. Furthermore, the chances are I will not see Big Butch for several years, if it is left to me, but he comes looking for me one night, and he seems to be all pleasured up about something.

"Say," Big Butch says to me, "you know I never give a copper credit for knowing any too much about anything, but I wish to say that this fat sergeant we run into the other night is a very, very smart duck. He is right about it being teeth that is ailing John Ignatius Junior, for what happens yesterday but John cuts in his first tooth."

Little Miss Marker

One evening along toward seven o'clock, many citizens are standing out on Broadway in front of Mindy's restaurant, speaking of one thing and another, and particularly about the tough luck they have playing the races in the afternoon, when who comes up the street with a little doll hanging onto his right thumb but a guy by the name of Sorrowful.

This guy is called Sorrowful because this is the way he always is about no matter what, and especially about the way things are with him when anybody tries to put the bite on him. In fact, if anybody who tries to put the bite on Sorrowful can listen to him for two minutes about how things are with him and not bust into tears, they must be very hard-hearted, indeed.

Regret, the horse player, is telling me that he once tries to put the bite on Sorrowful for a sawbuck, and by the time Sorrowful gets through explaining how things are with him, Regret feels so sorry for him that he goes out and puts the bite on somebody else for the saw and gives it to Sorrowful, although it is well known to one and all that Sorrowful has plenty of potatoes hid away somewhere.

He is a tall, skinny guy with a long, sad, mean-looking kisser, and a mournful voice. He is maybe sixty years old, give or take a couple of years, and for as long as I can remember he is running a handbook over in Forty-ninth Street next door to a chop-suey joint. In fact, Sorrowful is one of the largest handbook makers in this town.

Any time you see him he is generally by himself, because being by himself is not apt to cost him anything, and it is therefore a most surprising scene when he comes along Broadway with a little doll.

And there is much speculation among the citizens as to how this comes about, for no one ever hears of Sorrowful having any family, or relations of any kind, or even any friends.

The little doll is a very little doll indeed, the top of her noggin only coming up to Sorrowful's knee, although of course Sorrowful has very high knees, at that. Moreover, she is a very pretty little doll, with big blue eyes and fat pink cheeks, and a lot of yellow curls hanging down her back, and she has fat little legs and quite a large smile, although Sorrowful is lugging her along the street so fast that half the time her feet are dragging the sidewalk and she has a license to be bawling instead of smiling.

Sorrowful is looking sadder than somewhat, which makes his face practically heart-rending as he pulls up in front of Mindy's and motions us to follow him in. Anybody can see that he is worried about something very serious, and many citizens are figuring that maybe he suddenly discovers all his potatoes are counterfeit, because nobody can think of anything that will worry Sorrowful except money.

Anyway, four or five of us gather around the table where Sorrowful sits down with the little doll beside him, and he states a most surprising situation to us.

It seems that early in the afternoon a young guy who is playing the races with Sorrowful for several days pops into his place of business next door to the chop-suey joint, leading the little doll, and this guy wishes to know how much time he has before post in the first race at Empire.

Well, he only has about twenty-five minutes, and he seems very down-hearted about this, because he explains to Sorrowful that he has a sure thing in this race, which he gets the night before off a guy who is a pal of a close friend of Jockey Workman's valet.

The young guy says he is figuring to bet himself about a deuce on this sure thing, but he does not have such a sum as a deuce on him when he goes to bed, so he plans to get up bright and early in the morning and hop down to a spot on Fourteenth Street where he knows a guy who will let him have the deuce.

But it seems he oversleeps, and here it is almost post time, and it is too late for him to get to Fourteenth Street and back before the race is run off, and it is all quite a sad story indeed, although of course it does not make much impression on Sorrowful, as he is already sadder than somewhat himself just from thinking that somebody may beat him for a bet during the day, even though the races do not start anywhere as yet.

Well, the young guy tells Sorrowful he is going to try to get to Fourteenth Street and back in time to bet on the sure thing, because he says it will be nothing short of a crime if he has to miss such a wonderful opportunity.

"But," he says to Sorrowful, "to make sure I do not miss, you take my marker for a deuce, and I will leave the kid here with you as security until I get back."

Now, ordinarily, asking Sorrowful to take a marker will be considered great foolishness, as it is well known to one and all that Sorrowful will not take a marker from Andrew Mellon. In fact, Sorrowful can almost break your heart telling you about the poorhouses that are full of bookmakers who take markers in their time.

But it happens that business is just opening up for the day, and Sorrowful is pretty busy, and besides the young guy is a steady customer for several days, and has an honest pan, and Sorrowful figures a guy is bound to take a little doll out of hock for a deuce. Furthermore, while Sorrowful does not know much about kids, he can see the little doll must be worth a deuce, at least, and maybe more.

So he nods his head, and the young guy puts the little doll on a chair and goes tearing out of the joint to get the dough, while Sorrowful marks down a deuce bet on Cold Cuts, which is the name of the sure thing. Then he forgets all about the proposition for a while, and all the time the little doll is sitting on the chair as quiet as a mouse, smiling at Sorrowful's customers, including the Chinks from the chop-suey joint who come in now and then to play the races.

Well, Cold Cuts blows, and in fact is not even fifth, and along late in the afternoon Sorrowful suddenly realizes that the young guy never shows up again, and that the little doll is still sitting in the chair, although she is now playing with a butcher knife which one of the Chinks from the chop-suey joint gives her to keep her amused.

Finally it comes on Sorrowful's closing time, and the little doll is still there, so he can think of nothing else to do in this situation, but to bring her around to Mindy's and get a little advice from different citizens, as he does not care to leave her in his place of business alone, as Sorrowful will not trust anybody in there alone, not even himself.

"Now," Sorrowful says, after giving us this long spiel, "what are we to do about this proposition?"

Well, of course, up to this minute none of the rest of us know we are being cut in on any proposition, and personally I do not care for any part of it, but Big Nig, the crap shooter, speaks up as follows:

"If this little doll is sitting in your joint all afternoon," Nig says, "the best thing to do right now is to throw a feed into her, as the chances are her stomach thinks her throat is cut."

Now this seems to be a fair sort of an idea, so Sorrowful orders up a couple of portions of ham hocks and sauerkraut, which is a very tasty dish in Mindy's at all times, and the little doll tears into it very enthusiastically, using both hands, although a fat old doll who is sitting at the next table speaks up and says this is terrible fodder to be tossing into a child at such an hour and where is her mamma?

"Well," Big Nig says to the old doll, "I hear of many people getting a bust in the snoot for not minding their own business in this town, but you give off an idea, at that. Listen," Big Nig says to the little doll, "where is your mamma?"

But the little doll does not seem to know, or maybe she does not wish to make this information public, because she only shakes her head and smiles at Big Nig, as her mouth is too full of ham hocks and sauerkraut for her to talk.

"What is your name?" Big Nig asks, and she says something that Big Nig claims sounds like Marky, although personally I think she is trying to say Martha. Anyway, it is from this that she gets the name we always call her afterward, which is Marky.

"It is a good monicker," Big Nig says. "It is short for marker, and she is certainly a marker unless Sorrowful is telling us a large lie. Why," Big Nig says, "this is a very cute little doll, at that, and pretty smart. How old are you, Marky?"

She only shakes her head again, so Regret, the horse player, who claims he can tell how old a horse is by its teeth, reaches over and sticks his finger in her mouth to get a peek at her crockery, but she seems to think Regret's finger is a hunk of ham hock and shuts down on it so hard Regret lets out an awful squawk. But he says that before she tries to cripple him for life he sees enough of her teeth to convince him that she is maybe three, rising four, and this seems reasonable, at that. Anyway, she cannot be much older.

Well, about this time a guinea with a hand organ stops out in front of Mindy's and begins grinding out a tune while his ever-loving wife is passing a tambourine around among the citizens on the sidewalk and, on hearing this music, Marky slides off of her chair with her mouth still full of ham hock and sauerkraut, which she swallows so fast she almost chokes, and then she speaks as follows:

"Marky dance," she says.

Then she begins hopping and skipping around among the tables, holding her little short skirt up in her hands and showing a pair of white panties underneath. Pretty soon Mindy himself comes along and starts putting up a beef about making a dance hall of his joint, but a guy by the name of Sleep-out, who is watching Marky with much interest, offers to bounce a sugar bowl off of Mindy's sconce if he does not mind his own business.

So Mindy goes away, but he keeps muttering about the white panties being a most immodest spectacle, which of course is great nonsense, as many dolls older than Marky are known to do dances in Mindy's, especially on the late watch, when they stop by for a snack on their way home from the night clubs and the speaks, and I hear some of them do not always wear white panties, either.

Personally, I like Marky's dancing very much, although of course she is no Pavlowa, and finally she trips over her own feet and falls on her snoot. But she gets up smiling and climbs back on her chair and pretty soon she is sound asleep with her head against Sorrowful.

Well, now there is much discussion about what Sorrowful ought to do with her. Some claim he ought to take her to a police station, and others say the best thing to do is to put an ad in the Lost and Found columns of the morning bladders, the same as people do when they find Angora cats, and Pekes, and other animals which they do not wish to keep, but none of these ideas seems to appeal to Sorrowful.

Finally he says he will take her to his own home and let her sleep there while he is deciding what is to be done about her, so Sorrowful takes Marky in his arms and lugs her over to a fleabag in West Forty-ninth Street where he has a room for many years, and afterwards a bellhop tells me Sorrowful sits up all night watching her while she is sleeping.

Now what happens but Sorrowful takes on a great fondness for the little doll, which is most surprising, as Sorrowful is never before fond of anybody or anything, and after he has her overnight he cannot bear the idea of giving her up.

Personally, I will just as soon have a three-year-old baby wolf around me as a little doll such as this, but Sorrowful thinks she is the greatest thing that ever happens. He has a few inquiries made around and about to see if he can find out who she belongs to, and he is tickled silly when nothing comes of these inquiries, although nobody else figures anything will come of them anyway, as it is by no means uncommon in this town for little kids to be left sitting in chairs, or on doorsteps, to be chucked into orphan asylums by whoever finds them.

Anyway, Sorrowful says he is going to keep Marky, and his attitude causes great surprise, as keeping Marky is bound to be an expense, and it does not seem reasonable that Sorrowful will go to any expense for anything. When it commences to look as if he means what he says, many citizens naturally figure there must be an angle, and soon there are a great many rumors on the subject.

Of course one of these rumors is that the chances are Marky is Sorrowful's own offspring which is tossed back on him by the wronged mamma, but this rumor is started by a guy who does not know Sorrowful, and after he gets a gander at Sorrowful, the guy apologizes, saying he realizes that no wronged mamma will be daffy enough to permit herself to be wronged by Sorrowful. Personally, I always say that if Sorrowful wishes to keep Marky it is his own business, and most of the citizens around Mindy's agree with me.

But the trouble is Sorrowful at once cuts everybody else in on the management of Marky, and the way he talks to the citizens around Mindy's about her, you will think we are all personally responsible for her. As most of the citizens around Mindy's are bachelors, or are wishing they are bachelors, it is most inconvenient to them to suddenly find themselves with a family.

Some of us try to explain to Sorrowful that if he is going to keep Marky it is up to him to handle all her play, but right away Sorrowful starts talking so sad about all his pals deserting him and Marky just when they need them most that it softens all hearts, although up to this time we are about as pally with Sorrowful as a burglar with a copper. Finally every night in Mindy's is meeting night for a committee to decide something or other about Marky.

The first thing we decide is that the fleabag where Sorrowful lives is no place for Marky, so Sorrowful hires a big apartment in one of the swellest joints on West Fifty-ninth Street, overlooking Central Park, and spends plenty of potatoes furnishing it, although up to this time

Sorrowful never sets himself back more than about ten bobs per week for a place to live and considers it extravagance, at that. I hear it costs him five G's to fix up Marky's bedroom alone, not counting the solid gold toilet set that he buys for her.

Then he gets her an automobile and he has to hire a guy to drive it for her, and finally when we explain to Sorrowful that it does not look right for Marky to be living with nobody but him and a chauffeur, Sorrowful hires a French doll with bobbed hair and red cheeks by the name of Mam'selle Fifi as a nurse for Marky, and this seems to be quite a sensible move, as it insures Marky plenty of company.

In fact, up to the time that Sorrowful hires Mam'selle Fifi, many citizens are commencing to consider Marky something of a nuisance and are playing the duck for her and Sorrowful, but after Mam'selle Fifi comes along you can scarcely get in Sorrowful's joint of Fifty-ninth Street, or around his table in Mindy's when he brings Marky and Mam'selle Fifi in to eat. But one night Sorrowful goes home early and catches Sleep-out guzzling Mam'selle Fifi, and Sorrowful makes Mam'selle Fifi take plenty of breeze, claiming she will set a bad example to Marky.

Then he gets an old tomato by the name of Mrs. Clancy to be Marky's nurse, and while there is no doubt Mrs. Clancy is a better nurse than Mam'selle Fifi and there is practically no danger of her setting Marky a bad example, the play at Sorrowful's joint is by no means as brisk as formerly.

You can see that from being closer than a dead heat

with his potatoes, Sorrowful becomes as loose as ashes. He not only spends plenty on Marky, but he starts picking up checks in Mindy's and other spots, although up to this time picking up checks is something that is most repulsive to Sorrowful.

He gets so he will hold still for a bite, if the bite is not too savage and, what is more, a great change comes over his kisser. It is no longer so sad and mean-looking, and in fact it is almost a pleasant sight at times, especially as Sorrowful gets so he smiles now and then, and has a big hello for one and all, and everybody says the Mayor ought to give Marky a medal for bringing about such a wonderful change.

Now Sorrowful is so fond of Marky that he wants her with him all the time, and by and by there is much criticism of him for having her around his hand-book joint among the Chinks and the horse players, and especially the horse players, and for taking her around night clubs and keeping her out at all hours, as some people do not consider this a proper bringing-up for a little doll.

We hold a meeting in Mindy's on this proposition one night, and we get Sorrowful to agree to keep Marky out of his joint, but we know Marky is so fond of night clubs, especially where there is music, that it seems a sin and a shame to deprive her of this pleasure altogether, so we finally compromise by letting Sorrowful take her out one night a week to the Hot Box in Fifty-fourth Street, which is only a few blocks from where Marky lives, and Sorrowful can get her home fairly early. In fact, after this Sorrowful seldom keeps her out any later than 2 A.M.

The reason Marky likes night clubs where there is

music is because she can do her dance there, as Marky is practically daffy on the subject of dancing, especially by herself, even though she never seems to be able to get over winding up by falling on her snoot, which many citizens consider a very artistic finish, at that.

The Choo-Choo Boys' band in the Hot Box always play a special number for Marky in between the regular dances, and she gets plenty of applause, especially from the Broadway citizens who know her, although Henri, the manager of the Hot Box, once tells me he will just as soon Marky does not do her dancing there, because one night several of his best customers from Park Avenue, including two millionaires and two old dolls, who do not understand Marky's dancing, bust out laughing when she falls on her snoot, and Big Nig puts the slug on the guys, and is trying to put the slug on the old dolls, too, when he is finally headed off.

Now one cold, snowy night, many citizens are sitting around the tables in the Hot Box, speaking of one thing and another and having a few drams, when Sorrowful drops in on his way home, for Sorrowful has now become a guy who is around and about, and in and out. He does not have Marky with him, as it is not her night out and she is home with Mrs. Clancy.

A few minutes after Sorrowful arrives, a party by the name of Milk Ear Willie from the West Side comes in, this Milk Ear Willie being a party who is once a prize fighter and who has a milk ear, which is the reason he is called Milk Ear Willie, and who is known to carry a John Roscoe in his pants pocket. Furthermore, it is well known that he knocks off several guys in his time, so he is considered rather a suspicious character.

It seems that the reason he comes into the Hot Box is to shoot Sorrowful full of little holes, because he has a dispute with Sorrowful about a parlay on the races the day before, and the chances are Sorrowful will now be very dead if it does not happen that, just as Milk Ear outs with the old equalizer and starts taking dead aim at Sorrowful from a table across the room, who pops into the joint but Marky.

She is in a long nightgown that keeps getting tangled up in her bare feet as she runs across the dance floor and jumps into Sorrowful's arms, so if Milk Ear Willie lets go at this time he is apt to put a slug in Marky, and this is by no means Willie's intention. So Willie puts his rod back in his kick, but he is greatly disgusted and stops as he is going out and makes a large complaint to Henri about allowing children in a night club.

Well, Sorrowful does not learn until afterward how Marky saves his life, as he is too much horrified over her coming four or five blocks through the snow bare-footed to think of anything else, and everybody present is also horrified and wondering how Marky finds her way there. But Marky does not seem to have any good explanation for her conduct, except that she wakes up and discovers Mrs. Clancy asleep and gets to feeling lonesome for Sorrowful.

About this time, the Choo-Choo Boys start playing Marky's tune, and she slips out of Sorrowful's arms and runs out on the dance floor.

"Marky dance," she says.

Then she lifts her nightgown in her hands and starts

hopping and skipping about the floor until Sorrowful collects her in his arms again, and wraps her in an overcoat and takes her home.

Now what happens, but the next day Marky is sick from being out in the snow bare-footed and with nothing on but her nightgown, and by night she is very sick indeed, and it seems that she has pneumonia, so Sorrowful takes her to the Clinic hospital, and hires two nurses and two croakers, and wishes to hire more, only they tell him these will do for the present.

The next day Marky is no better, and the next night she is worse, and the management of the Clinic is very much upset because it has no place to put the baskets of fruit and candy and floral horseshoes and crates of dolls and toys that keep arriving every few minutes. Furthermore, the management by no means approves of the citizens who are tiptoeing along the hall on the floor where Marky has her room, especially such as Big Nig, and Sleep-out, and Wop Joey, and the Pale Face Kid and Guinea Mike and many other prominent characters, especially as these characters keep trying to date up the nurses.

Of course I can see the management's point of view, but I wish to say that no visitor to the Clinic ever brings more joy and cheer to the patients than Sleep-out, as he goes calling in all the private rooms and wards to say a pleasant word or two to the inmates, and I never take any stock in the rumor that he is looking around to see if there is anything worth picking up. In fact, an old doll from Rockville Center, who is suffering with yellow jaundice, puts up an awful holler when Sleep-out is heaved from her room, because she says he is right in the middle of a story about a traveling salesman and she wishes to learn what happens.

There are so many prominent characters in and around the Clinic that the morning bladders finally get the idea that some well-known mob guy must be in the hospital full of slugs, and by and by the reporters come buzzing around to see what is what. Naturally they find out that all this interest is in nothing but a little doll, and while you will naturally think that such a little doll as Marky can scarcely be worth the attention of the reporters, it seems they get more heated up over her when they hear the story than if she is Jack Diamond.

In fact, the next day all the bladders have large stories about Marky, and also about Sorrowful and about how all these prominent characters of Broadway are hanging around the Clinic on her account. Moreover, one story tells about Sleep-out entertaining the other patients in the hospital, and it makes Sleep-out sound like a very large-hearted guy.

It is maybe three o'clock on the morning of the fourth day Marky is in the hospital that Sorrowful comes into Mindy's looking very sad, indeed. He orders a sturgeon sandwich on pumpernickel, and then he explains that Marky seems to be getting worse by the minute and that he does not think his doctors are doing her any good, and at this Big Nig, the crap shooter, speaks up and states as follows:

"Well," Big Nig says, "if we are only able to get Doc Beerfeldt, the great pneumonia specialist, the chances are he will cure Marky like breaking sticks. But of course," Nig says, "it is impossible to get Doc Beerfeldt unless you are somebody like John D. Rockfeller, or maybe the President."

Naturally, everybody knows that what Big Nig says is very true, for Doc Beerfeldt is the biggest croaker in this town, but no ordinary guy can get close enough to Doc Beerfeldt to hand him a ripe peach, let alone get him to go out on a case. He is an old guy, and he does not practice much any more, and then only among a few very rich and influential people. Furthermore, he has plenty of potatoes himself, so money does not interest him whatever, and anyway it is great foolishness to be talking of getting Doc Beerfeldt out at such an hour as this.

"Who do we know who knows Doc Beerfeldt?" Sorrowful says. "Who can we call up who may have influence enough with him to get him to just look at Marky? I will pay any price," he says. "Think of somebody," he says.

Well, while we are all trying to think, who comes in but Milk Ear Willie, and he comes in to toss a few slugs at Sorrowful, but before Milk Ear can start blasting Sleep-out sees him and jumps up and takes him off to a corner table, and starts whispering in Milk Ear's good ear.

As Sleep-out talks to him Milk Ear looks at Sorrowful in great surprise, and finally he begins nodding his head, and by and by he gets up and goes out of the joint in a hurry, while Sleep-out comes back to our table and says like this:

"Well," Sleep-out says, "let us stroll over to the Clinic.

I just send Milk Ear Willie up to Doc Beerfeldt's house on Park Avenue to get the old Doc and bring him to the hospital. But, Sorrowful," Sleep-out says, "if he gets him, you must pay Willie the parlay you dispute with him, whatever it is. The chances are," Sleep-out says, "Willie is right. I remember once you out-argue me on a parlay when I know I am right."

Personally, I consider Sleep-out's talk about sending Milk Ear Willie after Doc Beerfeldt just so much nonsense, and so does everybody else, but we figure maybe Sleep-out is trying to raise Sorrowful's hopes, and anyway he keeps Milk Ear from tossing these slugs at Sorrowful, which everybody considers very thoughtful of Sleep-out, at least, especially as Sorrowful is under too great a strain to be dodging slugs just now.

About a dozen of us walk over to the Clinic, and most of us stand around the lobby on the ground floor, although Sorrowful goes up to Marky's floor to wait outside her door. He is waiting there from the time she is first taken to the hospital, never leaving except to go over to Mindy's once in a while to get something to eat, and occasionally they open the door a little to let him get a peek at Marky.

Well, it is maybe six o'clock when we hear a taxi stop outside the hospital and pretty soon in comes Milk Ear Willie with another character from the West Side by the name of Fats Finstein, who is well known to one and all as a great friend of Willie's, and in between them they have a little old guy with a Vandyke beard, who does not seem to have on anything much but a silk dressing gown and who seems somewhat agitated, especially as

Milk Ear Willie and Fats Finstein keep prodding him from behind.

Now it comes out that this little old guy is nobody but Doc Beerfeldt, the great pneumonia specialist, and personally I never see a madder guy, although I wish to say I never blame him much for being mad when I learn how Milk Ear Willie and Fats Finstein boff his butler over the noggin when he answers their ring, and how they walk right into old Doc Beerfeldt's bedroom and haul him out of the hay at the point of their Roscoes and make him go with them.

In fact, I consider such treatment most discourteous to a prominent croaker, and if I am Doc Beerfeldt I will start hollering copper as soon as I hit the hospital, and for all I know maybe Doc Beerfeldt has just such an idea, but as Milk Ear Willie and Fats Finstein haul him into the lobby who comes downstairs but Sorrowful. And the minute Sorrowful sees Doc Beerfeldt he rushes up to him and says like this:

"Oh, Doc," Sorrowful says, do something for my little girl. She is dying, Doc," Sorrowful says. "Just a little bit of a girl, Doc. Her name is Marky. I am only a gambler, Doc, and I do not mean anything to you or to anybody else, but please save the little girl."

Well, old Doc Beerfeldt sticks out his Vandyke beard and looks at Sorrowful a minute, and he can see there are large tears in old Sorrowful's eyes, and for all I know maybe the doc knows it has been many and many a year since there are tears in these eyes, at that. Then the doc looks at Milk Ear Willie and Fats Finstein and the rest of us, and at the nurses and internes who are commencing to come running up from every which way. Finally he speaks as follows:

"What is this?" he says. "A child? A little child? Why," he says, "I am under the impression that these gorillas are kidnapping me to attend to some other sick or wounded gorilla. A child? This is quite different. Why do you not say so in the first place? Where is the child?" Doc Beerfeldt says, "and," he says, "somebody get me some pants."

We all follow him upstairs to the door of Marky's room and we wait outside when he goes in, and we wait there for hours, because it seems that even old Doc Beerfeldt cannot think of anything to do in this situation no matter how he tries. And along toward ten-thirty in the morning he opens the door very quietly and motions Sorrowful to come in, and then he motions all the rest of us to follow, shaking his head very sad.

There are so many of us that we fill the room around a little high narrow bed on which Marky is lying like a flower against a white wall, her yellow curls spread out over her pillow. Old Sorrowful drops on his knees beside the bed and his shoulders heave quite some as he kneels there, and I hear Sleep-out sniffing as if he has a cold in his head. Marky seems to be asleep when we go in, but while we are standing around the bed looking down at her, she opens her eyes and seems to see us and, what is more, she seems to know us, because she smiles at each guy in turn and then tries to hold out one of her little hands to Sorrowful.

Now very faint, like from far away, comes a sound of music through a half-open window in the room, from a jazz band that is rehearsing in a hall just up the street from the hospital, and Marky hears this music because she holds her head in such a way that anybody can see she is listening, and then she smiles again at us and whispers very plain, as follows: "Marky dance."

And she tries to reach down as if to pick up her skirt as she always does when she dances, but her hands fall across her breast as soft and white and light as snowflakes, and Marky never again dances in this world.

Well, old Doc Beerfeldt and the nurses make us go outside at once, and while we are standing there in the hall outside the door, saying nothing whatever, a young guy and two dolls, one of them old, and the other not so old, come along the hall, much excited. The young guy seems to know Sorrowful, who is sitting down again in his chair just outside the door, because he rushes up to Sorrowful and says to him like this:

"Where is she?" he says. "Where is my darling child? You remember me?" he says. "I leave my little girl with you one day while I go on an errand, and while I am on this errand everything goes blank, and I wind up back in my home in Indianapolis with my mother and sister here, and recall nothing about where I leave my child, or anything else."

"The poor boy has amnesia," the old doll says. "The stories that he deliberately abandons his wife in Paris and his child in New York are untrue."

"Yes," the doll who is not old puts in. "If we do not see the stories in the newspapers about how you have the child in this hospital we may never learn where she is. But everything is all right now. Of course we never approve of Harold's marriage to a person of the stage, and we only recently learn of her death in Paris soon after their separation there and are very sorry. But everything is all right now. We will take full charge of the child."

Now while all this gab is going on, Sorrowful never glances at them. He is just sitting there looking at Marky's door. And now as he is looking at the door a very strange thing seems to happen to his kisser, for all of a sudden it becomes the sad, mean-looking kisser that it is in the days before he ever sees Marky, and furthermore it is never again anything else.

"We will be rich," the young guy says. "We just learn that my darling child will be sole heiress to her maternal grandpapa's fortune, and the old guy is only a hop ahead of the undertaker right now. I suppose," he says, "I owe you something?"

And then Sorrowful gets up off his chair, and looks at the young guy and at the two dolls, and speaks as follows:

"Yes," he says, "you owe me a two-dollar marker for the bet you blow on Cold Cuts, and," he says, "I will trouble you to send it to me at once, so I can wipe you off my books."

Now he walks down the hall and out of the hospital, never looking back again, and there is a very great silence behind him that is broken only by the sniffing of Sleep-out, and by some first-class sobbing from some of the rest of us, and I remember now that the guy who is doing the best job of sobbing of all is nodoby but Milk Ear Willie.

Dark Dolores

Waldo Winchester, the newspaper scribe, is saying to me the other night up in the Hot Box that it is a very great shame there are no dolls around such as in the old days to make good stories for the newspapers by knocking off guys right and left, because it seems that newspaper scribes consider a doll knocking off a guy very fine news indeed, especially if the doll or the guy belongs to the best people.

"Why," Waldo Winchester says, "if we only have a Cleopatra, or a Helen of Troy, or even a Queen Elizabeth around now guzzling guys every few minutes, think what a great thing it will be for the circulation of the newspapers, especially the tabloids. The best we get nowadays is some doll belting a guy with a sash weight, or maybe filling him full of slugs, and this is no longer exciting."

Then Waldo Winchester tells me about a doll by the name of Lorelei who hangs out in the Rhine River some time ago and stools sailors up to the rocks to get them wrecked, which I consider a dirty trick, although Waldo does not seem to make so much of it. Furthermore, he speaks of another doll by the name of Circe, who is quite a hand for luring guys to destruction, and by the time Waldo gets to Circe he is crying because there are no more dolls like her around to furnish news for the papers.

But of course the real reason Waldo is crying is not because he is so sorry about Circe. It is because he is full of the liquor they sell in the Hot Box, which is liquor that is apt to make anybody bust out crying on a very short notice. In fact, they sell the cryingest liquor in town up in the Hot Box.

Well, I get to thinking over these dolls Waldo Winchester speaks of, and thinks I, the chances are Dolores Dark connects up with one of them away back yonder, and maybe with all of them for all I know, Dolores Dark being the name of a doll I meet when I am in Atlantic City with Dave the Dude the time of the big peace conference.

Afterwards I hear she is called Dark Dolores in some spots on account of her complexion, but her name is really the other way around. But first I will explain how it is I am in Atlantic City with Dave the Dude at the time of the big peace conference as follows:

One afternoon I am walking along Broadway thinking of not much, when I come on Dave the Dude just getting in a taxicab with a suitcase in his duke, and the next thing I know Dave is jerking me into the cab and telling the jockey to go to the Penn Station. This is how I come to be in Atlantic City the time of the big peace conference, although of course I have nothing to do with the peace conference, and am only with Dave the Dude to keep him company.

I am a guy who is never too busy to keep people company, and Dave the Dude is a guy who just naturally loves company. In fact, he hates to go anywhere, or be anywhere, by himself, and the reason is because when he is by himself Dave the Dude has nobody to nod him yes, and if there is one thing Dave is very, very fond of, it is to have somebody to nod him yes. Why it is that Dave the Dude does not have Big Nig with him I do not know, for Big Nig is Dave's regular nod-guy.

But I am better than a raw hand myself at nodding. In fact, I am probably as good a nod-guy as there is in this town, where there must be three million nod-guys, and why not, because the way I look at it, it is no bother whatever to nod a guy. In fact, it saves a lot of conversation.

Anyway, there I am in Atlantic City the time of the big peace conference, although I wish to say right now that if I know in advance who is going to be at this peace conference, or that there is going to be any peace conference, I will never be anywhere near Atlantic City, because the parties mixed up in it are no kind of associates for a nervous guy like me.

It seems this peace conference is between certain citizens of St. Louis, such as Black Mike Marrio, Benny the Blond Jew and Scoodles Shea, who all have different mobs in St. Louis, and who are all ripping and tearing at each other for a couple of years over such propositions as to who shall have what in the way of business privileges of one kind and another, including alky, and liquor, and gambling.

From what I hear there is plenty of shooting going on between these mobs, and guys getting topped right and left. Also there is much heaving of bombs, and all that, until finally the only people making any dough in the town are the undertakers, and it seems there is no chance of anybody cutting in on the undertakers, though Scoodles Shea tries.

Well, Scoodles, who is a pretty smart guy, and who is once in the war in France, finally remembers that when all the big nations get broke, and sick and tired of fighting, they hold a peace conference and straighten things out, so he sends word to Black Mike and Benny the Blond Jew that maybe it will be a good idea if they do the same thing, because half their guys are killed anyway, and trade is strictly on the bum.

It seems Black Mike and Benny think very well of this proposition, and are willing to meet Scoodles in a peace conference, but Scoodles, who is a very suspicious character, asks where they will hold this conference. He says he does not wish to hold any conference with Black Mike and Benny in St. Louis, except maybe in his own cellar, because he does not know of any other place in St. Louis where he will be safe from being guzzled by some of Black Mike's or Benny's guys, and he says he does not suppose Black Mike and Benny will care to go into his cellar with him.

Well, he supposes a hundred percent right, although I hear Black Mike's cellar is not a bad place, as he keeps his wine there, but still from what I see of him personally, Black Mike is not such a guy as I will care to chum up with in a cellar.

So Scoodles Shea finally asks how about Atlantic City, and it seems this is agreeable to Black Mike because he has a cousin in Atlantic City by the name of Pisano that he does not see since they leave the old country.

Benny the Blond Jew says any place is okay with him

as long as it is not in the State of Missouri, because, he says, he does not care to be seen anywhere in the State of Missouri with Black Mike and Scoodles, as it will be a knock to his reputation. This seems to sound somewhat insulting, and almost busts up the peace conference before it starts, but finally Benny withdraws the bad crack, and says he does not mean the State of Missouri, but only St. Louis, so the negotiations proceed, and they settle on Atlantic City as the spot.

Then Black Mike says some outside guy must sit in with them as a sort of umpire, and help them iron out their arguments, and Benny says he will take President Hoover, Colonel Lindbergh, or Chief Justice Taft. Now of course this is great foolishness to think they can get any one of these parties, because the chances are President Hoover, Colonel Lindbergh and Chief Justice Taft are too busy with other things to bother about ironing out a mob war in St. Louis.

So finally Scoodles Shea suggests Dave the Dude. Both Black Mike and Benny say Dave is okay, though Benny holds out for some time for at least Chief Justice Taft. So Dave the Dude is asked to act as umpire for the St. Louis guys, and he is glad to do same, for Dave often steps into towns where guys are battling and straightens them out, and sometimes they do not start battling again for several weeks after he leaves town.

You see, Dave the Dude is friendly with everybody everywhere, and is known to one and all as a right guy, and one who always gives everybody a square rattle in propositions of this kind. Furthermore, it is a pleasure for Dave to straighten guys out in other towns, because the battling tangles up his own business interests in spots such as St. Louis.

Now it seems that on their way to the station to catch a train for Atlantic City, Scoodles Shea and Black Mike and Benny decide to call on a young guy by the name of Frankie Farrone, who bobs up all of a sudden in St. Louis with plenty of nerve, and who is causing them no little bother one way and another.

In fact, it seems that this Frankie Farrone is as good a reason as any other why Scoodles and Black Mike and Benny are willing to hold a peace conference, because Frankie Farrone is nobody's friend in particular and he is biting into all three wherever he can, showing no respect whatever to old-established guys.

It looks as if Frankie Farrone will sooner or later take the town away from them if they let him go far enough, and while each one of the three tries at different times to make a connection with him, it seems he is just naturally a lone wolf, and wishes no part of any of them. In fact, somebody hears Frankie Farrone say he expects to make Scoodles Shea and Black Mike and Benny jump out of a window before he is through with them, but whether he means one window, or three different windows, he does not say.

So there is really nothing to be done about Frankie Farrone but to call on him, especially as the three are now together, because the police pay no attention to his threats, and make no move to protect Scoodles and Black Mike and Benny, the law being very careless in St. Louis at this time.

Of course Frankie Farrone has no idea Scoodles and

Black Mike and Benny are friendly with each other, and he is probably very much surprised when they drop in on him on their way to the station. In fact, I hear there is a surprised look still on his face when they pick him up later.

He is sitting in a speak-easy reading about the Cardinals losing another game to the Giants when Scoodles Shea comes in the front door, and Black Mike comes in the back door, and Benny the Blond Jew slides in through a side entrance, it being claimed afterwards that they know the owner of the joint and get him to fix it for them so they will have no bother about dropping in on Frankie Farrone sort of unexpected like.

Well, anyway, the next thing Frankie Farrone knows he has four slugs in him, one from Scoodles Shea, one from Benny, and two from Black Mike, who seems to be more liberal than the others. The chances are they will put more slugs in him, only they leave their taxi a block away with the engine running, and they know the St. Louis taxi jockeys are terrible for jumping the meter on guys who keep them waiting.

So they go on to catch their train, and they are all at the Ritz Hotel in Atlantic City when Dave the Dude and I get there, and they have a nice layout of rooms looking out over the ocean, for these are high-class guys in every respect, and very good spenders.

They are sitting around a table with their coats off playing pinochle and drinking liquor when Dave and I show up, and right away Black Mike says: "Hello, Dave; where do we find the tomatoes?"

I can see at once that this Black Mike is a guy who

has little bringing-up, or he will not speak of dolls as tomatoes, although of course different guys have different names for dolls, such as broads, and pancakes, and cookies, and tomatoes, which I claim are not respectful.

This Black Mike is a Guinea, and not a bad-looking Guinea, at that, except for a big scar on one cheek which I suppose is done by somebody trying to give him a laughing mouth. Some Guins, especially Sicilians, can swing a shiv so as to give a guy a slash that leaves him looking as if he is always laughing out of his mouth, although generally this is only for dolls who are not on the level with their ever-loving guys.

Benny the Blond Jew is a tall pale guy, with soft light-colored hair and blue eyes, and if I do not happen to know that he personally knocks off about nine guys I will consider him as harmless a looking guy as I ever see. Scoodles Shea is a big red-headed muzzler with a lot of freckles and a big grin all over his kisser.

They are all maybe thirty-odd, and wear colored silk shirts, with soft collars fastened with gold pins, and Black Mike and Scoodles Shea are wearing diamond rings and wrist watches. Unless you know who they are you will never figure them to be gorills, even from St. Louis, although at the same time the chances are you will not figure them to be altar boys, unless you are very simple indeed.

They seem to be getting along first-rate together, which is not surprising, because it will be considered very bad taste indeed for guys such as these from one town to go into another town and start up any heat.

It will be regarded as showing no respect whatever for the local citizens. Anyway, Atlantic City is never considered a spot for anything but pleasure, and even guys from Philly who may be mad at each other, and who meet up in Atlantic City, generally wait until they get outside the city limits before taking up any arguments. Many a guy gets the old business on the roads outside Atlantic City who can be much more handily settled right in town if it will not be considered disrespectful to the local citizens.

Well, it seems that not only Black Mike wishes to meet up with some dolls, but Scoodles Shea and Benny are also thinking of such, because the first two things guys away from home think of are liquor and dolls, although personally I never give these matters much of a tumble. I am a nervous guy, and liquor and dolls are by no means good for the nerves, especially dolls.

Furthermore, I can see that Dave the Dude is not so anxious about them as you will expect, because Dave is now married to Miss Billy Perry, and if Miss Billy Perry hears that Dave is having any truck with liquor and dolls, especially dolls, it is apt to cause gossip around his house.

But Dave figures he is a sort of host in this territory, because the others are strangers to Atlantic City, and important people where they come from, so we go down to Joe Goss' joint, which is a big cabaret just off the Boardwalk, and in no time there are half a dozen dolls of different shapes and sizes from Joe Goss' chorus, and also several of Joe Goss' hostesses, for Joe Goss gets many tired business men from New York among his customers, and there is nothing a tired business man from New York appreciates more than a lively hostess. Furthermore, Joe Goss himself is sitting with us as a mark of respect to Dave the Dude.

Black Mike and Scoodles and Benny are talking with the dolls and dancing with them now and then, and a good time is being had by one and all, as far as I can see, including Dave the Dude after he gets a couple of slams of Joe Goss' liquor in him and commences to forget about Miss Billy Perry. In fact, Dave so far forgets about Miss Billy Perry that he gets out on the floor with one of the dolls, and dances some, which shows you what a couple of slams of Joe Goss' liquor will do to a guy.

Most of the dolls are just such dolls as you will find in a cabaret but there is one among them who seems to be a hostess, and whose name seems to be Dolores, and who is a lily for looks. It is afterwards that I find out her other name is Dark, and it is Dave the Dude who afterwards finds out that she is called Dark Dolores in spots.

She is about as good a looker as a guy will wish to clap an eye on. She is tall and limber, like a buggy whip, and she has hair as black as the ace of spades, and maybe blacker, and all smooth and shiny. Her eyes are black and as big as doughnuts, and she has a look in them that somehow makes me think she may know more than she lets on, which I afterwards find out is very true, indeed.

She does not have much to say, and I notice she does not drink, and does not seem to be so friendly with the other dolls, so I figure her a fresh-laid one around there, especially as Joe Goss himself does not act as familiar towards her as he does towards most of his dolls, although I can see him give her many a nasty look on account of her passing up drinks.

In fact, nobody gives her much of a tumble at all at first, because guys generally like gabby dolls in situations such as this. But finally I notice that Benny the Blond Jew is taking his peeks at her, and I figure it is because he has better judgment than the others, although I do not understand how Dave the Dude can overlook such a bet, because no better judge of dolls ever lives than Dave the Dude.

But even Benny does not talk to Dolores or offer to dance with her and at one time when Joe Goss is in another part of the joint chilling a beef from some customer about a check, or maybe about the liquor, which calls for at least a mild beef, and the others are out on the floor dancing, Dolores and I are left all alone at the table. We sit there quite a spell with plenty of silence between us, because I am never much of a hand to chew the fat with dolls, but finally, not because I wish to know or care a whoop but just to make small talk, I ask her how long she is in Atlantic City.

"I get here this afternoon, and go to work for Mr. Goss just this very night," she says. "I am from Detroit."

Now I do not ask her where she is from, and her sticking in this information makes me commence to think that maybe she is a gabby doll after all, but she dries up and does not say anything else until the others come back to the table.

Now Benny the Blond Jew moves into a chair alongside Dolores, and I hear him say:

"Are you ever in St. Louis? Your face is very familiar

to me."

"No," she says. "I am from Cleveland. I am never in St. Louis in my life."

"Well," Benny says, "you look like somebody I see before in St. Louis. It is very strange, because I cannot believe it possible for there to be more than one wonderful beautiful doll like you."

I can see Benny is there with the old stuff when it comes to carrying on a social conversation, but I am wondering how it comes this Dolores is from Detroit with me and from Cleveland with him. Still, I know a thousand dolls who cannot remember offhand where they are from if you ask them quick.

By and by Scoodles Shea and Black Mike notice Benny is all tangled in conversation with Dolores, which makes them take a second peek at her, and by this time they are peeking through plenty of Joe Goss' liquor, which probably makes her look ten times more beautiful than she really is. And I wish to say that any doll ten times more beautiful than Dolores is nothing but a dream.

Anyway, before long Dolores is getting much attention from Black Mike and Scoodles, as well as Benny, and the rest of the dolls finally take the wind, because nobody is giving them a tumble any more. And even Dave the Dude begins taking dead aim at Dolores until I remind him that he must call up Miss Billy Perry, so he spends the next half-hour in a phone booth explaining to Miss Billy Perry that he is in his hotel in the hay, and that he loves her very dearly.

Well, we are in Joe Goss' joint until five o'clock A.M., with Black Mike and Scoodles and Benny talking to

Dolores and taking turns dancing with her, and Dave the Dude is plumb wore out, especially as Miss Billy Perry tells him she knows he is a liar and a bum as she can hear an orchestra playing "I Get So Blue When It Rains" and for him to just wait until she sees him. Then we take Dolores and go to Childs' restaurant on the Boardwalk and have some coffee, and finally all hands escort her to a little flea-bag in North Carolina Avenue where she says she is stopping.

"What are you doing this afternoon, beautiful one?" asks Benny the Blond Jew as we are telling her good night, even though it is morning, and at this crack Black Mike and Scoodles Shea look at Benny very, very cross.

"I am going bathing in front of the Ritz," she says. "Do some of you boys wish to come along with me?"

Well, it seems that Black Mike and Scoodles and Benny all think this is a wonderful idea, but it does not go so big with Dave the Dude or me. In fact, by this time Dave the Dude and me are pretty sick of Dolores, and only wishing to get back to the hotel and give the old Ostermoor a strong play.

"Anyway," Dave says, "we must start our conference this afternoon and get through with it, because my ever-loving doll is already steaming, and I have plenty of business to look after in New York."

But the conference does not start this afternoon, or the next night or the next day, or the next day following, because in the afternoons Black Mike and Scoodles and Benny are in the ocean with Dolores and at night they are in Joe Goss' joint, and in between they are taking her riding in rolling chairs on the Boardwalk, or feeding her around the different hotels. No one guy is ever alone with her as far as I can see, except when she is dancing with one in Joe Goss' joint, and about the third night they are so jealous of each other they all try to dance with her at once.

Well, naturally even Joe Goss complains about this because it makes confusion on his dance floor, and looks unusual, so Dolores settles the proposition by not dancing with anybody, and I figure this is a good break for her, as no doll's dogs can stand all the dancing Black Mike and Scoodles and Benny wish to do.

The biggest rolling chair on the Boardwalk only takes in three guys, or two guys and one doll, or what is much better, one guy and two dolls, so when Dolores is in a rolling chair with a guy sitting on each side of her, the other walks alongside the chair, which is a peculiar sight, indeed. How they decide the guy who walks I never know, but I suppose Dolores fixes it. When she is in bathing in the ocean, Black Mike and Scoodles and Benny all stick so close to her that she is really quite crowded at times.

I doubt if even Waldo Winchester, the scribe, who hears of a lot of things, ever hears of such a situation as this with three guys all daffy over the same doll, and guys who do not think any too well of each other to begin with. I can see they are getting more and more hostile towards each other over her, but when they are not with Dolores, they stick close to each other for fear one will cop a sneak, and get her to himself.

I am very much puzzled because Black Mike and Scoodles and Benny do not get their rods out and start a shooting match among themselves over her, but I find that Dave the Dude makes them turn in their rods to him the second day because he does not care to have them doing any target practice around Atlantic City. So they cannot start a shooting match among themselves if they wish, and the reason they do not put the slug on each other is because Dolores tells them she hates tough guys who go around putting the slug on people. So they are being gentlemen, bar a few bad cracks passing among them now and then.

Well, it comes on a Friday, and there we are in Atlantic City since a Monday and nothing stirring on the peace conference as yet, and Dave the Dude is very much disgusted indeed, especially as Miss Billy Perry is laying the blast on him plenty every night over the telephone until Dave is sorry that he ever thinks of marrying Miss Billy Perry.

All night Friday and into Saturday morning we are in Joe Goss', and personally I can think of many other places I will rather be. To begin with, I never care to be around gorills when they are drinking, and when you take gorills who are drinking and get them all crazy about the same doll, they are apt to turn out to be no gentlemen any minute. The only reason I stick around is because Dave the Dude sticks, and the only reason Dave the Dude sticks is to keep these guys from giving Atlantic City a bad name.

I do not know who it is who suggests a daybreak swimming party, because I am half asleep, and so is Dave the Dude, but I hear afterwards it is Dolores. Anyway, the next thing anybody knows we are out on the beach and Dolores and Black Mike and Scoodles Shea and Benny the Blond Jew are in their bathing suits and the dawn is touching up the old ocean very beautiful.

Of course Dave the Dude and me are not in bathing suits, because in the first place neither of us is any hand for going in bathing, and in the second place, if we are going in bathing we will not go in bathing at such an hour. Furthermore, as far as I am personally concerned, I hope I am never in a bathing suit if I will look no better in it than Black Mike, while Scoodles Shea is no Gene Tunney in regards to shape. Benny the Blond Jew is the only one who looks human, and I do not give even him more than sixty-five points.

Dave the Dude and me stand around watching them, and mostly we are watching Dolores. She is in a red bathing suit, with a red rubber cap over her black hair, and while most dolls in bathing suits hurt my eyes, she is still beautiful. I will always claim she is the most beautiful thing I ever see, bar Blue Larkspur, and of course Blue Larkspur is a race horse and not a doll. I am very glad that Miss Billy Perry is not present to see the look in Dave the Dude's eyes as he watches Dolores in her bathing suit, for Miss Billy Perry is quick to take offense.

When she is in the water, Dolores slides around like a big beautiful red fish. You can see she loves it. The chances are I can swim better on my back than Black Mike or Scoodles Shea can on their stomachs and Benny the Blond Jew is no Gertrude Ederle, but of course I am allowing for them being well loaded with Joe Goss' liquor, and a load of Joe Goss' liquor is not apt to float well anywhere.

Well, after they paddle around in the ocean a while, Dolores and her three Romeos lay out on the sand, and Dave the Dude and me are just figuring on going to bed, when all of a sudden we see Dolores jump up and start running for the ocean with Black Mike and Benny head-and-head just behind her, and Scoodles Shea half a length back.

She tears into the water, kicking it every which way until she gets to where it is deep, when she starts to swim, heading for the open sea. Black Mike and Scoodles Shea and Benny the Blond Jew are paddling after her like blazes. We can see it is some kind of a chase, and we stand watching it. We can see Dolores' little red cap bouncing along over the water like a rubber ball on a sidewalk, with Black Mike and Scoodles and Benny staggering along behind her, for Joe Goss' liquor will make a guy stagger on land or sea.

She is away ahead of them at first, but then she seems to pull up and let them get closer to her. When Black Mike, who is leading the other two, gets within maybe fifty yards of her, the red cap bounces away again, always going farther out. It strikes me that Dolores is sort of swimming in wide circles, now half turning as if coming back to the beach, and then taking a swing that carries her seaward again. When I come to think it over afterwards, I can see that when you are watching her it does not look as if she is swimming away from the beach and yet all the time she is getting away from it.

One of her circles takes her almost back to Benny, who is a bad last to Black Mike and Scoodles Shea, and in fact she gets so close to Benny that he is lunging for her, when she slides away again, and is off faster than any fish I ever see afloat. Then she does the same to Black Mike and Scoodles. I figure they are playing tag in the water, or some such, and while this may be all right for guys who are full of liquor, and a light-headed doll, I do not consider it a proper amusement at such an hour for guys in their right senses, like Dave the Dude and me.

So I am pleased when he says we better go to bed, because by this time Dolores and Black Mike and Scoodles Shea and Benny seem to be very far out in the water indeed. As we are strolling along the Boardwalk, I look back again and there they are, no bigger than pin points on the water, and it seems to me that I can see only three pin points, at that, but I figure Dolores is so far out I cannot see her through the haze.

"They will be good and tuckered out by the time they get back," I say to Dave the Dude.

"I hope they drown," Dave says, but a few days later he apologizes for this crack, and explains he makes it only because he is tired and disgusted.

Well, I often think now that it is strange neither Dave the Dude or me see anything unnatural in the whole play, but we do not even mention Dolores or Black Mike or Scoodles Shea or Benny the Blond Jew until late in the afternoon when we are putting on the old grapefruit and ham and eggs in Dave's room and Dave is looking out over the ocean.

"Say," he says, as if he just happens to remember it, "do you know those guys are away out yonder the last we see of them? I wonder if they get back okay?"

And as if answering his question there is a knock on

the door, and who walks in but Dolores. She looks all fagged out, but she is so beautiful I will say she seems to light up the room, only I do not wish anybody to think I am getting romantic. Anyway, she is beautiful, but her voice is very tired as she says to Dave the Dude:

"Your friends from St. Louis will not return, Mister Dave the Dude. They do not swim so well, but better than I thought. The one that is called Black Mike and Scoodles Shea turn back when we are about three miles out, but they never reach the shore. I see them both go down for the last time. I make sure of this, Mister Dave the Dude. The pale one, Benny, lasts a little farther although he is the worst swimmer of them all, and he never turns back. He is still trying to follow me when a cramp gets him and he sinks. I guess he loves me the most, at that, as he always claims."

Well, naturally, I am greatly horrified by this news, especially as she tells it without batting one of her beautiful eyes.

"Do you mean to tell us you let these poor guys drown out there in all this salt water?" I say, very indignant. "Why, you are nothing but a cad."

But Dave the Dude makes a sign for me to shut up, and Dolores says:

"I come within a quarter of a mile of swimming the English Channel in 1927, as you will see by looking up the records," she says, "and I can swim the Mississippi one-handed, but I cannot pack three big guys such as these on my back. Even," she says, "if I care to, which I do not. Benny is the only one who speaks to me before he goes. The last time I circle back to him he waves his hand and says, 'I know all along I see you somewhere before. I remember now. You are Frankie Farrone's doll.' "

"And you are?" asks Dave the Dude.

"His widow," says Dolores. "I promise him as he lays in his coffin that these men will die, and they are dead. I spend my last dollar getting to this town by airplane, but I get here, and I get them. Only it is more the hand of Providence," she says. "Now I will not need this."

And she tosses out on the table among our breakfast dishes a little bottle that we find out afterwards is full of enough cyanide to kill forty mules, which always makes me think that this Dolores is a doll who means business.

"There is only one thing I wish to know," Dave the Dude says. "Only one thing. How do you coax these fatheads to follow you out in the water?"

"This is the easiest thing of all," Dolores says. "It is an inspiration to me as we lay out on the beach. I tell them I will marry the first one who reaches me in the water. I do not wish to seem hard-hearted, but it is a relief to me when I see Black Mike sink. Can you imagine being married to such a bum?"

It is not until we are going home that Dave the Dude has anything to say about the proposition, and then he speaks to me as follows:

"You know," Dave says, "I will always consider I get a very lucky break that Dolores does not include me in her offer, or the chances are I will be swimming yet."

All Horse Players Die Broke

It is during the last race meeting at Saratoga, and one evening I am standing out under the elms in front of the Grand Union Hotel thinking what a beautiful world it is, to be sure, for what do I do in the afternoon at the track but grab myself a piece of a ten-to-one shot. I am thinking what a beautiful moon it is, indeed, that is shining down over the park where Mr. Dick Canfield once deals them higher than a cat's back, and how pure and balmy the air is, and also what nice-looking Judys are wandering around and about, although it is only the night before that I am standing in the same spot wondering where I can borrow a Betsy with which to shoot myself smack-dab through the pimple.

In fact, I go around to see a character I know by the name of Solly something, who owns a Betsy, but it seems he has only one cartridge to his name for this Betsy and he is thinking some of either using the cartridge to shoot his own self smack-dab through the pimple, or of going out to the race course and shooting an old catfish by the name of Pair of Jacks that plays him false in the fifth race, and therefore Solly is not in a mood to lend his Betsy to anybody else. So we try to figure out a way we can make one cartridge do for two pimples, and in the meantime Solly outs with a bottle of applejack, and after a couple of belts at this bottle we decide that the sensible thing to do is to take the Betsy out and peddle it for whatever we can, and maybe get a taw for the next day.

Well, it happens that we run into an Italian party from Passaic, N. J., by the name of Guiseppe Palladino, who is called Joe for short, and this Joe is in the money very good at the moment, and he is glad to lend us a pound note on the Betsy, because Joe is such a character as never knows when he may need an extra Betsy, and anyway it is the first time in his experience around the race tracks that anybody ever offers him collateral for a loan. So there Solly and I are with a deuce apiece after we spend the odd dollar for breakfast the next day, and I run my deuce up to a total of twenty-two slugs on the ten-to-one shot in the last heat of the day, and everything is certainly all right with me in every respect.

Well, while I am standing there under the elms, who comes along but a raggedy old Dutchman by the name of Unser Fritz, who is maybe sventy-five years old, come next grass, and who is following the giddyaps since the battle of Gettysburg, as near as anybody can figure out. In fact, Unser Fritz is quite an institution around the race tracks, and is often written up by the newspaper scribes as a terrible example of what a horse player comes to, although personally I always say that what Unser Fritz comes to is not so tough when you figure that he does not do a tap of work in all these years. In his day, Unser Fritz is a most successful handicapper, a handicapper being a character who can dope out from the form what horses ought to win the races, and as long as his figures turn out all right, a handicapper is spoken of most respectfully by one and all, although of course when he begins missing out for any length of time as handicappers are bound to do, he is no longer spoken of respectifully, or even as a handicapper. He is spoken of as a bum.

It is a strange thing how a handicapper can go along for years doing everything right, and then all of a sudden he finds himself doing everything wrong, and this is the way it is with Unser Fritz. For a long time his figures on the horse races are considered most remarkable, indeed, and as he will bet till the cows come home on his own figures, he generally has plenty of money, and a fiancée by the name of Emerald Em. She is called Emerald Em because she has a habit of wearing a raft of emeralds in rings, and pins, and bracelets, and one thing and another, which are purchased for her by Unser Fritz to express his love, an emerald being a green stone that is considered most expressive of love, if it is big enough. It seems that Emerald Em is very fond of emeralds, especially when they are surrounded by large, coarse diamonds. I hear the old-timers around the race tracks say that when Emerald Em is young, she is a tall, goodlooking Judy with yellow hair that is by no means a phony yellow, at that, and with a shape that does not require a bustle such as most Judys always wear in those days.

But then nobody ever hears an old timer mention any Judy that he remembers from back down the years who is not good-looking, and in fact beautiful. To hear the old-timers tell it, every pancake they ever see when they are young is a double Myrna Loy, though the chances are, figuring in the law of averages, that some of them are bound to be rutabagas, the same as now. Anyway, for years this Emerald Em is known on every race track from coast to coast as Unser Fritz's fiancée, and is considered quite a remarkable scene, what with her emeralds, and not requiring any bustle, and everything else.

Then one day Unser Fritz's figures run plumb out on him, and so does his dough, and so does Emerald Em, and now Unser Fritz is an old pappy guy, and it is years since he is regarded as anything but a crumbo around the race tracks, and nobody remembers much of his story, or cares a cuss about it, for if there is anything that is a drug on the market around the tracks it is the story of a broker. How he gets from place to place, and how he lives after he gets there, is a very great mystery to one and all, although I hear he often rides in the horsecars with the horses, when some owner or trainer happens to be feeling tenderhearted, or he hitchhikes in automobiles, and sometimes he even walks, for Unser Fritz is still fairly nimble, no matter how old he is.

He always has under his arm a bundle of newspapers that somebody throws away, and every night he sits down and handicaps the horses running the next day according to his own system, but he seldom picks any winners and even if he does pick any winners, he seldom has anything to bet on them. Sometimes he promotes a stranger, who does not know he is bad luck to a good hunting dog, to put down a few dibs on one of his picks, and once in a while the pick wins, and Unser Fritz gets a small stake, and sometimes an old timer who feels sorry for him will slip him something. But whatever Unser Fritz gets hold of, he bets off right away on the next race that comes up, so naturally he never is holding anything very long.

Well, Unser Fritz stands under the elms with me a while, speaking of this and that, and especially of the races, and I am wondering to myself if I will become as disheveled as Unser Fritz if I keep on following the races, when he gazes at the Grand Union Hotel, and says to me like this:

"It looks nice," he says. "It looks cheery-like, with the lights, and all this and that. It brings back memories to me. Emma always lives in this hotel whenever we make Saratoga for the races back in the days when I am in the money. She always has a suite of two or three rooms on this side of the hotel. Once she has four. I often stand here under these trees," Unser Fritz says, "watching her windows to see what time she puts out her lights, because, while I trust Emma implicitly, I know she has a restless nature, and sometimes she cannot resist returning to scenes of gaiety after I bid her good night, especially," he says, "with a party by the name of Pete Shovelin, who runs the restaurant where she once deals them off the arm."

"You mean she is a biscuit shooter?" I say.

"A waitress," Unser Fritz says. "A good waitress. She comes of a family of farm folks in this very section, although I never know much about them," he says. "Shovelin's is a little hole-in-the-wall up the street here somewhere which long since disappears. I go there for my morning java in the old days. I will say one thing for

Shovelin," Unser Fritz says, "he always has good java. Three days after I first clap eyes on Emma, she is wearing her first emerald, and is my fiancée. Then she moves into a suite in the Grand Union. I only wish you can know Emma in those days," he says. "She is beautiful. She is a fine character. She is always on the level, and I love her dearly."

"What do you mean—always on the level?" I say. "What about this Shovelin party you just mention?"

"Ah," Unser Fritz says, "I suppose I am dull company for a squab, what with having to stay in at night to work on my figures, and Emma likes to go around and about. She is a highly nervous type, and extremely restless, and she cannot bear to hold still very long at a time. But," he says, "in those days it is not considered proper for a young Judy to go around and about without a chaperon, so she goes with Shovelin for her chaperon. Emma never goes anywhere without a chaperon," he says.

Well, it seems that early in their courtship, Unser Fritz learns that he can generally quiet her restlessness with emeralds, if they have diamonds on the side. It seems that these stones have a very soothing effect on her, and this is why he purchases them for her by the bucket. "Yes," Unser Fritz says, "I always think of Emma whenever I am in New York City, and look down Broadway at night with the go lights on."

But it seems from what Unser Fritz tells me that even with the emeralds her restless spells come on her very bad, and especially when he finds himself running short of ready, and is unable to purchase more emeralds for her at the moment, although Unser Fritz claims this is nothing unusual. In fact, he says anybody with any experience with nervous female characters knows that it becomes very monotonous for them to be around people who are short of ready. "But," he says, "not all of them require soothing with emeralds. Some require pearls," he says.

Well, it seems that Emma generally takes a trip without Unser Fritz to break the monotony of his running short of ready, but she never takes one of these trips without a chaperon, because she is very careful about her good name, and Unser Fritz's, too. It seems that in those days Judys have to be more careful about such matters than they do now.

He remembers that once when they are in San Francisco she takes a trip through the Yellowstone with Jockey Gus Kloobus as her chaperon, and is gone three weeks and returns much refreshed, especially as she gets back just as Unser Fritz makes a nice score and has a seidel of emeralds waiting for her. He remembers another time she goes to England with a trainer by the name of Blootz as her chaperon and comes home with an English accent that sounds right cute, to find Unser Fritz going like a house afire at Belmont. "She takes a lot of other trips without me during the time we are engaged," Unser Fritz says, "but," he says, "I always know Emma will return to me as soon as she hears I am back in the money and can purchase more emeralds for her. In fact," he says, "this knowledge is all that keeps me struggling now."

"Look, Fritz," I say, "what do you mean, keeps you going? Do you mean you think Emma may return to you again?"

"Why, sure," Unser Fritz says. "Why, certainly, if I get my rushes again. Why not?" he says. "She knows there will be a pail of emeralds waiting for her. She knows I love her and always will," he says.

Well, I ask him when he sees Emerald Em last, and he says it is 1908 in the old Waldorf-Astoria the night he blows a hundred and sixty thousand betting on a hide called Sir Martin to win the Futurity, and it is all the dough Unser Fritz has at the moment. In fact, he is cleaner than a jay bird, and he is feeling somewhat discouraged. It seems he is waiting on his floor for the elevator, and when it comes down Emerald Em is one of the several passengers, and when the door opens, and Unser Fritz starts to get in, she raises her foot and plants it in his stomach, and gives him a big push back out the door and the elevator goes on down without him.

"But, of course," Unser Fritz says, "Emma never likes to ride in the same elevator with me, because I am not always tidy enough to suit her in those days, what with having so much work to do on my figures, and she claims it is a knock to her socially. Anyway," he says, "this is the last I see of Emma."

"Why, Fritz," I say, "nineteen-eight is nearly thirty years back, and if she ever thinks of returning to you, she will return long before this."

"No," Unser Fritz says. "You see, I never make a scratch since then. I am never since in the money, so there is no reason for Emma to return to me. But," he says, "wait until I get going good again and you will see."

Well, I always figure Unser Fritz must be more or

less of an old screwball for going on thinking there is still a chance for him around the tracks, and now I am sure of it, and I am about to bid him good evening, when he mentions that he can use about two dollars if I happen to have a deuce on me that is not working, and I will say one thing for Unser Fritz, he seldom comes right out and asks anybody for anything unless things are very desperate with him, indeed. "I need it to pay something on account of my landlady," he says. "I room with old Mrs. Crob around the corner for over twenty years, and," he says, "she only charges me a finnif a week, so I try to keep from getting too far to the rear with her. I will return it to you the first score I make."

Well, of course I know this means practically never, but I am feeling so good about my success at the track that I slip him a deucer, and it is half an hour later before I fully realize what I do, and go looking for Fritz to get anyway half of it back. But by this time he disappears, and I think no more of the matter until the next day out at the course when I hear Unser Fritz bets two dollars on a thing by the name of Speed Cart, and it bows down at fifty to one, so I know Mrs. Crob is still waiting for hers.

Now there is Unser Fritz with one hundred slugs, and this is undoubtedly more money than he enjoys since Hickory Slim is a two-year-old. And from here on the story becomes very interesting, and in fact remarkable, because up to the moment Speed Cart hits the wire, Unser Fritz is still nothing but a crumbo, and you can say it again, while from now on he is somebody to point out and say can you imagine such a thing happening?

He bets a hundred on a centipede called Marchesa, and down pops Marchesa like a trained pig at twenty to one. Then old Unser Fritz bets two hundred on a caterpillar by the name of Merry Soul, at four to one, and Merry Soul just laughs his way home. Unser Fritz winds up the day betting two thousand more on something called Sharp Practice, and when Sharp Practice wins by so far it looks as if he is a shoo-in, Fritz finds himself with over twelve thousand slugs, and the way the bookmakers in the betting ring are sobbing is really most distressing to hear.

Well, in a week Unser Fritz is a hundred thousand dollars in front, because the way he sends it in is quite astonishing to behold, although the old timers tell me it is just the way he sends it when he is younger. He is betting only on horses that he personally figures out, and what happens is that Unser Fritz's figures suddenly come to life again, and he cannot do anything wrong. He wins so much dough that he even pays off a few old touches, including my two, and he goes so far as to lend Joe Palladino three dollars on the Betsy that Solly and I hock with Joe for the pound note, as it seems that by this time Joe himself is practically on his way to the poorhouse, and while Unser Fritz has no use whatsoever for a Betsy he cannot bear to see a character such as Joe go to the poorhouse.

But with all the dough Unser Fritz carries in his pockets, and plants in a safe-deposit box in the jug downtown, he looks just the same as ever, because he claims he cannot find time from working on his figures to buy new clothes and dust himself off, and if you tell anybody who does not know who he is that this old crutch is stone rich, the chances are they will call you a liar.

In fact, on a Monday around noon, the clerk in the branch office that a big Fifth Avenue jewelry firm keeps in the lobby of the States Hotel is all ready to yell for the constables when Unser Fritz leans up against the counter and asks to see some jewelry on display in a showcase, as Unser Fritz is by no means the clerk's idea of a customer for jewelry. I am standing in the lobby of the hotel on the off chance that some fresh money may arrive in the city on the late trains that I may be able to connect up with before the races, when I notice Unser Fritz and observe the agitation of the clerk, and presently I see Unser Fritz waving a fistful of bank notes under the clerk's beak, and the clerk starts setting out the jewelry with surprising speed.

I go over to see what is coming off, and I can see that the jewelry Unser Fritz is looking at consists of a necklace of emeralds and diamonds, with a centerpiece the size of the home plate, and some eardrops, and bracelets, and clips of same, and as I approach the scene I hear Unser Fritz ask how much for the lot as if he is dickering for a basket of fish.

"One hundred and one thousand dollars, sir," the clerk says. "You see, sir, it is a set, and one of the finest things of the kind in the country. We just got it in from our New York store to show a party here, and," he says, "she is absolutely crazy about it, but she states she cannot give us a final decision until five o'clock this afternoon. Confidentially, sir," the clerk says, "I think the real trouble is financial, and doubt that we will hear from her again. In fact," he says, "I am so strongly of this opinion that I am prepared to sell the goods without waiting on her. It is really a bargain at the price," he says.

"Dear me," Unser Fritz says to me, "this is most unfortunate as the sum mentioned is just one thousand dollars more than I possess in all this world. I have twenty thousand on my person, and eighty thousand over in the box in the jug, and not another dime. But," he says, "I will be back before five o'clock and take the lot. In fact," he says, "I will run in right after the third race, and pick it up." Well, at this, the clerk starts putting the jewelry back in the case, and anybody can see that he figures he is on a lob and that he is sorry he wastes so much time, but Unser Fritz says to me like this: "Emma is returning to me," he says.

"Emma who?" I say.

"Why," Unser Fritz says, "my Emma. The one I tell you about not long ago. She must hear I am in the money again, and she is returning just as I always say she will."

"How do you know?" I say. "Do you hear from her, or what?"

"No," Unser Fritz says, "I do not hear from her direct, but Mrs. Crob knows some female relative of Emma's that lives at Ballston Spa a few miles from here, and this relative is in Saratoga this morning to do some shopping, and she tells Mrs. Crob and Mrs. Crob tells me. Emma will be here tonight. I will have these emeralds waiting for her." Well, what I always say is that every guy knows his own business best, and if Unser Fritz wishes to toss his dough off on jewelry, it is none of my put-in, so all I remark is that I have no doubt Emma will be very much surprised, indeed. "No," Unser Fritz says. "She will be expecting them. She always expects emeralds when she returns to me. I love her," he says. "You have no idea how I love her. But let us hasten to the course," he says. "Cara Mia is a right good thing in the third, and I will make just one bet today to win the thousand I need to buy these emeralds."

"But, Fritz," I say, "you will have nothing left for operating expenses after you invest in the emeralds."

"I am not worrying about operating expenses now," Unser Fritz says. "The way my figures are standing up, I can run a spool of thread into a pair of pants in no time. But I can scarcely wait to see the expression on Emma's face when she sees her emeralds. I will have to make a fast trip into town after the third to get my dough out of the box in the jug and pick them up," he says. "Who knows but what this other party that is interested in the emeralds may make her mind up before five o'clock and pop in there and nail them?"

Well, after we get to the race track, all Unser Fritz does is stand around waiting for the third race. He has his figures on the first two races, and ordinarily he will be betting himself a gob on them, but he says he does not wish to take the slightest chance on cutting down his capital at this time, and winding up short of enough dough to buy the emeralds. It turns out that both of the horses Unser Fritz's figures make on top in the first and second races bow down, and Unser Fritz will have his thousand if he only bets a couple of hundred on either of them, but Unser Fritz says he is not sorry he does not bet. He says the finishes in both races are very close, and prove that there is an element of risk in these races. And Unser Fritz says he cannot afford to tamper with the element of risk at this time.

He states that there is no element of risk whatever in the third race, and what he states is very true, as everybody realizes that this mare Cara Mia is a stick-out. In fact, she is such a stick-out that it scarcely figures to be a contest. There are three other horses in the race, but it is the opinion of one and all that if the owners of these horses have any sense they will leave them in the barn and save them a lot of unnecessary lather.

The opening price offered by the bookmakers on Cara Mia is two to five, which means that if you wish to wager on Cara Mia to win you will have to put up five dollars to a bookmaker's two dollars, and everybody agrees that this is a reasonable thing to do in this case unless you wish to rob the poor bookmaker. In fact, this is considered so reasonable that everybody starts running at the bookmakers all at once, and the bookmakers can see if this keeps up they may get knocked off their stools in the betting ring and maybe seriously injured, so they make Cara Mia one to six, and out, as quickly as possible to halt the rush and give them a chance to breathe.

This one to six means that if you wish to wager on Cara Mia to win, you must wager six of your own dollars to one of the bookmaker's dollars, and means that the bookies are not offering any prices whatsoever on Cara Mia running second, or third. You can get almost any price you can think of right quick against any of the other horses winning the race, and place and show prices, too, but asking the bookmakers to lay against Cara Mia running second or third will be something like asking them to bet that Mr. Roosevelt is not President of the United States. Well, I am expecting Unser Fritz to step in and partake of the two to five on Cara Mia for all the dough he has on his person the moment it is offered, because he is very high indeed on this mare, and in fact I never see anybody any higher on any horse, and it is a price Unser Fritz will not back off from when he is high on anything.

Moreover, I am pleased to think he will make such a wager, because it will give him plenty over and above the price of the emeralds, and as long as he is bound to purchase the emeralds, I wish to see him have a little surplus, because when anybody has a surplus there is always a chance for me. It is when everybody runs out of surpluses that I am handicapped no little. But instead of stepping in and partaking, Unser Fritz keeps hesitating until the opening price gets away from him, and finally he says to me like this:

"Of course," he says, "my figures show Cara Mia cannot possibly lose this race, but," he says, "to guard against any possibility whatever of her losing, I will make an absolute cinch of it. I will bet her third."

"Why, Fritz," I say, "I do not think there is anybody in this world outside of an insane asylum who will give you a price on the peek. Furthermore," I say, "I am greatly surprised at this sign of weakening on your part on your figures."

"Well," Unser Fritz says, "I cannot afford to take a chance on not having the emeralds for Emma when she arrives. Let us go through the betting ring, and see what we can see," he says. So we walk through the betting ring, and by this time it seems that many of the books are so loaded with wagers on Cara Mia to win that they will not accept any more under any circumstances, and I figure that Unser Fritz blows the biggest opportunity of his life in not grabbing the opening. The bookmakers who are loaded are now looking even sadder than somewhat, and this makes them a pitiful spectacle, indeed.

Well, one of the saddest-looking is a character by the name of Slow McCool, but he is a character who will usually give you a gamble and he is still taking Cara Mia at one to six, and Unser Fritz walks up to him and whispers in his ear, and what he whispers is he wishes to know if Slow McCool cares to lay him a price on Cara Mia third. But all that happens is that Slow McCool stops looking sad a minute and looks slightly perplexed, and then he shakes his head and goes on looking sad again. Now Unser Fritz steps up to another sad-looking bookmaker by the name of Pete Phozzler and whispers in his ear, and Pete also shakes his head and after we leave him I look back and see that Pete is standing up on his stool watching Unser Fritz, and still shaking his head. Well, Unser Fritz approaches maybe a dozen other sad-looking bookmakers, and whispers to them, and all he gets is the old head shake, but none of them seem to become angry with Unser Fritz, and I always say that this proves that bookmakers are better than some people think, because, personally, I claim they have a right to get angry with Unser Fritz for insulting their intelligence, and trying to defraud them, too, by asking a price on Cara Mia third.

Finally we come to a character by the name of Willie

the Worrier, who is called by this name because he is always worrying about something, and what he is generally worrying about is a short bank roll, or his ever-loving wife, and sometimes both, though mostly it is his wife. Personally, I always figure she is something to worry about, at that, though I do not consider details necessary. She is a red-headed Judy about half as old as Willie the Worrier, and this alone is enough to start any guy worrying, and what is more she is easily vexed, especially by Willie. In fact, I remember Solly telling me that she is vexed with Willie no longer ago than about 11 A.M. this very day, and gives him a public reprimanding about something or other in the telegraph office downtown when Solly happens to be in there hoping maybe he will receive an answer from a mark in Pittsfield, Mass., that he sends a tip on a horse. Solly says the last he hears Willie the Worrier's wife say is that she will leave him for good this time, but I just see her over on the clubhouse lawn wearing some right classy-looking garments, so I judge she does not leave him as yet, as the clubhouse lawn is not a place to be waiting for a train.

Well, when Unser Fritz sees that he is in front of Willie's stand, he starts to move on, and I nudge him and motion at Willie, and ask him if he does not notice that Willie is another bookmaker, and Unser Fritz says he notices him all right, but that he does not care to offer him any business, because Willie insults him ten years ago. He says Willie calls him a dirty old Dutch bum, and while I am thinking what a wonderful memory Unser Fritz has to remember insults from bookmakers for ten years, Willie the Worrier, sitting there on his stool looking out over the crowd, spots Unser Fritz and yells at him as follows:

"Hellow, Dirty Dutch," he says. "How is the soap market? What are you looking for around here, Dirty Dutch? Santa Claus?"

Well, at this, Unser Fritz pushes his way through the crowd around Willie the Worrier's stand, and gets close to Willie, and says:

"Yes," he says, "I am looking for Santa Claus. I am looking for a show price on number two horse, but," he says, "I do not expect to get it from the shoemakers who are booking nowadays."

Now the chances are Willie the Worrier figures Unser Fritz is just trying to get sarcastic with him for the benefit of the crowd around his stand in asking for such a thing as a price on Cara Mia third, and in fact the idea of anybody asking a price third on a horse that some bookmakers will not accept any more wagers on first, or even second, is so humorous that many characters laugh right out loud. "All right," Willie the Worrier says. "No one can ever say he comes to my store looking for a market on anything and is turned down. I will quote you a show price, Dirty Dutch," he says. "You can have one to one hundred." This means that Willie the Worrier is asking Unser Fritz for one hundred dollars to the book's one dollar, if Unser Fritz wishes to bet on Cara Mia dropping in there no worse than third, and of course Willie has no idea Unser Fritz or anybody else will ever take such a price, and the chances are if Willie is not sizzling a little at Unser Fritz, he will not offer such a price, because it sounds foolish.

Furthermore, the chances are if Unser Fritz offers Willie a comparatively small bet at this price, such as may enable him to chisel just a couple of hundred out of Willie's book, Willie will find some excuse to wiggle off, but Unser Fritz leans over and says in a low voice to Willie the Worrier: "A hundred thousand."

Willie nods his head and turns to a clerk alongside him, and his voice is as low as Unser Fritz's as he says to the clerk: "A thousand to a hundred thousand, Cara Mia third."

The clerk's eyes pop open and so does his mouth, but he does not say a word. He just writes something on a pad of paper in his hand, and Unser Fritz offers Willie the Worrier a package of thousand-dollar bills, and says:

"Here is twenty," he says. "The rest is in the jug."

"All right, Dutch," Willie says. "I know you have it, although," he says, "this is the first crack you give me at it. You are on, Dutch," he says. "P. S.," Willie says, "the Dirty does not go any more."

Well, you understand Unser Fritz is betting one hundred thousand dollars against a thousand dollars that Cara Mia will run in the money, and personally I consider this wager a very sound business proposition, indeed, and so does everybody else, for all it amounts to is finding a thousand dollars in the street. There is really nothing that can make Cara Mia run out of the money, the way I look at it, except what happens to her, and what happens is she steps in a hole fifty yards from the finish when she is on top by ten, and breezing, and down she goes all spread out, and of course the other three horses run on past her to the wire, and all this is quite a disaster to many members of the public, including Unser Fritz.

I am standing with him on the rise of the grandstand lawn watching the race, and it is plain to be seen that he is slightly surprised at what happens, and personally, I am practically dumbfounded because, to tell the truth, I take a nibble at the opening price of two to five on Cara Mia with a total of thirty slugs, which represents all my capital, and I am thinking what a great injustice it is for them to leave holes in the track for horses to step in, when Unser Fritz says like this:

"Well," he says, "it is horse racing."

And this is all he ever says about the matter, and then he walks down to Willie the Worrier, and tells Willie if he will send a clerk with him, he will go to the jug and get the balance of the money that is now due Willie. "Dutch," Willie says, "it will be a pleasure to accompany you to the jug in person." As Willie is getting down off his stool, somebody in the crowd who hears of the wager gazes at Unser Fritz, and remarks that he is really a game guy, and Willie says:

"Yes," he says, "he is a game guy at that. But," he says, "what about me?" And he takes Unser Fritz by the arm, and they walk away together, and anybody can see that Unser Fritz picks up anyway twenty years or more, and a slight stringhalt, in the last few minutes.

Then it comes on night again in Saratoga, and I am standing out under the elms in front of the Grand Union, thinking that this world is by no means as beautiful as formerly, when I notice a big, fat old Judy with snow-white hair and spectacles standing near me, looking up and down the street. She will weigh a good two hundred pounds, and much of it is around her ankles, but she has a pleasant face, at that, and when she observes me looking at her, she comes over to me, and says:

"I am trying to fix the location of a restaurant where I work many years ago," she says. "It is a place called Shovelin's. The last thing my husband tells me is to see if the old building is still here, but," she says, "it is so long since I am in Saratoga I cannot get my bearings."

"Ma'am," I say, "is your name Emma by any chance, and do they ever call you Emerald Em?"

Well, at this the old Judy laughs, and says:

"Why, yes," she says. "That is what they call me when I am young and foolish. But how do you know?" she says. "I do not remember ever seeing you before in my life."

"Well," I say, "I know a party who once knows you. A party by the name of Unser Fritz."

"Unser Fritz?" she says. "Unser Fritz? Oh," she says, "I wonder if you mean a crazy Dutchman I run around with many years ago? My gracious," she says, "I just barely remember him. He is a great hand for giving me little presents, such as emeralds. When I am young, I think emeralds are right pretty, but," she says, "otherwise I cannot stand him."

"Then you do not come here to see him?" I say.

"Are you crazy, too?" she says. "I am on my way to Ballston Spa to see my grandchildren. I live in Macon, Georgia. If ever you are in Macon, Georgia, drop in at Shovelin's restaurant and get some real Southern fried chicken. I am Mrs. Joe Shovelin," she says. "By the way," she says, "I remember more about that crazy Dutchman.

He is a horse player. I always figure he must die long ago and that the chances are he dies broke, too. I remember I hear people say all horse players die broke."

"Yes," I say, "he dies all right, and he dies as you suggest, too," for it is only an hour before that they find old Unser Fritz in a vacant lot over near the railroad station with the Betsy he gets off Joe Palladino in his hand and a bullet hole smack-dab through his pimple.

Nobody blames him much for taking this out, and in fact I am standing there thinking long after Emerald Em goes on about her business that it will be a good idea if I follow his example, only I cannot think where I can find another Betsy, when Solly comes along and stands there with me. I ask Solly if he knows anything new.

"No," Solly says, "I do not know anything new, except," he says, "I hear Willie the Worrier and his ever-loving make up again, and she is not going to leave him after all. I hear Willie takes home a squarer in the shape of a batch of emeralds and diamonds that she orders sent up here when Willie is not looking, and that they are fighting about all day. Well," Solly says, "maybe this is love."

A Story Goes with It

One night I am in a gambling joint in Miami watching the crap game and thinking what a nice thing it is, indeed, to be able to shoot craps without having to worry about losing your potatoes.

Many of the high shots from New York and Detroit and St. Louis and other cities are around the table, and there is quite some action in spite of the hard times. In fact, there is so much action that a guy with only a few bobs on him, such as me, will be considered very impolite to be pushing into this game, because they are packed in very tight around the table.

I am maybe three guys back from the table, and I am watching the game by standing on tiptoe peeking over their shoulders, and all I can hear is Goldie, the stick man, hollering money-money-money every time some guy makes a number, so I can see the dice are very warm indeed, and that the right betters are doing first-rate.

By and by a guy by the name of Guinea Joe, out of Trenton, picks up the dice and starts making numbers right and left, and I know enough about this Guinea Joe to know that when he starts making numbers anybody will be very foolish indeed not to follow his hand, although personally I am generally a wrong better against the dice, if I bet at all.

Now all I have in my pocket is a sawbuck, and the hotel stakes are coming up on me the next day, and I need this saw, but with Guinea Joe hotter than a forty-five it will be overlooking a big opportunity not to go along with him, so when he comes out on an eight, which is a very easy number for Joe to make when he is hot, I dig up my sawbuck, and slide it past the three guys in front of me to the table, and I say to Lefty Park, who is laying against the dice, as follows: "I will take the odds, Lefty."

Well, Lefty looks at my sawbuck and nods his head, for Lefty is not such a guy as will refuse any bet, even though it is as modest as mine, and right away Goldie yells money-money-money, so there I am with twenty-two dollars.

Next Guinea Joe comes out on a nine, and naturally I take thirty to twenty for my sugar, because nine is nothing for Joe to make when he is hot. He makes the nine just as I figure, and I take two to one for my half a yard when he starts looking for a ten, and when he makes the ten I am right up against the table, because I am now a guy with means.

Well, the upshot of the whole business is that I finally find myself with three hundred bucks, and when it looks as if the dice are cooling off, I take out and back off from the table, and while I am backing off I am trying to look like a guy who loses all his potatoes, because there are always many wolves waiting around crap games and one thing and another in Miami this season, and what they are waiting for is to put the bite on anybody who happens to make a little scratch.

In fact, nobody can remember when the bite is as painful as it is in Miami this season, what with the unemployment situation among many citizens who come to Miami expecting to find work in the gambling joints, or around the race track. But almost as soon as these citizens arrive, the gambling joints are all turned off, except in spots, and the bookmakers are chased off the track and the mutuels put in, and the consequences are the suffering is most intense. It is not only intense among the visiting citizens, but it is quite intense among the Miami landlords, because naturally if a citizen is not working, nobody can expect him to pay any room rent, but the Miami landlords do not seem to understand this situation, and are very unreasonable about their room rent.

Anyway, I back through quite a crowd without anybody biting me, and I am commencing to figure I may escape altogether and get to my hotel and hide my dough before the news gets around that I win about five G's, which is what my winning is sure to amount to by the time the rumor reaches all quarters of the city.

Then, just as I am thinking I am safe, I find I am looking a guy by the name of Hot Horse Herbie in the face, and I can tell from Hot Horse Herbie's expression that he is standing there watching me for some time, so there is no use in telling him I am washed out in the game. In fact, I cannot think of much of anything to tell Hot Horse Herbie that may keep him from putting the bite on me for at least a few bobs, and I am greatly astonished when he does not offer to bite me at all, but says to me like this:

"Well," he says, "I am certainly glad to see you make

such a nice score. I will be looking for you tomorrow at the track, and will have some big news for you."

Then he walks away from me and I stand there with my mouth open looking at him, as it is certainly a most unusual way for Herbie to act. It is the first time I ever know Herbie to walk away from a chance to bite somebody, and I can scarcely understand such actions, for Herbie is such a guy as will not miss a bite, even if he does not need it.

He is a tall, thin guy, with a sad face and a long chin, and he is called Hot Horse Herbie because he nearly always has a very hot horse to tell you about. He nearly always has a horse that is so hot it is fairly smoking, a hot horse being a horse that cannot possibly lose a race unless it falls down dead, and while Herbie's hot horses often lose without falling down dead, this does not keep Herbie from coming up with others just as hot.

In fact, Hot Horse Herbie is what is called a hustler around the race tracks, and his business is to learn about these hot horses, or even just suspect about them, and then get somebody to bet on them, which is a very legitimate business indeed, as Herbie only collects a commission if the hot horses win, and if they do not win Herbie just keeps out of sight awhile from whoever he gets to bet on the hot horses. There are very few guys in this world who can keep out of sight better than Hot Horse Herbie, and especially from old Cap Duhaine, of the Pinkertons, who is always around pouring cold water on hot horses.

In fact, Cap Duhaine, of the Pinkertons, claims that guys such as Hot Horse Herbie are nothing but touts, and sometimes he heaves them off the race track altogether, but of course Cap Duhaine is a very unsentimental old guy and cannot see how such characters as Hot Horse Herbie add to the romance of the turf.

Anyway, I escape from the gambling joint with all my scratch on me, and hurry to my room and lock myself in for the night, and I do not show up in public until along about noon the next day, when it is time to go over to the coffee shop for my java. And of course by this time the news of my score is all over town, and many guys are taking dead aim at me.

But naturally I am now able to explain to them that I have to wire most of the three yards I win to Nebraska to save my father's farm from being seized by the sheriff, and while everybody knows I do not have a father, and that if I do have a father I will not be sending him money for such a thing as saving his farm, with times what they are in Miami, nobody is impolite enough to doubt my word except a guy by the name of Pottsville Legs, who wishes to see my receipts from the telegraph office when I explain to him why I cannot stake him to a double sawbuck.

I do not see Hot Horse Herbie until I get to the track, and he is waiting for me right inside the grandstand gate, and as soon as I show up he motions me off to one side and says to me like this:

"Now," Herbie says, "I am very smart indeed about a certain race today. In fact," he says, "if any guy knowing what I know does not bet all he can rake and scrape together on a certain horse, such a guy ought to cut his own throat and get himself out of the way forever. What

I know," Herbie says, "is enough to shake the foundations of this country if it gets out. Do not ask any questions," he says, "but get ready to bet all the sugar you win last night on this horse I am going to mention to you, and all I ask you in return is to bet fifty on me. And," Herbie says, "kindly do not tell me you leave your money in your other pants, because I know you do not have any other pants."

"Now, Herbie," I say, "I do not doubt your information, because I know you will not give out information unless it is well founded. But," I say, "I seldom stand for a tip, and as for betting fifty for you, you know I will not bet fifty even for myself if somebody guarantees me a winner. So I thank you, Herbie, just the same," I say, "but I must do without your tip," and with this I start walking away.

"Now," Herbie says, "wait a minute. A story goes with it," he says.

Well, of course this is a different matter entirely. I am such a guy as will always listen to a tip on a horse if a story goes with the tip. In fact, I will not give you a nickel for a tip without a story, but it must be a first-class story, and most horse players are the same way. In fact, there are very few horse players who will not listen to a tip if a story goes with it, for this is the way human nature is. So I turn and walk back to Hot Horse Herbie, and say to him like this:

"Well," I say, "let me hear the story, Herbie."

"Now," Herbie says, dropping his voice away down low, in case old Cap Duhaine may be around somewhere listening, "it is the third race, and the horse is a horse by the name of Never Despair. It is a boat race," Herbie says. "They are going to shoo in Never Despair. Everything else in the race is a cooler," he says.

"Well," I say, "this is just an idea, Herbie, and not a story."

"Wait a minute," Herbie says. "The story that goes with it is a very strange story indeed. In fact," he says, "it is such a story as I can scarcely believe myself, and I will generally believe almost any story, including," he says, "the ones I make up out of my own head. Anyway, the story is as follows:

"Never Despair is owned by an old guy by the name of Seed Mercer," Herbie says. "Maybe you remember seeing him around. He always wears a black slouch hat and gray whiskers," Herbie says, "and he is maybe a hundred years old, and his horses are very terrible horses indeed. In fact," Herbie says, "I do not remember seeing any more terrible horses in all the years I am around the track, and," Herbie says, "I wish to say I see some very terrible horses indeed.

"Now," Herbie says, "old Mercer has a granddaughter who is maybe sixteen years old, come next grass, by the name of Lame Louise, and she is called Lame Louise because she is all crippled up from childhood by infantile what-is-this, and can scarcely navigate, and," Herbie says, "her being crippled up in such a way makes old Mercer feel very sad, for she is all he has in the world, except these terrible horses."

"It is a very long story, Herbie," I say, "and I wish to see Moe Shapoff about a very good thing in the first race."

"Never mind Moe Shapoff," Herbie says. "He will only tell you about a bum by the name of Zachary in the first race, and Zachary has no chance whatever. I make Your John a standout in the first," he says.

"Well," I say, "let us forget the first and go on with your story, although it is commencing to sound all mixed up to me."

"Now," Herbie says, "it not only makes old man Mercer very sad because Lame Louise is all crippled up, but," he says, "it makes many of the jockeys and other guys around the race track sad, because," he says, "they know Lame Louise since she is so high and she always has a smile for them, and especially for Jockey Scroon. In fact," Herbie says, "Jockey Scroon is even more sad about Lame Louise than old man Mercer, because Jockey Scroon loves Lame Louise."

"Why," I say, very indignant, "Jockey Scroon is nothing but a little burglar. Why," I say, "I see Jockey Scroon do things to horses I bet on that he will have to answer for on the Judgment Day, if there is any justice at such a time. Why," I say, "Jockey Scroon is nothing but a Gerald Chapman in his heart, and so are all other jockeys."

"Yes," Hot Horse Herbie says, "what you say is very, very true, and I am personally in favor of the electric chair for all jockeys, but," he says, "Jockey Scroon loves Lame Louise just the same, and is figuring on making her his ever-loving wife when he gets a few bobs together, which," Herbie says, "makes Louise eight to five in my line to be an old maid. Jockey Scroon rooms with me downtown," Herbie says, "and he speaks freely to me about his love for Louise. Furthermore," Herbie says, "Jockey Scroon is personally not a bad little guy, at that, although of course being a jockey he is sometimes greatly misunderstood by the public.

"Anyway," Hot Horse Herbie says, "I happen to go home early last night before I see you at the gambling joint, and I hear voices coming out of my room, and naturally I pause outside the door to listen, because for all I know it may be the landlord speaking about the room rent, although," Herbie says, "I do not figure my landlord to be much worried at this time because I see him sneak into my room a few days before and take a lift at my trunk to make sure I have belongings in the same, and it happens I nail the trunk to the floor beforehand, so not being able to lift it, the landlord is bound to figure me a guy with property.

"These voices," Herbie says, "are mainly soprano voices, and at first I think Jockey Scroon is in there with some dolls, which is by no means permissible in my hotel, but, after listening awhile, I discover they are the voices of young boys, and I make out that these boys are nothing but jockeys, and they are the six jockeys who are riding in the third race, and they are fixing up this race to be a boat race, and to shoo in Never Despair, which Jockey Scroon is riding.

"And," Hot Horse Herbie says, "the reason they are fixing up this boat race is the strangest part of the story. It seems," he says, "that Jockey Scroon hears old man Mercer talking about a great surgeon from Europe who is a shark on patching up cripples such as Lame Louise, and who just arrives at Palm Beach to spend the winter, and old man Mercer is saying how he wishes he has dough enough to take Lame Louise to this guy so he can operate on her, and maybe make her walk good again.

"But of course," Herbie says, "it is well known to one and all that old man Mercer does not have a quarter, and that he has no way of getting a quarter unless one of his terrible horses accidentally wins a purse. So," Herbie says, "it seems these jockeys get to talking it over among themselves, and they figure it will be a nice thing to let old man Mercer win a purse such as the thousand bucks that goes with the third race today, so he can take Lame Louise to Palm Beach, and now you have a rough idea of what is coming off.

"Furthermore," Herbie says, "these jockeys wind up their meeting by taking a big oath among themselves that they will not tell a living soul what is doing so nobody will bet on Never Despair, because," he says, "these little guys are smart enough to see if there is any betting on such a horse there may be a very large squawk afterwards. And," he says, "I judge they keep their oath because Never Despair is twenty to one in the morning line, and I do not hear a whisper about him, and you have the tip all to yourself."

"Well," I say, "so what?" For this story is now commencing to make me a little tired, especially as I hear the bell for the first race, and I must see Moe Shapoff.

"Why," Hot Horse Herbie says, "so you bet every nickel you can rake and scrape together on Never Despair, including the twenty you are to bet for me for giving you this tip and the story that goes with it."

"Herbie," I say, "it is a very interesting story indeed,

and also very sad, but," I say, "I am sorry it is about a horse Jockey Scroon is to ride, because I do not think I will ever bet on anything Jockey Scroon rides if they pay off in advance. And," I say, "I am certainly not going to bet twenty for you or anybody else."

"Well," Hot Horse Herbie says, "I will compromise with you for a pound note, because I must have something going for me on this boat race."

So I give Herbie a fiver, and the chances are this is about as strong as he figures from the start, and I forget all about his tip and the story that goes with it, because while I enjoy a story with a tip, I feel that Herbie overdoes this one.

Anyway, no handicapper alive can make Never Despair win the third race off the form, because this race is at six furlongs, and there is a barrel of speed in it, and anybody can see that old man Mercer's horse is away over his head. In fact, The Dancer tells me that any one of the other five horses in this race can beat Never Despair doing anything from playing hockey to putting the shot, and everybody else must think the same thing because Never Despair goes to forty to one.

Personally, I like a horse by the name of Loose Living, which is a horse owned by a guy by the name of Bill Howard, and I hear Bill Howard is betting plenty away on his horse, and any time Bill Howard is betting away on his horse a guy will be out of his mind not to bet on this horse, too, as Bill Howard is very smart indeed. Loose Living is two to one in the first line, but by and by I judge the money Bill Howard bets away commences to come back to the track, and Loose Living winds up seven to ten, and while I am generally not a seven-to-ten guy, I can see that here is a proposition I cannot overlook.

So, naturally, I step up to the mutuel window and invest in Loose Living. In fact, I invest everything I have on me in the way of scratch, amounting to a hundred and ten bucks, which is all I have left after taking myself out of the hotel stakes and giving Hot Horse Herbie the finnif, and listening to what Moe Shapoff has to say about the first race, and also getting beat a snoot in the second.

When I first step up to the window, I have no idea of betting all my scratch on Loose Living, but while waiting in line there I get to thinking what a cinch Loose Living is, and how seldom such an opportunity comes into a guy's life, so I just naturally set it all in.

Well, this is a race which will be remembered by one and all to their dying day, as Loose Living beats the barrier a step, and is two lengths in front before you can say Jack Robinson, with a thing by the name of Callipers second by maybe half a length, and with the others bunched except Never Despair, and where is Never Despair but last, where he figures.

Now any time Loose Living busts on top there is no need worrying any more about him, and I am thinking I better get in line at the pay-off window right away, so I will not have to wait long to collect my sugar. But I figure I may as well stay and watch the race, although personally I am never much interested in watching races. I am interested only in how a race comes out.

As the horses hit the turn into the stretch, Loose Living is just breezing, and anybody can see that he is going to laugh his way home from there. Callipers is still second, and a thing called Goose Pimples is third, and I am surprised to see that Never Despair now struggles up to fourth with Jockey Scroon belting away at him with his bat quite earnestly. Furthermore, Never Despair seems to be running very fast, though afterwards I figure this may be because the others are commencing to run very slow.

Anyway, a very strange spectacle now takes place in the stretch, as all of a sudden Loose Living seems to be stopping, as if he is waiting for a street car, and what is all the more remarkable Callipers and Goose Pimples also seem to be hanging back, and the next thing anybody knows, here comes Jockey Scroon on Never Despair sneaking through on the rail, and personally it looks to me as if the jock on Callipers moves over to give Jockey Scroon plenty of elbow room, but of course the jock on Callipers may figure Jockey Scroon has diphtheria, and does not wish to catch it.

Loose Living is out in the middle of the track, anyway, so he does not have to move over. All Loose Living has to do is to keep on running backwards as he seems to be doing from the top of the stretch, to let Jockey Scroon go past on Never Despair to win the heat by a length.

Well, the race is practically supernatural in many respects, and the judges are all upset over it, and they haul all the jocks up in the stand and ask them many questions, and not being altogether satisfied with the answers, they ask these questions over several times. But all the jocks will say is that Never Despair sneaks past them very unexpectedly indeed, while Jockey Scroon, who is a pretty fresh duck at that, wishes to know if he is supposed to blow a horn when he is slipping through a lot of guys sound asleep.

But the judges are still not satisfied, so they go prowling around investigating the betting, because naturally when a boat race comes up there is apt to be some reason for it, such as the betting, but it seems that all the judges find is that one five-dollar win ticket is sold on Never Despair in the mutuels, and they cannot learn of a dime being bet away on the horse. So there is nothing much the judges can do about the proposition, except give the jocks many hard looks, and the jocks are accustomed to hard looks from the judges, anyway.

Personally, I am greatly upset by this business, especially when I see that Never Despair pays $86.34, and for two cents I will go right up in the stand and start hollering copper on these little Jesse Jameses for putting on such a boat race and taking all my hard-earned potatoes away from me, but before I have time to do this, I run into The Dancer, and he tells me that Dedicate in the next race is the surest thing that ever goes to the post, and at five to one, at that. So I have to forget everything while I bustle about to dig up a few bobs to bet on Dedicate, and when Dedicate is beat a whisker, I have to do some bustling to dig up a few bobs to bet on Vesta in the fifth, and by this time the third race is such ancient history that nobody cares what happens in it.

It is nearly a week before I see Hot Horse Herbie again, and I figure he is hiding out on everybody because he has this dough he wins off the fiver I give him, and personally I consider him a guy with no manners not to be kicking back the fin, at least. But before I can mention the fin, Herbie gives me a big hello, and says to me like this:

"Well," he says, "I just see Jockey Scroon, and Jockey Scroon just comes back from Palm Beach, and the operation is a big success, and Lame Louise will walk as good as anybody again, and old Mercer is tickled silly. But," Herbie says, "do not say anything out loud, because the judges may still be trying to find out what comes off in the race."

"Herbie," I say, very serious, "do you mean to say the story you tell me about Lame Louise, and all this and that, the other day is on the level?"

"Why," Herbie says, "certainly it is on the level, and I am sorry to hear you do not take advantage of my information. But," he says, "I do not blame you for not believing my story, because it is a very long story for anybody to believe. It is not such a story," Herbie says, "as I will tell to any one if I expect them to believe it. In fact," he says, "it is so long a story that I do not have the heart to tell it to anybody else but you, or maybe I will have something running for me on the race.

"But," Herbie says, "never mind all this. I will be plenty smart about a race tomorrow. Yes," Herbie says, "I will be wiser than a treeful of owls, so be sure and see me if you happen to have any coconuts."

"There is no danger of me seeing you," I say, very sad, because I am all sorrowed up to think that the story he tells me is really true. "Things are very terrible with me at this time," I say, "and I am thinking maybe you can hand me back my finnif, because you must do all right for yourself with the fiver you have on Never Despair at such a price."

Now a very strange look comes over Hot Horse Herbie's face, and he raises his right hand, and says to me like this:

"I hope and trust I drop down dead right here in front of you," Herbie says, "if I bet a quarter on the horse. It is true," he says, "I am up at the window to buy a ticket on Never Despair, but the guy who is selling the tickets is a friend of mine by the name of Heeby Rosenbloom, and Heeby whispers to me that Big Joe Gompers, the guy who owns Callipers, just bets half a hundred on his horse, and," Herbie says, "I know Joe Gompers is such a guy as will not bet half a hundred on anything he does not get a Federal Reserve guarantee with it.

"Anyway," Herbie says, "I get to thinking about what a bad jockey this Jockey Scroon is, which is very bad indeed, and," he says, "I figure that even if it is a boat race it is no even-money race they can shoo him in, so I buy a ticket on Callipers."

"Well," I say, "somebody buys one five-dollar ticket on Never Despair, and I figure it can be nobody but you."

"Why," Hot Horse Herbie says, "do you not hear about this? Why," he says, "Cap Duhaine, of the Pinkertons, traces this ticket and finds it is bought by a guy by the name of Steve Harter, and the way this guy Harter comes to buy it is very astonishing. It seems," Herbie says, "that this Harter is a tourist out of Indiana who comes to Miami for the sunshine, and who loses all his dough but six bucks against the faro bank at Hollywood.

"At the same time," Herbie says, "the poor guy gets a telegram from his ever-loving doll back in Indiana saying she no longer wishes any part of him.

"Well," Herbie says, "between losing his dough and his doll, the poor guy is practically out of his mind, and he figures there is nothing left for him to do but knock himself off.

"So," Herbie says, "this Harter spends one of his six bucks to get to the track, figuring to throw himself under the feet of the horses in the first race and let them kick him to a jelly. But he does not get there until just as the third race is coming up and," Herbie says, "he sees this name 'Never Despair,' and he figures it may be a hunch, so he buys himself a ticket with his last fiver. Well, naturally," Herbie says, "when Never Despair pops down, the guy forgets about letting the horses kick him to a jelly, and he keeps sending his dough along until he runs nothing but a nubbin into six G's on the day.

"Then," Herbie says, "Cap Duhaine finds out that the guy, still thinking of Never Despair, calls his ever-loving doll on the phone, and finds she is very sorry she sends him the wire and that she really loves him more than somewhat, especially," Herbie says, "when she finds out about the six G's. And the last anybody hears of the matter, this Harter is on his way home to get married, so Never Despair does quite some good in this wicked old world, after all.

"But," Herbie says, "let us forget all this, because tomorrow is another day. Tomorrow," he says, "I will tell you about a thing that goes in the fourth which is just the same as wheat in the bin. In fact," Hot Horse Herbie says, "if it does not win, you can never speak to me again."

"Well," I say, as I start to walk away, "I am not interested in any tip at this time."

"Now," Herbie says, "wait a minute. A story goes with it."

"Well," I say, coming back to him, "let me hear the story."

A Light in France

In the summer of 1936, a personality by the name of Blond Maurice is found buried in a pit of quicklime up in Sullivan County, or, anyway, what is found is all that is left of Maury, consisting of a few odds and ends in the way of bones, and a pair of shoes which have Brown the shoemaker's name in them, and which Brown identifies as a pair of shoes he makes for Maury some months before, when Maury is in the money and is able to have his shoes made to order.

It is common gossip in all circles along Broadway that Maury is placed in this quicklime by certain parties who do not wish him well, and it is also the consensus of opinion that placing him there is by no means a bad idea, at that, as Maury is really quite a scamp and of no great credit to the community. In fact, when it comes out that there is nothing left of him but a pair of shoes, it is agreed by one and all that it is two shoes too many.

Well, knowing that Maury is quicklimed, it is naturally something of a surprise to me to come upon him in Mindy's restaurant one evening in the spring of 1943, partaking of cheese blintzes. At first I think I am seeing a ghost, but, of course, I know that ghosts never come in Mindy's, and, if they do, they never eat cheese blintzes, so I realize that it is nobody but Maury himself.

Consequently I step over to his table and give him a medium hello, and he looks up and gives me a medium hello right back, for, to tell the truth, Maury and I are never bosom friends. In fact, I always give him plenty of the back of my neck because I learn long ago that it is best not to associate with such harum-scarum personalities unless, of course, you need them.

But naturally I am eager to hear of his experiences in the quicklime as I never before meet a guy who returns from being buried in this substance, so I draw up a chair and speak to him as follows:

"Well, Maury," I say, "where are you all this time that I do not see you around and about?"

"I am in a place called France," Maury says. "I leave there on account of the war. Perhaps you hear of the war?"

"Yes," I say, "I hear rumors of it from time to time."

"It is a great nuisance," Maury says.

"But, Maury," I say, "how do you come to go to a place where there is a war?"

"Oh," Maury says, "there is no war when I go there. The war is here in New York. This city is very unsettled at the time, what with the unpleasantness between my employer, the late Little Kishke, and Sammy Downtown developing cases for the medical examiner all over the layout. I am pleased to find on my return that law and order now prevail."

"But, Maury," I say, "how do you stand with reference to law and order?"

"I am in favor of both," Maury says. "Oh, I am all right. Immediately upon my return, I call on the D.A. in

Manhattan to see if he has anything he wishes me to plead guilty to, and he cannot find a thing, although he seems somewhat regretful, at that.

"Then," Maury says, "I go over to Brooklyn and call on the D.A. there, and he consults the books of Murder, Incorporated, and he states that all he can find entered under my name is that I am deceased, and that he hopes and trusts I will remain so. I am as clean as a whistle, and," Maury says, "maybe cleaner."

"Well," I say, "I am glad to hear this, Maury. I always know you are sound at bottom. By the way, do you run into Girondel on your travels? We hear that he is over there also. At least, he is absent quite a spell. Girondel is always a great one for going around and about in foreign lands."

"No," Maury says, "I do not see him there. But if you care to listen, I will now relate to you my adventures in France."

Well [Maury says] I go to France when things come up that convince me that I am not as popular as formerly with Sammy Downtown and his associates, and, furthermore, I am tired out and feel that I can use a little rest and peace.

And the reason I pick this France as a place to go to is because I take a fancy to the country when I am there once on a pleasure trip all over Europe as a guest of the late Drums Capello, who is in the importing business, and what he imports is such merchandise as morphine and heroin and sometimes a little opium.

But I wish to state that I have no part of Drums' play in this respect and no part of his fall when the Brush finally catches up with him. And, furthermore, I wish to state that I never approve of his enterprise in any way whatever, but I must say he is a fine host and takes me all over England and Germany, and introduces me to many of his friends and business associates, and you can have them.

Now, the exact spot in France to which I go is a sleepy little town on the seacoast, but I cannot reveal the name at this time as it is a military secret and, anyway, I am unable to pronounce it. The main drag of this town faces a small harbor, and you can stand in front of any place of business along the stem and almost flip a dime into the water—if you happen to have a dime to spare.

It is an old fishing spot, and when I first go there, it is infested by fishermen with hay on their chins, and while most of them inhabit dinky little houses in the town, others live on farms about the size of napkins just outside the burg, and they seem to divide their time between chasing fish and cows. But it is quiet and peaceful there, and very restful after you get used to not hearing the Broadway traffic.

I reside in a tiny gaff that is called a hotel on the main street, and this gaff is run by a French bim by the name of Marie. In fact, all bims in France seem to be named Marie when they are not named Yvonne. I occasionally notice an old sack in the background who may be Marie's mamma or her aunt or some such, but Marie is strictly the boss of the trap and operates it in first-class style. She is the chief clerk and the headwaiter and she is also the bartender in the little smoky barroom that opens directly on the street, so, if the door is left open, you get herring with your cognac.

I know she makes the beds and dusts up the three tiny bedrooms in the joint, so you can see she is an all-around personality. She is maybe twenty years old, and I will not attempt to describe her except to say that if I am interested in the hugging and kissing department, I will most certainly take my business to Marie, especially as she speaks English, and you will not have to waste time with the sign language.

Well, it is very pleasant, to be sure, strolling around the little town talking to the fishermen or wandering out into the country and observing the agriculturists, who seem to be mostly female personalities who are all built in such a way that they will never be able to sit down in a washtub with comfort, and who really have very little glamor.

It is also very pleasant to nuzzle a dram or two in the cool of the evening at a little table in front of Marie's hotel and it is there I make the acquaintance of the only other roomer in the hotel. He is a fat old guy who is nobody but Thaddeus T. Blackman, a rich zillionaire from the city of New York and a lam-master from the Brush boys back home for over twenty years on an income-tax beef.

It seems that Thaddeus T. is mixed up in a large scandal about oil lands, and a grand jury hands out readers right and left among some of the best people in the U.S.A., although all they do is swindle the government, and it is a great shock to them to learn that this is against the law.

Anyway, Thaddeus T. starts running as soon as he

gets wind of the beef and does not pause for breath until he arrives in this little town in France, and there he lives all these years. It seems the Brush cannot touch him there, and why this is I do not know, but I suppose it is because he is smart enough to take his zillions with him, and naturally this kind of moolouw is protection on land or sea.

He discusses his case with me once and gives me to understand that it is a bum beef as far as he is concerned and that he only takes the fall for others, but of course this is by no means an unfamiliar tale to me, and, as he never mentions why he does not try to chill the beef by paying the government the dough, I do not consider it tactful to bring the matter up.

He is up in the paint-cards in age when I meet him, being maybe close to seventy, and he is a fashion plate of the fashion of about 1922. Moreover, he seems to be a lonely old gee, though how anybody can be lonely with all his zillions is a great mystery to me. He always has a short briar pipe in his mouth and is generally lighting it with little wax matches, and, in fact, I never see a pipe man who is not generally lighting his pipe, and if ever I get time I will invent a pipe that stays lit and make a fortune.

Anyway, Thaddeus T. and I become good friends over the little table in front of the hotel, and then one day who shows up but an old pal of mine out of the city of Boston, Mass., who is also an absentee from a small charge of homicide in his home town.

He is called by the name of Mike the Mugger because it seems his occupation is reaching out of doorways on dark nights and taking passers-by by the neck and pulling them in close to him with one hand and examining into their pockets with the other hand, the idea of the hand around the neck being to keep them from complaining aloud until he is through with them.

Personally, I do not consider this occupation at all essential or even strictly ethical, but I always say every guy to his own taste and naturally I have to respect Mike as the very top guy in his profession who never makes a mistake except the one time he clasps a customer too tight and too long and becomes involved in this difficulty I mention.

He is about thirty-odd and is a nifty-drifty in his dress and very good company, except that he is seldom holding anything and is generally leaning on me. However, I am personally loaded at this time and I am not only pleased to okay Mike with Marie for the last of her three rooms, but I stake him to walk-about money, which is money for his pocket, and he is grateful to me in every respect.

Naturally, Mike joins out with Thaddeus T. and me in strolling here and there and in sitting at the little table in front of the hotel or in the barroom, talking and playing cards, and what we generally talk about, of course, is the good old U.S.A., which is a subject of great interest to all three of us.

A few fishermen and small merchants of the town are also usually in the barroom, and Marie is always behind the bar, and it is not long before I notice that both Thaddeu T. and Mike the Mugger are paying considerable attention to her. In fact, Mike tells me he is in love with her and is surprised that I am not in the same condition.

"But," Mike says, "of course I will never mention my love to Marie because I am undoubtedly a low-class personality with a tough beef against me and am unfit to associate with a nice lady saloonkeeper."

As far as I can see, Thaddeus T.'s interest in Marie is more fatherly than anything else, which is very nice if you like an old wolf for a father. He tells me he wishes he has her for his daughter because, he says, the one of his own back in the U.S.A. is a dingbat and so is her mamma, and from the way he carries on about them, I can see that Thaddeus T.'s former home life is far from being a plug for matrimony.

Now it comes on 1939 and with it the war, and Thaddeus T., who can gabble the frog language quite fluently and is always around on the Ear-ie finding out what is going on, tells me that the people of the town are pretty much worked up and that some of the guys are going away to join the army, but it makes little difference in our lives, as we seem to be outside the active war zone, and all we know about any actual fighting is what we hear.

We still sit out in front of the hotel in the afternoon and in the barroom at night, though I observe Marie now pays more attention to other customers than she does to us and is always chattering to them in a most excited manner, and Thaddeus T. says it is about the war. He says Marie is taking it to heart no little and quite some.

But it is not until the summer of 1940 that Thaddeus T. and me and even Mike really notice the war, because overnight the little town fills up with German soldiers and other German guys who are not soldiers but seem to be working gees, and it is plain to be seen that something big is doing. Thaddeus T. says he hears they are making a submarine base of the harbor because it is a very handy spot for the subs to sneak out of and knock off the British ships, and in fact after a while we see many subs and other shipping along the quays.

Anyway, the Germans pay very little attention to us at first except to examine our papers, and the officers who come into Marie's bar for drinks are quite polite and nod to us and sometimes talk to Thaddeus T., who speaks German better than he does French. Presently we are practically ignoring the presence of the Germans in our midst, although naturally Marie has no fancy for them whatever and is always making faces at them behind their backs and spitting on the ground when they pass, until I tell her that this is unlady like.

Well, on coming home one night from a little stroll, I hear a commotion in the kitchen, which is just off the barroom, and on entering I observe Marie wrestling with a big blubber in civilian clothes who is wearing a small scrubby mustache and a derby hat and who has practically no neck whatever.

They are knocking kitchen utensils right and left, including a pot of spaghetti which I know Marie prepares for my dinner and which vexes me no little. Marie is sobbing and I can see that the blubber is outwrestling her and in fact has a strangle hold on her that figures to win him the fall very shortly. I am standing there, admiring his technique in spite of my vexation over the spaghetti, when Marie sees me and calls to me as follows:

"Please help me, Chauncey," which, as I forget to tell you before, is at this time my monicker, and I am then in possession of passports and other papers to prove same.

Naturally, I pay no attention to her, as I do not know on what terms she is wrestling the blubber, but finally I see she is in some distress, so I step forward and tap the bloke on the shoulder and say to him like this:

"I beg your pardon," I say, "but the strangle hold is illegal. If you are going to wrestle, you must obey the rules."

At this, the guy lets go of Marie and steps back and I say to her in English, "Who is this plumber?"

"He is Herr Klauber," Marie says back to me in English. "He is the head of the Gestapo in this district."

Well, then I get a good glaum at the gee and I see that he is nobody but the same Klauber that Drums Capello does business with in Hamburg the time I am Drums' guest, only in those days he is not usually called by the name of Klauber. He is called the Vasserkopf, which is a way of saying "waterhead" in German, because he has an extra large sconce piece that is practically a deformity and as the Vasserkopf he is known far and wide on two continents, and especially here in New York, where he once operates, as a very sure-footed merchant in morphine, heroin, opium and similar commodities.

Naturally, it is a great pleasure to me to behold a familiar puss in a strange place, even if it is only the Vasserkopf's puss, so I give him a sizable hello and speak to him as follows:

"Well, Vasser," I say, "this is an unexpected privilege, to be sure. There you are and here I am, and much water runs over the dam since last we met, and how are you anyway?"

"Who are you?" the Vasserkopf says in English and in a most unfriendly manner.

"Come, come, Vasser," I say. "Let us not waste time in shadowboxing. Do you know our old pal Drums finally takes a fall in Milwaukee, Wis., for a sixer?"

Then the Vasserkopf comes close to me and speaks to me in a low voice like this: "Listen," he says, "it is in my mind to throw you in the jail house."

"Tut-tut, Vass," I say, "if you throw me in the jail house, I will be compelled to let out a bleat. I will be compelled to remember the time you ship the cargo of Santa Clauses out of Nuremburg and each Santa contains enough of the white to junk up half of the good old U.S.A. I hear your Fuehrer is a strait-laced gee, and what will he say if he hears one of his big coppers peddles junk and maybe uses it?"

I can see the Vasserkopf turns a little pale around the guzzle at this statement and he says: "Come outside. We will talk."

So I go outside the gaff with him, and we stand in the street in the darkness and have quite a chat and the Vasserkopf becomes more friendly and tells me that he is now a real high-muck-a-muck with the Gestapo and the greatest spy catcher in the racket. Then he wishes to know what I am doing in these parts, and I tell him quite frankly that I am there for my health and explain my ailment to him. I also tell him why Thaddeus T. and

Mike the Mugger are there because I know that, as a former underworld personality, the Vasserkopf is apt to be understanding and sympathetic in such situations, especially when he knows my hole card is my knowledge of his background in junk.

"Now, Vass," I say, "all we wish is to be let alone, and if you can assist us in any way, I will personally be much obliged. What is more," I say, "I will see that you are well rewarded, if a member of the Gestapo takes."

"Sure," the Vasserkopf says. "Only let us understand one thing right off the reel. The broad belongs to me. I am crazy about her. But there is talk today at headquarters of closing this place and putting her out of business because of her attitude, and because one of our officers becomes ill after drinking cognac in here last night.

"I will tell the dumb military he probably has a touch of ptomaine," he continues. "I will tell them I need this hotel as a listening post to find out what is going on among the people around here. I will advise them not to molest you, as you are neutrals, and it may make trouble with your government, although," the Vasserkopf says, "I can see that the only trouble your government may make will be for you. But the Reich is not interested in American lammeroos, and neither am I as long as you remember the dame is mine and see that I collect a hundred a week in your money. I can scarcely sleep nights thinking of her."

Now this seems to me to be a very reasonable proposition all the way around, except for the hundred a week. The way I look at it, the Vasserkopf is at least entitled to Marie for his trouble because, to tell the truth, it will be most inconvenient for Thaddeus T. and Mike the Mugger and me to leave this spot at the moment, as there is no other place we can go and no way of getting there if there is such a place.

So I shave the Vasserkopf to half a C every week, and then I go back into the hotel to find Marie in the bar with Thaddeus T. and Mike, and I can see that she is quite agitated by her recent experience with the Vasserkopf. I also learn from her that it is not his first visit.

"He is here several times before," Marie says. "He comes to me first with news of my brother who is a prisoner in a camp near Hamburg. Herr Klauber tells me he can make things easier for Henri and perhaps get him released. He comes again and again on different excuses. I am frightened because I fear his motive." Then all of a sudden Marie puts her finger to her lips and says, "Hark!"

We hark, and I hear away off somewhere a sound that I know must come from a lot of planes, and as this sound grows louder and louder, and then dies away again, Marie says:

"English bombers," she says. "Every night they pass over here and go on up the coast to drop their bombs. They do not know what is going on here. Oh, if we can only show a light here to let them know this is a place to strike—this nest of snakes."

"A light?" I say. "Why, if you show a light around here, these squareheads will settle you in no time. Besides," I say, "it may get me and my friends in a jam, and we are Americans and very neutral. Let us not even think of showing a light and, Marie," I say, "kindly cease sizzling every time you serve a German, and, Mike, if you have any more Mickey Finns on your person, please take them yourself instead of dropping them in officers' drinks."

"Who? Me?" Mike the Mugger says.

Well, I see the Vasserkopf in the hotel almost every day after this talking to Marie, and he always gives me an E-flat hello and I give him the same, and, while I can see that Marie is afraid of him, she says he is now very polite to her and does not try to show her any more holds.

Of course, I do not tell Marie about my deal with the Vasserkopf and I do not tell Mike either, though I inform Thaddeus T., as I expect him to kick with some of the dough, and he says okay and that he is glad to learn that the Vasseropf is on the take, only he thinks the half a C is enough without throwing in Marie. But he says a deal is a deal, and I can count on his co-operation.

From now on as far as we are concerned, everything seems to be almost the same as before there is any war whatever, except that we cannot go near the water front where the Germans are working and everything has to be blacked out good after dark, and you cannot as much as strike a match in the street, which is a great nuisance to Thaddeus T., as he is always striking matches. In fact, he almost gets his toupée blown off by sentries before he can break himself of the habit of striking matches outdoors at night.

I can see that the Vasserkopf must be keeping his

agreement to front for us at headquarters, all right, and I am greasing him every week per our arrangement, but I find myself bored by the place, and I have a feeling that it is time for Mike the Mugger and maybe Thaddeus T., too, to leave, especially as the Vasserkopf accidentally drops a hint one day that he finds himself impeded in his progress with Marie by our constant presence in the hotel and that he thinks he is getting the short end of the deal. Finally, I have a conference with Thaddeus T., and state my views to him.

"Yes," Thaddeus T. says, "you are a hundred per cent right. But," he says, "leaving here is not a simple matter for us now. I am reliably informed that the military is likely to oppose our departure for the present, because the sub base here is a great secret and they do not care to run the risk of having us noise it about.

"In fact," he says, "I am told that they are sorry they do not chase us when they first come here, but now that they make this mistake, they are not going to make another by letting us depart, and other information that I hesitate to credit is that they may wind up clapping us in a detention camp somewhere."

"Thaddeus T.," I say, "I am an American and so is Mike and so are you, and our country is not concerned in this war. No one can hold us here against our wishes."

Well, at this, Thaddeus T. lets out a large laugh, and I can see his point and laugh with him, and then he informs me that for some days he is personally laying plans for our departure and that he buys a slightly tubercular motorboat from a certain personality and has it hidden at this very moment in a little cove about a mile up the coast and that all he now needs is a little petrol, which is a way of saying gasoline, to run the boat with the three of us in it out to sea, where we will have the chance of being picked up.

Thaddeus T. explains to me that all the petrol in this vicinity is in the hands of the Germans, but he says that where there is a will, there is a way. Consequently, he makes arrangements with the same personality who sells him the boat for a supply of gasoline, and who is this personality but the Vasserkopf, and Thaddeus is paying him more per gill for the gas than the old Vass ever gets per ounce for his hop, and, as I am personally paying him regularly, I can see that he is getting his coming and going and, naturally, I have to admire his enterprise.

However, Thaddeus states that the Vasserkopf is really most co-operative in every respect, and that he is to deliver the gas at the hotel the following night, and moreover that he is going to escort us to the cove so we will not be molested by any sentries we may encounter in that vicinity, which I say is very nice of the Vasserkopf though I seem to remember that there are never any sentries in that vicinity anyway, as it is part of the coast that does not seem to interest the Germans in any manner.

Then I get to meditating more and more on the Vasserkopf and on what a big heart he has, to be sure, and as I am meditating I am also sauntering late the next evening in a roundabout way up the coast as I wish to confirm the presence of the boat in the cove because, of course, there is the possibility of it getting away after the Vasserkopf has it placed there.

My roundabout saunter carries me across the fields of the little farms beyond the town that in some places run almost down to the sea, and it is a route that the Germans are not apt to suspect as taking me on any considerable journey, even if they notice me sauntering, which I take care they do not.

Finally, I saunter through a field to a slight rise of ground that overlooks the little cove, and there is just enough daylight left by now for me to see a boat floating just offshore, and at this same moment, I am surprised to scent the odor of fresh-turned earth near at hand, and the reason I am surprised is because it is now winter and by no means plowing time.

Consequently, I look around and I am further surprised to observe on this rise a newly made trench in the ground of a size and shape that brings back many memories to me. So I saunter back in a more roundabout way still meditating no little and quite some on the Vasserkopf.

But, sure enough, he shows up this very night around nine o'clock after Marie closes her place, and he brings with him two five-gallon cans of gasoline which he delivers to Thaddeus T. in the bar where Thaddeus and me and Mike the Mugger are waiting to receive the gas. Then, after handing over the cans, the Vass goes looking for Marie, saying he wishes to speak to her before escorting us to the boat.

As soon as he leaves the bar, Mike the Mugger outs with his pocketknife and stabs holes in two corners of the can and speaks as follows, "It smells like gasoline on the outside, but we smear the outside of cans with booze in the old bootleg days for the liquor smell when there is only water inside the cans. I hear the Vasserkopf is an old booter and he may remember the trick, and, besides, I do not trust him on general principles."

Now Mike lifts the can up as if it is no more than a demitasse and he holds it to his mouth so he can get a swig of the contents through one of the holes, when all of a sudden who comes into the bar all out of breath but Marie, and who is right behind her but the Vasserkopf, and there is no doubt that Marie is greatly flustered, and the Vasserkopf is much perturbed.

"So," he says to me, "you are double-crosing me and are going to take this omelet with you, hey? Well, it is a good thing I walk in on her as she is packing a keister, and I am now arresting her as a dangerous spy."

Marie begins to weep and wail and to carry on as bims will do when they are flustered, and naturally Thaddeus T. and me and Mike the Mugger are quite perplexed by this situation and, in fact, Mike is so perplexed that he is still holding the can in his hands and his cheeks are bulged out on each side from gasoline in his mouth as if he has the mumps.

I am about to say something to cool the Vasserkopf off, for, to tell the truth, up to this minute I have no idea Marie is going with us, though I can see from the way Thaddeus T. and Mike the Mugger look that it is undoubtedly their idea. And, before I can say anything, Mike steps up to the Vasserkopf and gives a huge ploo-oo-oo and spews his mouthful of gasoline right in the Vasserkopf's kisser and, as he gets his mouth clear, Mike says, "Why, you muzzler, it is somewhat watered, just as I suspect."

Well, naturally, the gasoline runs off the Vasserkopf's face and down over his clothes and he is standing there looking quite nonplused, and, as Mike the Mugger sees me gazing at him disapprovingly, he becomes embarrassed and self-conscious and, maybe to cover his confusion, he lifts the can of gasoline and holds it over the Vasserkopf's head, and the gas pours out and splashes off the old Vass' derby hat and splatters over his shoulders while he just stands there nonplused.

Thaddeus T. Blackman is leaning against the bar and, as usual, he is lighting his pipe with a little wax match and watching the Vasserkopf, and Marie has stopped crying and is laughing, and I am just standing there, when we again hear the sound of the planes high overhead and Thaddeus T. speaks as follows:

"A light you say, Marie?" he says. "A light for the English?"

Then he flips the lighted match on the Vasserkopf, whose clothes burst into flames at once and, almost as if they plan it all out beforehand, Mike jumps to the front door and opens it, and Thaddeus T. pushes the Vasserkopf, all ablaze, out the door into the street and yells at him:

"Run for the water!" he yells. "Run, run, run!"

The Vasserkopf seems to see what he means and starts galloping lickity-split toward the water front with Thaddeus T. puffing along behind him and giving him a shove whenever he shows signs of lagging, and Mike the Mugger runs up behind the Vasserkopf and keeps throwing little spurts of gasoline on him by jerking the can at him and, from the way it burns on the Vasserkopf, I think Mike's statement of its dilution may be a slight exaggeration.

As he runs and burns, the Vasserkopf is letting out loud cries which bring soldiers from every which way, and presently they start shooting off their rifles in different directions. He is really quite a bonfire there in the darkness, and now I hear once more far overhead the drone of planes and I figure the English bombers see the light and turn back over the town.

All of a sudden, there is a whistling sound and then a big *ker-bloom,* and then more whistling and more *ker-blooms,* and there is no doubt in my mind that it is Katie-bar-the-door for the water front and the subs lying along the quays.

I can see the Vasserkopf still blazing and I can hear Thaddeus T. still urging him to run, and now the bombs are shellacking the surrounding buildings, and presently I hear, in between the blasts of the bombs, some rifle shots, and I know the soldiers are firing at Thaddeus T. and Mike the Mugger and maybe at the Vasserkopf, too, for making the light.

In fact, by the glow shed by the Vasserkopf, I see old Thaddeus stumble and fall, and Mike the Mugger go down right afterward with his can of gasoline blazing over him, but the Vasserkopf continues on still in flames until he falls off the quay into the water and, the chances are, goes out with a zizz.

Well, when I think of Marie, I turn from these unusual scenes to the little hotel, but it is no longer there, because a bomb flattens it, too, and it is now nothing but a pile of miscellany. I do not have much time to look for Marie, as the German soldiers are all over the layout, trying to learn what happens, but I finally locate her with a big beam across her chest, and I can see that there is nothing I can do for her except kiss her and say goodby, and when I do this, she murmurs, "Thanks," but I am sure it is only for Thaddeus T. and Mike the Mugger and the light.

You will scarcely believe the difficulty I experience in getting away from this unpleasant situation and out of the country. In fact, I have only a vague recollection of my adventures now, but I will always remember very clearly how neatly I slip past four German soldiers sitting in the new-made trench on the rise of ground above the cove, with a machine gun covering the cove itself, and how I get in the boat and cut it loose and work it, with my hands for paddles, to open water, before they realize what is going on.

And I can never again have any respect for the memory of the Vasserkopf when I take to meditating on his unsportsmanlike conduct in trying to double-cinch a sure thing with a machine gun, although there are times before I am picked up at sea by an English destroyer that I find myself wishing that Mike the Mugger does not waste all the gasoline on the Vass, even if it is watered.

And this is all there is to the story [Maury says].

"But, Maury," I say, "do you not know that some remainders found in a pit of quicklime up in Sullivan County are supposed to be yours? They have on your shoes, which are identified by Brown the shoemaker. Are you ever in a quicklime pit in Sullivan County and, if so, what is it like?"

"Oh," Maury says, "I am in Sullivan County, all right, but never in a quicklime pit. I go to Sullivan County at the invitation of Girondel, and the purpose of his invitation is to discuss ways and means of getting me straightened out with his chief, Sammy Downtown.

"But one day," Maury says, "Girondel invites me to a stroll in the woods with him and, while we are strolling, he is talking about the beauties of the landscape and calling my attention to the flowers and the birds, which is all very interesting, to be sure, but something tells me that Girondel is by no means the nature lover he seems.

"Finally," Maury says, "he strolls me to a spot in the deep, tangled wildwood, and all of a sudden I catch an odor of something I never scent but once before in my life but will never again forget, and that is the time we lay the late Bugs Wonder to rest in Greenvale Cemetery. It is the odor of the fresh-turned earth from Bugs' last resting place.

"And as I catch this again in the woods," Maury says, "I realize that somebody does some digging around there lately, so I quietly give Girondel a boff over his pimple with a blackjack and flatten him like a welcome mat. Then I examine my surroundings and, sure enough, there, hidden by the shrubbery, I find a deep freshmade hole lined with quicklime, and I place Girondel in it and cover him up and leave him with my best wishes.

"But, first," Maury says, "I change shoes with him because my own are badly worn and, besides, I know that if ever he is found, the shoes will outlast the quicklime and be traced as mine, and I wish Girondel's connection to think I am no more. By the way," he says, "the odor I mention is the same I notice on the rise of ground at the cove in France which causes me to distrust the Vasserkopf. I guess I am just naturally allergic to the odor of newmade graves."

Romance in the Roaring Forties

Only a rank sucker will think of taking two peeks at Dave the Dude's doll, because while Dave may stand for the first peek, figuring it is a mistake, it is a sure thing he will get sored up at the second peek, and Dave the Dude is certainly not a man to have sored up at you.

But this Waldo Winchester is one hundred per cent sucker, which is why he takes quite a number of peeks at Dave's doll. And what is more, she takes quite a number of peeks right back at him. And there you are. When a guy and a doll get to taking peeks back and forth at each other, why, there you are indeed.

This Waldo Winchester is a nice-looking young guy who writes pieces about Broadway for the *Morning Item*. He writes about the goings-on in night clubs, such as fights, and one thing and another, and also about who is running around with who, including guys and dolls.

Sometimes this is very embarrassing to people who may be married and are running around with people who are not married, but of course Waldo Winchester cannot be expected to ask one and all for their marriage certificates before he writes his pieces for the paper.

The chances are if Waldo Winchester knows Miss Billy Perry is Dave the Dude's doll, he will never take more than his first peek at her, but nobody tips him off until his second or third peek, and by this time Miss Billy Perry is taking her peeks back at him and Waldo Winchester is hooked.

In fact, he is plum gone, and being a sucker, like I tell you, he does not care whose doll she is. Personally, I do not blame him much, for Miss Billy Perry is worth a few peeks, especially when she is out on the floor of Miss Missouri Martin's Sixteen Hundred Club doing her tap dance. Still, I do not think the best tap dancer that ever lives can make me take two peeks at her if I know she is Dave the Dude's doll, for Dave somehow thinks more than somewhat of his dolls.

He especially thinks plenty of Miss Billy Perry, and sends her fur coats, and diamond rings, and one thing and another, which she sends back to him at once, because it seems she does not take presents from guys. This is considered most surprising all along Broadway, but people figure the chances are she has some other angle.

Anyway, this does not keep Dave the Dude from liking her just the same, and so she is considered his doll by one and all, and is respected accordingly until this Waldo Winchester comes along.

It happens that he comes along while Dave the Dude is off in the Modoc on a little run-down to the Bahamas to get some goods for his business, such as Scotch and champagne, and by the time Dave gets back, Miss Billy Perry and Waldo Winchester are at the stage where they sit in corners between her numbers and hold hands.

Of course nobody tells Dave the Dude about this, because they do not wish to get him excited. Not even Miss

Missouri Martin tells him, which is most unusual because Miss Missouri Martin, who is sometimes called "Mizzoo" for short, tells everything she knows as soon as she knows it, which is very often before it happens.

You see, the idea is when Dave the Dude is excited he may blow somebody's brains out, and the chances are it will be nobody's brains but Waldo Winchester's, although some claim that Waldo Winchester has no brains or he will not be hanging around Dave the Dude's doll.

I know Dave is very, very fond of Miss Billy Perry, because I hear him talk to her several times, and he is most polite to her and never gets out of line in her company by using cuss words, or anything like this. Furthermore, one night when One-eyed Solly Abrahams is a little stewed up he refers to Miss Billy Perry as a broad, meaning no harm whatever, for this is the way many of the boys speak of the dolls.

But right away Dave the Dude reaches across the table and bops One-eyed Solly right in the mouth, so everybody knows from then on that Dave thinks well of Miss Billy Perry. Of course Dave is always thinking fairly well of some doll as far as this goes, but it is seldom he gets to bopping guys in the mouth over them.

Well, one night what happens but Dave the Dude walks into the Sixteen Hundred Club, and there in the entrance, what does he see but this Waldo Winchester and Miss Billy Perry kissing each other back and forth friendly. Right away Dave reaches for the old equalizer to shoot Waldo Winchester, but it seems Dave does not happen to have the old equalizer with him, not expecting to have to shoot anybody this particular evening.

So Dave the Dude walks over and, as Waldo Winchester hears him coming and lets go his strangle hold on Miss Billy Perry, Dave nails him with a big right hand on the chin. I will say for Dave the Dude that he is a fair puncher with his right hand, though his left is not so good, and he knocks Waldo Winchester bowlegged. In fact, Waldo folds right up on the floor.

Well, Miss Billy Perry lets out a screech you can hear clear to the Battery and runs over to where Waldo Winchester lights, and falls on top of him squalling very loud. All anybody can make out of what she says is that Dave the Dude is a big bum, although Dave is not so big, at that, and that she loves Waldo Winchester.

Dave walks over and starts to give Waldo Winchester the leather, which is considered customary in such cases, but he seems to change his mind, and instead of booting Waldo around, Dave turns and walks out of the joint looking very black and mad, and the next anybody hears of him he is over in the Chicken Club doing plenty of drinking.

This is regarded as a very bad sign indeed, because while everybody goes to the Chicken Club now and then to give Tony Bertazzola, the owner, a friendly play, very few people care to do any drinking there, because Tony's liquor is not meant for anybody to drink except the customers.

Well, Miss Billy Perry gets Waldo Winchester on his pegs again, and wipes his chin off with her handkerchief, and by and by he is all okay except for a big lump on his chin. And all the time she is telling Waldo Winchester what a big bum Dave the Dude is, although afterwards Miss Missouri Martin gets hold of Miss Billy Perry and puts the blast on her plenty for chasing a two-handed spender such as Dave the Dude out of the joint.

"You are nothing but a little sap," Miss Missouri Martin tells Miss Billy Perry. "You cannot get the right time off this newspaper guy, while everybody knows Dave the Dude is a very fast man with a dollar."

"But I love Mr. Winchester," says Miss Billy Perry. "He's so romantic. He is not a bootlegger and a gunman like Dave the Dude. He puts lovely pieces in the paper about me, and he is a gentleman at all times."

Now of course Miss Missouri Martin is not in a position to argue about gentlemen, because she meets very few in the Sixteen Hundred Club and anyway, she does not wish to make Waldo Winchester mad as he is apt to turn around and put pieces in his paper that will be a knock to the joint, so she lets the matter drop.

Miss Billy Perry and Waldo Winchester go on holding hands between her numbers, and maybe kissing each other now and then, as young people are liable to do, and Dave the Dude plays the chill for the Sixteen Hundred Club and everything seems to be all right. Naturally we are all very glad there is no more trouble over the proposition, because the best Dave can get is the worst of it in a jam with a newspaper guy.

Personally, I figure Dave will soon find himself another doll and forget all about Miss Billy Perry, because now that I take another peek at her, I can see where she is just about the same as any other tap dancer, except that she is red-headed. Tap dancers are generally blackheads, but I do not know why.

Moosh, the doorman at the Sixteen Hundred Club, tells me Miss Missouri Martin keeps plugging for Dave the Dude with Miss Billy Perry in a quiet way, because he says he hears Miss Missouri Martin make the following crack one night to her: "Well, I do not see any Simple Simon on your lean and linger."

This is Miss Missouri Martin's way of saying she sees no diamond on Miss Billy Perry's finger, for Miss Missouri Martin is an old experienced doll, who figures if a guy loves a doll he will prove it with diamonds. Miss Missouri Martin has many diamonds herself, though how any guy can ever get himself heated up enough about Miss Missouri Martin to give her diamonds is more than I can see.

I am not a guy who goes around much, so I do not see Dave the Dude for a couple of weeks, but late one Sunday afternoon little Johnny McGowan, who is one of Dave's men, comes and says to me like this: "What do you think? Dave grabs the scribe a little while ago and is taking him out for an airing!"

Well, Johnny is so excited it is some time before I can get him cooled out enough to explain. It seems that Dave the Dude gets his biggest car out of the garage and sends his driver, Wop Joe, over to the *Item* office where Waldo Winchester works, with a message that Miss Billy Perry wishes to see Waldo right away at Miss Missouri Martin's apartment on Fifty-ninth Street.

Of course this message is nothing but the phonus bolonus, but Waldo drops in for it and gets in the car. Then Wop Joe drives him up to Miss Missouri Martin's apartment, and who gets in the car there but Dave the Dude.

And away they go.

Now this is very bad news indeed, because when Dave the Dude takes a guy out for an airing the guy very often does not come back. What happens to him I never ask, because the best a guy can get by asking questions in this man's town is a bust in the nose.

But I am much worried over this proposition, because I like Dave the Dude, and I know that taking a newspaper guy like Waldo Winchester out for an airing is apt to cause talk, especially if he does not come back. The other guys that Dave the Dude takes out for airings do not mean much in particular, but here is a guy who may produce trouble, even if he is a sucker, on account of being connected with a newspaper.

I know enough about newspapers to know that by and by the editor or somebody will be around wishing to know where Waldo Winchester's pieces about Broadway are, and if there are no pieces from Waldo Winchester, the editor will wish to know why. Finally it will get around to where other people will wish to know, and after a while many people will be running around saying: "Where is Waldo Winchester?"

And if enough people in this town get to running around saying where is So-and-so, it becomes a great mystery and the newspapers hop on the cops and the cops hop on everybody, and by and by there is so much heat in town that it is no place for a guy to be.

But what is to be done about this situation I do not know. Personally, it strikes me as very bad indeed, and while Johnny goes away to do a little telephoning, I am trying to think up some place to go where people will see me, and remember afterwards that I am there in case it is necessary for them to remember.

Finally Johnny comes back, very excited, and says: "Hey, the Dude is up at the Woodcock Inn on the Pelham Parkway, and he is sending out the word for one and all to come at once. Good Time Charley Bernstein just gets the wire and tells me. Something is doing. The rest of the mob are on their way, so let us be moving."

But here is an invitation which does not strike me as a good thing at all. The way I look at it, Dave the Dude is no company for a guy like me at this time. The chances are he either does something to Waldo Winchester already, or is getting ready to do something to him which I wish no part of.

Personally, I have nothing against newspaper guys, not even the ones who write pieces about Broadway. If Dave the Dude wishes to do something to Waldo Winchester, all right, but what is the sense of bringing outsiders into it? But the next thing I now, I am in Johnny McGowan's roadster, and he is zipping along very fast indeed, paying practically no attention to traffic lights or anything else.

As we go busting out the Concourse, I get to thinking the situation over, and I figure that Dave the Dude probably keeps thinking about Miss Billy Perry, and drinking liquor such as they sell in the Chicken Club, until finally he blows his topper. The way I look at it, only a guy who is off his nut will think of taking a newspaper guy out for an airing over a doll, when dolls are a dime a dozen in this man's town.

Still, I remember reading in the papers about a lot of

different guys who are considered very sensible until they get tangled up with a doll, and maybe loving her, and the first thing anybody knows they hop out of windows, or shoot themselves, or somebody else, and I can see where even a guy like Dave the Dude may go daffy over a doll.

I can see that little Johnny McGowan is worried, too, but he does not say much, and we pull up in front of the Woodcock Inn in no time whatever, to find a lot of other cars there ahead of us, some of which I recognize as belonging to different parties.

The Woodcock Inn is what is called a roadhouse, and is run by Big Nig Skolsky, a very nice man indeed, and a friend of everybody's. It stands back a piece off the Pelham Parkway and is a very pleasant place to go to, what with Nig having a good band and a floor show with a lot of fair-looking dolls, and everything else a man can wish for a good time. It gets a nice play from nice people, although Nig's liquor is nothing extra.

Personally, I never go there much, because I do not care for roadhouses, but it is a great spot for Dave the Dude when he is pitching parties, or even when he is only drinking single-handed. There is a lot of racket in the joint as we drive up, and who comes out to meet us but Dave the Dude himself with a big hello. His face is very red, and he seems heated up no little, but he does not look like a guy who is meaning any harm to anybody, especially a newspaper guy.

"Come in, guys!" Dave the Dude yells. "Come right in!"

So we go in, and the place is full of people sitting at

tables, or out on the floor dancing, and I see Miss Missouri Martin with all her diamonds hanging from her in different places, and Good Time Charley Bernstein, and Feet Samuels, and Tony Bertazzola, and Skeets Boliver, and Nick the Greek, and Rochester Red, and a lot of other guys and dolls from around and about.

In fact, it looks as if everybody from all the joints on Broadway are present, including Miss Billy Perry, who is all dressed up in white and is lugging a big bundle of orchids and so forth, and who is giggling and smiling and shaking hands and going on generally. And finally I see Waldo Winchester, the scribe, sitting at a ringside table all by himself, but there is nothing wrong with him as far as I can see. I mean, he seems to be all in one piece so far.

"Dave," I say to Dave the Dude, very quiet, "what is coming off here? You know a guy cannot be too careful what he does around this town, and I will hate to see you tangled up in anything right now."

"Why," Dave says, "what are you talking about? Nothing is coming off here but a wedding, and it is going to be the best wedding anybody on Broadway ever sees. We are waiting for the preacher now."

"You mean somebody is going to be married?" I ask, being somewhat confused.

"Certainly," Dave the Dude says. "What do you think? What is the idea of a wedding, anyway?"

"Who is going to be married?" I ask.

"Nobody but Billy and the scribe," Dave says. "This is the greatest thing I ever do in my life. I run into Billy the other night and she is crying her eyes out because she loves this scribe and wishes to marry him, but it seems the scribe has nothing he can use for money. So I tell Billy to leave it to me, because you know I love her myself so much I wish to see her happy at all times, even if she has to marry to be that way.

"So I frame this wedding party, and after they are married I am going to stake them to a few G's so they can get a good running start," Dave says. "But I do not tell the scribe and I do not let Billy tell him as I wish it to be a big surprise to him. I kidnap him this afternoon and bring him out here and he is scared half to death thinking I am going to scrag him.

"In fact," Dave says, "I never see a guy so scared. He is still so scared nothing seems to cheer him up. Go over and tell him to shake himself together, because nothing but happiness for him is coming off here."

Well, I wish to say I am greatly relieved to think that Dave intends doing nothing worse to Waldo Winchester than getting him married up, so I go over to where Waldo is sitting. He certainly looks somewhat alarmed. He is all in a huddle with himself, and he has what you call a vacant stare in his eyes. I can see that he is indeed frightened, so I give him a jolly slap on the back and I say: "Congratulations, pal! Cheer up, the worst is yet to come!"

"You bet it is," Waldo Winchester says, his voice so solemn I am greatly surprised.

"You are a fine-looking bridegroom," I say. "You look as if you are at a funeral instead of a wedding. Why do you not laugh ha-ha, and maybe take a dram or two and go to cutting up some?"

"Mister," says Waldo Winchester, "my wife is not going to care for me getting married to Miss Billy Perry."

"Your wife?" I say, much astonished. "What is this you are speaking of? How can you have any wife except Miss Billy Perry? This is great foolishness."

"I know," Waldo says, very sad. "I know. But I got a wife just the same, and she is going to be very nervous when she hears about this. My wife is very strict with me. My wife does not allow me to go around marrying people. My wife is Lola Sapola of the Rolling Sapolas, the acrobats, and I am married to her for five years. She is the strong lady who juggles the other four people in the act. My wife just gets back from a year's tour of the Interstate time, and she is at the Marx Hotel right this minute. I am upset by this proposition."

"Does Miss Billy Perry know about this wife?" I ask.

"No," he says. "No. She thinks I am single-o."

"But why do you not tell Dave the Dude you are already married when he brings you out here to marry you off to Miss Billy Perry?" I ask. "It seems to me a newspaper guy must know it is against the law for a guy to marry several different dolls unless he is a Turk, or some such."

"Well," Waldo says, "if I tell Dave the Dude I am married after taking his doll away from him, I am quite sure Dave will be very much excited, and maybe do something harmful to my health."

Now there is much in what the guy says, to be sure. I am inclined to think, myself, that Dave will be somewhat disturbed when he learns of this situation, especially when Miss Billy Perry starts in being unhappy about it.

But what is to be done I do not know, except maybe to let the wedding go on, and then when Waldo is out of reach of Dave, to put in a claim that he is insane, and that the marriage does not count. It is a sure thing I do not wish to be around when Dave the Dude hears Waldo is already married.

I am thinking that maybe I better take it on the lam out of there, when there is a great row at the door and I hear Dave the Dude yelling that the preacher arrives. He is a very nice-looking preacher, at that, though he seems somewhat surprised by the goings-on, especially when Miss Missouri Martin steps up and takes charge of him. Miss Missouri Martin tells him she is fond of preachers, and is quite used to them, because she is twice married by preachers, and twice by justices of the peace, and once by a ship's captain at sea.

By this time one and all present, except maybe myself and Waldo Winchester, and the preacher and maybe Miss Billy Perry, are somewhat corned. Waldo is still sitting at his table looking very sad and saying "Yes" and "No" to Miss Billy Perry whenever she skips past him, for Miss Billy Perry is too much pleasured up with happiness to stay long in one spot.

Dave the Dude is more corned than anybody else, because he has two or three days' running start on everybody. And when Dave the Dude is corned I wish to say that he is a very unreliable guy as to temper, and he is apt to explode right in your face any minute. But he seems to be getting a great bang out of the doings.

Well, by and by Nig Skolsky has the dance floor cleared, and then he moves out on the floor a sort of arch of very beautiful flowers. The idea seems to be that Miss Billy Perry and Waldo Winchester are to be married under this arch. I can see that Dave the Dude must put in several days planning this whole proposition, and it must cost him plenty of the old do-re-mi, especially as I see him showing Miss Missouri Martin a diamond ring as big as a cough drop.

"It is for the bride," Dave the Dude says. "The poor loogan she is marrying will never have enough dough to buy her such a rock, and she always wishes a big one. I get it off a guy who brings it in from Los Angeles. I am going to give the bride away myself in person, so how do I act, Mizzoo? I want Billy to have everything according to the book."

Well, while Miss Missouri Martin is trying to remember back to one of her weddings to tell him, I take another peek at Waldo Winchester to see how he is making out. I once see two guys go to the old warm squativoo up in Sing Sing, and I wish to say both are laughing heartily compared to Waldo Winchester at this moment.

Miss Billy Perry is sitting with him and the orchestra leader is calling his men dirty names because none of them can think of how "Oh, Promise Me" goes, when Dave the Dude yells: "Well, we are all set! Let the happy couple step forward!"

Miss Billy Perry bounces up and grabs Waldo Winchester by the arm and pulls him up out of his chair. After a peek at his face I am willing to lay six to five he does not make the arch. But he finally gets there with everybody laughing and clapping their hands, and the preacher comes forward, and Dave the Dude looks happier than I ever see him look before in his life as they all get together under the arch of flowers.

Well, all of a sudden there is a terrible racket at the front door of the Woodcock Inn, with some doll doing a lot of hollering in a deep voice that sounds like a man's, and naturally everybody turns and looks that way. The doorman, a guy by the name of Slugsy Sachs, who is a very hard man indeed, seems to be trying to keep somebody out, but pretty soon there is a heavy bump and Slugsy Sachs falls down, and in comes a doll about four feet high and five feet wide.

In fact, I never see such a wide doll. She looks all hammered down. Her face is almost as wide as her shoulders, and makes me think of a great big full moon. She comes in bounding-like, and I can see that she is all churned up about something. As she bounces in, I hear a gurgle, and I look around to see Waldo Winchester slumping down to the floor, almost dragging Miss Billy Perry with him.

Well, the wide doll walks right up to the bunch under the arch and says in a large bass voice: "Which one is Dave the Dude?"

"I am Dave the Dude," says Dave the Dude, stepping up. "What do you mean by busting in here like a walrus and gumming up our wedding?"

"So you are the guy who kidnaps my ever-loving husband to marry him off to this little red-headed pancake here, are you?" the wide doll says, looking at Dave the Dude, but pointing at Miss Billy Perry.

Well now, calling Miss Billy Perry a pancake to Dave the Dude is a very serious proposition, and Dave the

Dude gets very angry. He is usually rather polite to dolls, but you can see he does not care for the wide doll's manner whatever.

"Say, listen here," Dave the Dude says, "you better take a walk before somebody clips you. You must be drunk," he says. "Or daffy," he says. "What are you talking about, anyway?"

"You will see what I am talking about," the wide doll yells. "The guy on the floor there is my lawful husband. You probably frighten him to death, the poor dear. You kidnap him to marry this red-headed thing, and I am going to get you arrested as sure as my name is Lola Sapola, you simple-looking tramp!"

Naturally, everybody is greatly horrified at a doll using such language to Dave the Dude, because Dave is known to shoot guys for much less, but instead of doing something to the wide doll at once, Dave says: "What is this talk I hear? Who is married to who? Get out of here!" Dave says, grabbing the wide doll's arm.

Well, she makes out as if she is going to slap Dave in the face with her left hand, and Dave naturally pulls his kisser out of the way. But instead of doing anything with her left, Lola Sapola suddenly drives her right fist smack-dab into Dave the Dude's stomach, which naturally comes forward as his face goes back.

I wish to say I see many a body punch delivered in my life, but I never see a prettier one than this. What is more, Lola Sapola steps in with the punch, so there is plenty on it.

Now a guy who eats and drinks like Dave the Dude does cannot take them so good in the stomach, so Dave goes "oof," and sits down very hard on the dance floor, and as he is sitting there he is fumbling in his pants pockets for the old equalizer, so everybody around tears for cover except Lola Sapola, and Miss Billy Perry, and Waldo Winchester.

But before he can get his pistol out, Lola Sapola reaches down and grabs Dave by the collar and hoists him to his feet. She lets go her hold on him, leaving Dave standing on his pins but teetering around somewhat, and then she drives her right hand to Dave's stomach a second time.

The punch drops Dave again, and Lola steps up to him as if she is going to give him the foot. But she only gathers up Waldo Winchester from off the floor and slings him across her shoulder like he is a sack of oats, and starts for the door. Dave the Dude sits up on the floor again and by this time he has the old equalizer in his duke.

"Only for me being a gentleman I will fill you full of slugs," he yells.

Lola Sapola never even looks back, because by this time she is petting Waldo Winchester's head and calling him loving names and saying what a shame it is for bad characters like Dave the Dude to be abusing her precious one. It all sounds to me as if Lola Sapola thinks well of Waldo Winchester.

Well, after she gets out of sight, Dave the Dude gets up off the floor and stands there looking at Miss Billy Perry, who is out to break all crying records. The rest of us come out from under cover, including the preacher, and we are wondering how mad Dave the Dude is going to be about the wedding being ruined. But Dave the Dude seems only disappointed and sad.

"Billy," he says to Miss Billy Perry, "I am mighty sorry you do not get your wedding. All I wish is for your happiness, but I do not believe you can ever be happy with this scribe if he also has to have his lion tamer around. As Cupid I am a total bust. This is the only nice thing I ever try to do in my whole life, and it is too bad it does not come off. Maybe if you wait until he can drown her, or something—"

"Dave," says Miss Billy Perry, dropping so many tears that she seems to finally wash herself right into Dave the Dude's arms, "I will never, never be happy with such a guy as Waldo Winchester. I can see now you are the only man for me."

"Well, well, well," Dave the Dude says, cheering right up. "Where is the preacher? Bring on the preacher and let us have our wedding anyway."

I see Mr. and Mrs. Dave the Dude the other day, and they seem very happy. But you never can tell about married people, so of course I am never going to let on to Dave the Dude that I am the one who telephones Lola Sapola at the Marx Hotel, because maybe I do not do Dave any too much of a favor, at that.

The Snatching of Bookie Bob

Now it comes on the spring of 1931, after a long hard winter, and times are very tough indeed, what with the stock market going all to pieces, and banks busting right and left, and the law getting very nasty about this and that, and one thing and another, and many citizens of this town are compelled to do the best they can.

There is very little scratch anywhere and along Broadway many citizens are wearing their last year's clothes and have practically nothing to bet on the races or anything else, and it is a condition that will touch anybody's heart.

So I am not surprised to hear rumors that the snatching of certain parties is going on in spots, because while snatching is by no means a high-class business, and is even considered somewhat illegal, it is something to tide over the hard times.

Furthermore, I am not surprised to hear that this snatching is being done by a character by the name of Harry the Horse, who comes from Brooklyn, and who is a character who does not care much what sort of business he is in, and who is mobbed up with other characters from Brooklyn such as Spanish John and Little Isadore, who do not care what sort of business they are in, either.

In fact, Harry the Horse and Spanish John and Little Isadore are very hard characters in every respect, and there is considerable indignation expressed around and about when they move over from Brooklyn into Manhattan and start snatching, because the citizens of Manhattan feel that if there is any snatching done in their territory, they are entitled to do it themselves.

But Harry the Horse and Spanish John and Little Isadore pay no attention whatever to local sentiment and go on the snatch on a pretty fair scale, and by and by I am hearing rumors of some very nice scores. These scores are not extra large scores, to be sure, but they are enough to keep the wolf from the door, and in fact from three different doors, and before long Harry the Horse and Spanish John and Little Isadore are around the race tracks betting on the horses, because if there is one thing they are all very fond of, it is betting on the horses.

Now many citizens have the wrong idea entirely of the snatching business. Many citizens think that all there is to snatching is to round up the party who is to be snatched and then just snatch him, putting him away somewhere until his family or friends dig up enough scratch to pay whatever price the snatchers are asking. Very few citizens understand that the snatching business must be well organized and very systematic.

In the first place, if you are going to do any snatching, you cannot snatch just anybody. You must know who you are snatching, because naturally it is no good snatching somebody who does not have any scratch to settle with. And you cannot tell by the way a party looks or how he lives in town if he has any scratch, because many a party who is around in automobiles, and wearing good clothes, and chucking quite a swell is nothing but the phonus bolonus and does not have any real scratch whatever.

So of course such a party is no good for snatching, and of course guys who are on the snatch cannot go around inquiring into bank accounts, or asking how much this and that party has in a safe-deposit vault, because such questions are apt to make citizens wonder why, and it is very dangerous to get citizens to wondering why about anything. So the only way guys who are on the snatch can find out about parties worth snatching is to make a connection with some guy who can put the finger on the right party.

The finger guy must know the party he fingers has plenty of ready scratch to begin with, and he must also know that this party is such a party as is not apt to make too much disturbance about being snatched, such as telling the gendarmes. The party may be a legitimate party, such as a business guy, but he will have reasons why he does not wish it to get out that he is snatched, and the finger must know these reasons. Maybe the party is not leading the right sort of life, such as running around with blondes when he has an ever-loving wife and seven children in Mamaroneck, but does not care to have his habits known, as is apt to happen if he is snatched, especially if he is snatched when he is with a blonde.

And sometimes the party is such a party as does not care to have matches run up and down the bottom of his feet, which often happens to parties who are snatched and who do not seem to wish to settle their bill promptly, because many parties are very ticklish on the bottom of the feet, especially if the matches are lit. On the other hand, maybe the party is not a legitimate guy, such as a party who is running a crap game or a swell speakeasy, or who has some other dodge he does not care to have come out, and who also does not care about having his feet tickled.

Such a party is very good indeed for the snatching business, because he is pretty apt to settle without any argument. And after a party settles one snatching, it will be considered very unethical for anybody else to snatch him again very soon, so he is not likely to make any fuss about the matter. The finger guy gets a commission of twenty-five per cent of the settlement, and one and all are satisfied and much fresh scratch comes into circulation, which is very good for the merchants. And while the party who is snatched may know who snatches him, one thing he never knows is who puts the finger on him, this being considered a trade secret.

I am talking to Waldo Winchester, the newspaper scribe, one night and something about the snatching business comes up, and Waldo Winchester is trying to tell me that it is one of the oldest dodges in the world, only Waldo calls it kidnaping, which is a title that will be very repulsive to guys who are on the snatch nowadays. Waldo Winchester claims that hundreds of years ago guys are around snatching parties, male and female, and holding them for ransom, and furthermore Waldo Winchester says they even snatch very little children and

Waldo states that it is all a very, very wicked proposition.

Well, I can see where Waldo is right about it being wicked to snatch dolls and little children, but of course no guys who are on the snatch nowadays will ever think of such a thing, because who is going to settle for a doll in these times when you can scarcely even give them away? As for little children, they are apt to be a great nuisance, because their mammas are sure to go running around hollering bloody murder about them, and furthermore little children are very dangerous, indeed, what with being apt to break out with measles and mumps and one thing and another any minute and give it to everybody in the neighborhood.

Well, anyway, knowing that Harry the Horse and Spanish John and Little Isadore are now on the snatch, I am by no means pleased to see them come along one Tuesday evening when I am standing at the corner of Fiftieth and Broadway, although of course I give them a very jolly hello, and say I hope and trust they are feeling nicely.

They stand there talking to me a few minutes, and I am very glad indeed that Johnny Brannigan, the strong-arm cop, does not happen along and see us, because it will give Johnny a very bad impression of me to see me in such company, even though I am not responsible for the company. But naturally I cannot haul off and walk away from this company at once, because Harry the Horse and Spanish John and Little Isadore may get the idea that I am playing the chill for them, and will feel hurt.

"Well," I say to Harry the Horse, "how are things going, Harry?"

"They are going no good," Harry says. "We do not beat a race in four days. In fact," he says, "we go overboard today. We are washed out. We owe every bookmaker at the track that will trust us, and now we are out trying to raise some scratch to pay off. A guy must pay his bookmaker no matter what."

Well, of course this is very true, indeed, because if a guy does not pay his bookmaker it will lower his business standing quite some, as the bookmaker is sure to go around putting the blast on him, so I am pleased to hear Harry the Horse mention such honorable principles.

"By the way," Harry says, "do you know a guy by the name of Bookie Bob?"

Now I do not know Bookie Bob personally, but of course I know who Bookie Bob is, and so does everybody else in this town that ever goes to a race track, because Bookie Bob is the biggest bookmaker around and about, and has plenty of scratch. Furthermore, it is the opinion of one and all that Bookie Bob will die with this scratch, because he is considered a very close guy with his scratch. In fact, Bookie Bob is considered closer than a dead heat.

He is a short fat guy with a bald head, and his head is always shaking a little from side to side, which some say is a touch of palsy, but which most citizens believe comes of Bookie Bob shaking his head "No" to guys asking for credit in betting on the races. He has an ever-loving wife, who is a very quiet little old doll with gray hair and a very sad look in her eyes, but nobody can blame her for this when they figure that she lives with Bookie Bob for many years.

I often see Bookie Bob and his ever-loving wife eating in different joints along in the Forties, because they seem to have no home except a hotel, and many a time I hear Bookie Bob giving her a going-over about something or other, and generally it is about the price of something she orders to eat, so I judge Bookie Bob is as tough with his ever-loving wife about scratch as he is with everybody else. In fact, I hear him bawling her out one night because she has on a new hat which she says costs her six bucks, and Bookie Bob wishes to know if she is trying to ruin him with her extravagances.

But of course I am not criticizing Bookie Bob for squawking about the hat, because for all I know six bucks may be too much for a doll to pay for a hat, at that. And furthermore, maybe Bookie Bob has the right idea about keeping down his ever-loving wife's appetite, because I know many a guy in this town who is practically ruined by dolls eating too much on him.

"Well," I say to Harry the Horse, "if Bookie Bob is one of the bookmakers you owe, I am greatly surprised to see that you seem to have both eyes in your head, because I never before hear of Bookie Bob letting anybody owe him without giving him at least one of their eyes for security. In fact," I say, "Bookie Bob is such a guy as will not give you the right time if he has two watches."

"No," Harry the Horse says, "we do not owe Bookie Bob. But," he says, "he will be owing us before long. We are going to put the snatch on Bookie Bob."

Well, this is most disquieting news to me, not because I care if they snatch Bookie Bob or not, but because somebody may see me talking to them who will remember about it when Bookie Bob is snatched. But of course it will not be good policy for me to show Harry the Horse and Spanish John and Little Isadore that I am nervous, so I only speak as follows:

"Harry," I say, "every man knows his own business best, and I judge you know what you are doing. But," I say, "you are snatching a hard guy when you snatch Bookie Bob. A very hard guy, indeed. In fact," I say, "I hear the softest thing about him is his front teeth, so it may be very difficult for you to get him to settle after you snatch him."

"No," Harry the Horse says, "we will have no trouble about it. Our finger gives us Bookie Bob's hole card, and it is a most surprising thing, indeed. But," Harry the Horse says, "you come upon many surprising things in human nature when you are on the snatch. Bookie Bob's hole card is his ever-loving wife's opinion of him.

"You see," Harry the Horse says, "Bookie Bob has been putting himself away with his ever-loving wife for years as a very important guy in this town, with much power and influence, although of course Bookie Bob knows very well he stands about as good as a broken leg. In fact," Harry the Horse says, "Bookie Bob figures that his ever-loving wife is the only one in the world who looks on him as a big guy, and he will sacrifice even his scratch, or anyway some of it, rather than let her know that guys have such little respect for him as to put the snatch on him. It is what you call psychology," Harry the Horse says.

Well, this does not make good sense to me, and I am

thinking to myself that the psychology that Harry the Horse really figures to work out nice on Bookie Bob is tickling his feet with matches, but I am not anxious to stand there arguing about it, and pretty soon I bid them all good evening, very polite, and take the wind, and I do not see Harry the Horse or Spanish John or Little Isadore again for a month.

In the meantime, I hear gossip here and there that Bookie Bob is missing for several days, and when he finally shows up again he gives it out that he is very sick during his absence, but I can put two and two together as well as anybody in this town and I figure that Bookie Bob is snatched by Harry the Horse and Spanish John and Little Isadore, and the chances are it costs him plenty.

So I am looking for Harry the Horse and Spanish John and Little Isadore to be around the race track with plenty of scratch and betting them higher than a cat's back, but they never show up, and what is more I hear they leave Manhattan and are back in Brooklyn working every day handling beer. Naturally this is very surprising to me, because the way things are running, beer is a tough dodge just now, and there is very little profit in same, and I figure that with the scratch they must make off Bookie Bob, Harry the Horse and Spanish John and Little Isadore have a right to be taking things easy.

Now one night I am in Good Time Charley Bernstein's little speak in Forty-eighth Street, talking of this and that with Charley, when in comes Harry the Horse looking very weary and by no means prosperous. Naturally I give him a large hello, and by and by we get to gabbing together and I ask him whatever becomes of the Bookie Bob matter, and Harry the Horse tells me as follows:

Yes [Harry the Horse says], we snatch Bookie Bob all right. In fact, we snatch him the very next night after we are talking to you, or on a Wednesday night. Our finger tells us Bookie Bob is going to a wake over in his old neighborhood on Tenth Avenue, near Thirty-eighth Street, and this is where we pick him up.

He is leaving the place in his car along about midnight, and of course Bookie Bob is alone as he seldom lets anybody ride with him because of the wear and tear on his car cushions, and Little Isadore swings our flivver in front of him and makes him stop. Naturally Bookie Bob is greatly surprised when I poke my head into his car and tell him I wish the pleasure of his company for a short time, and at first he is inclined to argue the matter, saying I must make a mistake, but I put the old convincer on him by letting him peek down the snozzle of my John Roscoe.

We lock his car and throw the keys away, and then we take Bookie Bob in our car and go to a certain spot on Eighth Avenue where we have a nice little apartment all ready. When we get there I tell Bookie Bob that he can call up anybody he wishes and state that the snatch is on him and that it will require twenty-five G's, cash money, to take it off, but of course I also tell Bookie Bob that he is not to mention where he is or something may happen to him.

Well, I will say one thing for Bookie Bob, although everybody is always weighing in the sacks on him and saying he is no good—he takes it like a gentleman, and very calm and businesslike.

Furthermore, he does not seem alarmed, as many citizens are when they find themselves in such a situation. He recognizes the justice of our claim at once, saying as follows:

"I will telephone my partner, Sam Salt," he says. "He is the only one I can think of who is apt to have such a sum as twenty-five G's cash money. But," he says, "if you gentlemen will pardon the question, because this is a new experience to me, how do I know everything will be okay for me after you get the scratch?"

"Why," I say to Bookie Bob, somewhat indignant, "it is well known to one and all in this town that my word is my bond. There are two things I am bound to do," I say, "and one is to keep my word in such a situation as this, and the other is to pay anything I owe a bookmaker, no matter what, for these are obligations of honor with me."

"Well," Bookie Bob says, "of course I do not know you gentlemen, and, in fact, I do not remember ever seeing any of you, although your face is somewhat familiar, but if you pay your bookmaker you are an honest guy, and one in a million. In fact," Bookie Bob says, "if I have all the scratch that is owing to me around this town, I will not be telephoning anybody for such a sum as twenty-five G's. I will have such a sum in my pants pocket for change."

Now Bookie Bob calls a certain number and talks to somebody there but he does not get Sam Salt, and he seems much disappointed when he hangs up the receiver again.

"This is a very tough break for me," he says. "Sam Salt goes to Atlantic City an hour ago on very important business and will not be back until tomorrow evening, and they do not know where he is to stay in Atlantic City. And," Bookie Bob says, "I cannot think of anybody else to call to get this scratch, especially anybody I will care to have know I am in this situation."

"Why not call your ever-loving wife?" I say. "Maybe she can dig up this kind of scratch."

"Say," Bookie Bob says, "you do not suppose I am chump enough to give my ever-loving wife twenty-five G's, belonging to me, do you? I give my ever-loving wife ten bucks per week for spending money," Bookie Bob says, "and this is enough scratch for any doll, especially when you figure I pay for her meals."

Well, there seems to be nothing we can do except wait until Sam Salt gets back, but we let Bookie Bob call his ever-loving wife, as Bookie Bob says he does not wish to have her worrying about his absence, and tells her a big lie about having to go to Jersey City to sit up with a sick Brother Elk.

Well, it is now nearly four o'clock in the morning, so we put Bookie Bob in a room with Little Isadore to sleep, although, personally, I consider making a guy sleep with Little Isadore very cruel treatment, and Spanish John and I take turns keeping awake and watching out that Bookie Bob does not take the air on us before paying us off. To tell the truth, Little Isadore and Spanish John are somewhat disappointed that Bookie Bob agrees to settle so promptly, because they are looking forward to tickling his feet with great relish.

Now Bookie Bob turns out to be very good company when he wakes up the next morning, because he knows a lot of race-track stories and plenty of scandal, and he keeps us much interested at breakfast. He talks along with us as if he knows us all his life, and he seems very nonchalant indeed, but the chances are he will not be so nonchalant if I tell him about Spanish John's thought.

Well, about noon Spanish John goes out of the apartment and comes back with a racing sheet, because he knows Little Isadore and I will be wishing to know what is running in different spots although we do not have anything to bet on these races, or any way of betting on them, because we are overboard with every bookmaker we know.

Now Bookie Bob is also much interested in the matter of what is running, especially at Belmont, and he is bending over the table with me and Spanish John and Little Isadore, looking at the sheet, when Spanish John speaks as follows:

"My goodness," Spanish John says, "a spot such as this fifth race with Questionnaire at four to five is like finding money in the street. I only wish I have a few bobs to bet on him at such a price," Spanish John says.

"Why," Bookie Bob says, very polite, "if you gentlemen wish to bet on these races I will gladly book to you. It is a good way to pass away the time while we are waiting for Sam Salt, unless you will rather play pinochle?"

"But," I say, "we have no scratch to play the races, at least not much."

"Well," Bookie Bob says, "I will take your markers, because I hear what you say about always paying your bookmaker, and you put yourself away with me as an honest guy, and these other gentlemen also impress me as honest guys."

Now what happens but we begin betting Bookie Bob on the different races, not only at Belmont, but at all the other tracks in the country, for Little Isadore and Spanish John and I are guys who like plenty of action when we start betting on the horses. We write out markers for whatever we wish to bet and hand them to Bookie Bob, and Bookie Bob sticks these markers in an inside pocket, and along in the late afternoon it looks as if he has a tumor on his chest.

We get the race results by phone off a poolroom downtown as fast as they come off, and also the prices, and it is a lot of fun, and Little Isadore and Spanish John and Bookie Bob and I are all little pals together until all the races are over and Bookie Bob takes out the markers and starts counting himself up.

It comes out then that I owe Bookie Bob ten G's, and Spanish John owes him six G's, and Little Isadore owes him four G's, as Little Isadore beats him a couple of races out west.

Well, about this time, Bookie Bob manages to get Sam Salt on the phone, and explains to Sam that he is to go to a certain safe-deposit box and get out twenty-five G's, and then wait until midnight and hire himself a taxicab and start riding around the block between Fifty-first and Fifty-second, from Eighth to Ninth Avenues, and to keep riding until somebody flags the cab and takes the scratch off him.

Naturally Sam Salt understands right away that the snatch is on Bookie Bob, and he agrees to do as he is told, but he says he cannot do it until the following night because he knows there is not twenty-five G's in the box and he will have to get the difference at the track the next day. So there we are with another day in the apartment and Spanish John and Little Isadore and I are just as well pleased because Bookie Bob has us hooked and we naturally wish to wiggle off.

But the next day is worse than ever. In all the years I am playing the horses I never have such a tough day, and Spanish John and Little Isadore are just as bad. In fact, we are all going so bad that Bookie Bob seems to feel sorry for us and often lays us a couple of points above the track prices, but it does no good. At the end of the day, I am in a total of twenty G's, while Spanish John owes fifteen, and Little Isadore fifteen, a total of fifty G's among the three of us. But we are never any hands to hold postmortems on bad days, so Little Isadore goes out to a delicatessen store and lugs in a lot of nice things to eat, and we have a fine dinner, and then we sit around with Bookie Bob telling stories, and even singing songs together until time to meet Sam Salt.

When it comes on midnight Spanish John goes off and lays for Sam, and gets a little valise off Sam Salt. Then Spanish John comes back to the apartment and we open the valise and the twenty-five G's are there okay, and we cut this scratch three ways.

Then I tell Bookie Bob he is free to go about his business, and good luck to him, at that, but Bookie Bob looks at me as if he is very much surprised, and hurt, and says to me like this:

"Well, gentlemen, thank you for your courtesy, but what about the scratch you owe me? What about these markers? Surely, gentlemen, you will pay your bookmaker?"

Well, of course we owe Bookie Bob these markers, all right, and of course a man must pay his bookmaker, no matter what, so I hand over my bit and Bookie Bob puts down something in a little notebook that he takes out of his kick.

Then Spanish John and Little Isadore hand over their dough, too, and Bookie Bob puts down something more in the little notebook.

"Now," Bookie Bob says, "I credit each of your accounts with these payments, but you gentlemen still owe me a matter of twenty-five G's over and above the twenty-five I credit you with, and I hope and trust you will make arrangements to settle this at once because," he says, "I do not care to extend such accommodations over any considerable period."

"But," I say, "we do not have any more scratch after paying you the twenty-five G's on account."

"Listen," Bookie Bob says, dropping his voice down to a whisper, "what about putting the snatch on my partner, Sam Salt, and I will wait over a couple of days with you and keep booking to you, and maybe you can pull yourselves out. But of course," Bookie Bob whispers, "I will be entitled to twenty-five per cent of the snatch for putting the finger on Sam for you."

But Spanish John and Little Isadore are sick and tired

of Bookie Bob and will not listen to staying in the apartment any longer, because they say he is a jinx to them and they cannot beat him in any manner, shape or form. Furthermore, I am personally anxious to get away because something Bookie Bob says reminds me of something.

It reminds me that besides the scratch we owe him, we forget to take out six G's two-fifty for the party who puts the finger on Bookie Bob for us, and this is a very serious matter indeed, because everybody will tell you that failing to pay a finger is considered a very dirty trick. Furthermore, if it gets around that you fail to pay a finger, nobody else will ever finger for you.

So [Harry the Horse says] we quit the snatching business because there is no use continuing while this obligation is outstanding against us, and we go back to Brooklyn to earn enough scratch to pay our just debts.

We are paying off Bookie Bob's IOU a little at a time, because we do not wish to ever have anybody say we welsh on a bookmaker, and furthermore we are paying off the six G's two-fifty commission we owe our finger.

And while it is tough going, I am glad to say our honest effort is doing somebody a little good, because I see Bookie Bob's ever-loving wife the other night all dressed up in new clothes, very happy indeed.

And while a guy is telling me she is looking so happy because she gets a large legacy from an uncle who dies in Switzerland, and is now independent of Bookie Bob, I only hope and trust [Harry the Horse says] that it never gets out that our finger in this case is nobody but Bookie Bob's ever-loving wife.

The Lily of St. Pierre

There are four of us sitting in Good Time Charley Bernstein's little joint in Forty-eighth Street one Tuesday morning about four o'clock, doing a bit of quartet singing, very low, so as not to disturb the copper on the beat outside, a very good guy by the name of Carrigan, who likes to get his rest at such an hour.

Good Time Charley's little joint is called the Crystal Room, although of course there is no crystal whatever in the room, but only twelve tables, and twelve hostesses, because Good Time Charley believes in his customers having plenty of social life.

So he has one hostess to a table, and if there are twelve different customers, which is very seldom, each customer has a hostess to talk with. And if there is only one customer, he has all twelve hostesses to gab with and buy drinks for, and no customer can ever go away claiming he is lonesome in Good Time Charley's.

Personally, I will not give you a nickel to talk with Good Time Charley's hostesses, one at a time or all together, because none of them are anything much to look at, and I figure they must be all pretty dumb or they will not be working as hostesses in Good Time Charley's little joint. I happen to speak of this to Good Time Charley, and he admits that I may be right, but he says it is very difficult to get any Peggy Joyces for twenty-five bobs per week.

Of course I never buy any drinks in Good Time Charley's for hostesses, or anybody else, and especially for myself, because I am a personal friend of Good Time Charley's, and he will not sell me any drinks even if I wish to buy any, which is unlikely, as Good Time Charley figures that anybody who buys drinks in his place is apt to drink these drinks, and Charley does not care to see any of his personal friends drinking drinks in his place. If one of his personal friends wishes to buy a drink, Charley always sends him to Jack Fogarty's little speak down the street, and in fact Charley will generally go with him.

So I only go to Good Time Charley's to talk with him, and to sing in quartet with him. There are very seldom any customers in Good Time Charley's until along about five o'clock in the morning after all the other places are closed, and then it is sometimes a very hot spot indeed, and it is no place to sing in quartet at such hours, because everybody around always wishes to join in, and it ruins the harmony. But just before five o'clock it is okay, as only the hostesses are there, and of course none of them dast to join in our singing, or Good Time Charley will run them plumb out of the joint.

If there is one thing I love to do more than anything else, it is to sing in quartet. I sing baritone, and I wish to say I sing a very fine baritone, at that. And what we are singing—this morning I am talking about—is a lot of songs such as "Little White Lies," and "The Old Oaken Bucket," and "My Dad's Dinner Pail," and "Chloe," and

"Melancholy Baby," and I do not know what else, including "Home, Sweet Home," although we do not go so good on this because nobody remembers all the words, and half the time we are all just going ho-hum-hum-ho-hum-hum, like guys nearly always do when they are singing "Home, Sweet Home."

Also we sing "I Can't Give You Anything but Love, Baby," which is a very fine song for quartet singing, especially when you have a guy singing a nice bass, such as Good Time Charley, who can come in on every line with a big bum-bum, like this:

I can't give you anything but luh-huh-vuh,
Bay-hay-bee!
BUM-BUM!

I am the one who holds these last words, such as love, and baby, and you can hear my fine baritone very far indeed, especially when I give a little extra roll like bay-hay-ay-ay-BEE! Then when Good Time Charley comes in with his old bum-bum, it is worth going a long way to hear.

Well, naturally, we finally get around to torch songs, as guys who are singing in quartet are bound to do, especially at four o'clock in the morning, a torch song being a song which guys sing when they have the big burned-up feeling inside themselves over a battle with their dolls.

When a guy has a battle with his doll, such as his sweetheart, or even his ever-loving wife, he certainly feels burned up inside himself, and can scarcely think of anything much. In fact, I know guys who are carrying the torch to walk ten miles and never know they go an inch. It is surprising how much ground a guy can cover just walking around and about, wondering if his doll is out with some other guy, and everybody knows that at four o'clock in the morning the torch is hotter than at any other time of the day.

Good Time Charley, who is carrying a torch longer than anybody else on Broadway, which is nearly a year, or ever since his doll, Big Marge, gives him the wind for a rich Cuban, starts up a torch song by Tommy Lyman, which goes as follows, very, very slow, and sad:

Gee, but it's tough
When the gang's gone home.
Out on the corner
You stand alone.

Of course there is no spot in this song for Good Time Charley's bum-bum, but it gives me a great chance with my fine baritone, especially when I come to the line that says Gee, I wish I had my old gal back again.

I do not say I can make people bust out crying and give me money with this song like I see Tommy Lyman do in night clubs, but then Tommy is a professional singer, besides writing this song for himself, so naturally he figures to do a little better with it than me. But I wish to say it is nothing for me to make five or six of the hostesses in Good Time Charley's cry all over the joint when I hit this line about Gee, I wish I had my old gal back again, and making five or six hostesses out of twelve cry is a fair average anywhere, and especially Good Time Charley's hostesses.

Well, all of a sudden who comes popping into Good Time Charley's by way of the front door, looking here and there, and around and about, but Jack O'Hearts, and he no sooner pokes his snozzle into the joint than a guy by the name of Louie the Lug, who is singing a very fair tenor with us, jumps up and heads for the back door.

But just as he gets to the door, Jack O'Hearts outs with the old equalizer and goes whangity-whang-whang at Louie the Lug. As a general proposition, Jack O'Hearts is a fair kind of a shot, but all he does to Louie the Lug is to knock his right ear off. Then Louie gets the back door open and takes it on the lam through an areaway, but not before Jack O'Hearts gets one more crack at him, and it is this last crack which brings Louie down half an hour later on Broadway, where a copper finds him and sends him to the Polyclinic.

Personally, I do not see Louie's ear knocked off, because by the second shot I am out the front door, and on my way down Forty-eighth Street, but they tell me about it afterwards.

I never know Jack O'Hearts is even mad at Louie, and I am wondering why he takes these shots at him, but I do not ask any questions, because when a guy goes around asking questions in this town people may get the idea he is such a guy as wishes to find things out.

Then the next night I run into Jack O'Hearts in Bobby's chophouse, putting on the hot meat, and he asks me to sit down and eat with him, so I sit down and order a hamburger steak, with plenty of onions, and while I am sitting there waiting for my hamburger, Jack O'Hearts says to me like this:

"I suppose," he says, "I owe you guys an apology for busting up your quartet when I toss those slugs at Louie the Lug?"

"Well," I say, "some considers it a dirty trick at that, Jack, but I figure you have a good reason, although I am wondering what it is."

"Louie the Lug is no good," Jack says.

Well, of course I know this much already, and so does everybody else in town for that matter, but I cannot figure what it has to do with Jack shooting off ears in this town for such a reason, or by and by there will be very few people left with ears.

"Let me tell you about Louie the Lug," Jack O'Hearts says. "You will see at once that my only mistake is I do not get my shots an inch to the left. I do not know what is the matter with me lately."

"Maybe you are letting go too quick," I say, very sympathetic, because I know how it annoys him to blow easy shots.

"Maybe," he says. "Anyway, the light in Charley's dump is no good. It is only an accident I get Louie with the last shot, and it is very sloppy work all around. But now I will tell you about Louie the Lug."

It is back in 1924 [Jack O'Hearts says] that I go to St. Pierre for the first time to look after some business matters for John the Boss, rest his soul, who is at this time one of the largest operators in high-grade merchandise in the United States, especially when it comes to

Scotch. Maybe you remember John the Boss, and the heat which develops around and about when he is scragged in Detroit? John the Boss is a very fine character, and it is a terrible blow to many citizens when he is scragged.

Now if you are never in St. Pierre, I wish to say you miss nothing much, because what is it but a little squirt of a burg sort of huddled up alongside some big rocks off Newfoundland, and very hard to get to, any way you go. Mostly you go there from Halifax by boat, though personally I go there in 1924 in John the Boss's schooner by the name of the *Maude,* in which we load a thousand cases of very nice merchandise for the Christmas trade.

The first time I see St. Pierre I will not give you eight cents for the whole layout, although of course it is very useful to parties in our line of business. It does not look like much, and it belongs to France, and nearly all the citizens speak French, because most of them are French, and it seems it is the custom of the French people to speak French no matter where they are, even away off up yonder among the fish.

Well, anyway, it is on this trip to St. Pierre in 1924 that I meet an old guy by the name of Doctor Armand Dorval, for what happens to me but I catch pneumonia, and it looks as if maybe I am a gone gosling, especially as there is no place in St. Pierre where a guy can have pneumonia with any comfort. But this Doctor Armand Dorval is a friend of John the Boss, and he takes me into his house and lets me be as sick there as I please, while he does his best to doctor me up.

Now this Doctor Armand Dorval is an old Frenchman

with whiskers, and he has a little granddaughter by the name of Lily, who is maybe twelve years old at the time I am talking about, with her hair hanging down her back in two braids. It seems her papa, who is Doctor Armand's son, goes out one day looking for cod on the Grand Banks when Lily is nothing but a baby, and never comes back, and then her mamma dies, so old Doc raises up Lily and is very fond of her indeed.

They live alone in the house where I am sick with this pneumonia, and it is a nice, quiet little house and very old-fashioned, with a good view of the fishing boats, if you care for fishing boats. In fact, it is the quietest place I am ever in in my life, and the only place I ever know any real peace. A big fat old doll who does not talk English comes in every day to look after things for Doctor Armand and Lily, because it seems Lily is not old enough to keep house as yet, although she makes quite a nurse for me.

Lily talks English very good, and she is always bringing me things, and sitting by my bed and chewing the rag with me about this and that, and sometimes she reads to me out of a book which is called *Alice in Wonderland*, and which is nothing but a pack of lies, but very interesting in spots. Furthermore, Lily has a big, blond, dumb-looking doll by the name of Yvonne, which she makes me hold while she is reading to me, and I am very glad indeed that the *Maude* goes on back to the United States and there is no danger of any of the guys walking in on me while I am holding this doll, or they will think I blow my topper.

Finally, when I am able to sit up around the house of

an evening I play checkers with Lily, while old Doctor Armand Dorval sits back in a rocking chair, smoking a pipe and watching us, and sometimes I sing for her. I wish to say I sing a first-class tenor, and when I am in the war business in France with the Seventy-seventh Division I am always in great demand for singing a quartet. So I sing such songs to Lily as "There's a Long, Long Trail," and "Mademoiselle from Armentières," although of course when it comes to certain spots in this song I just go dum-dum-dee-dum and do not say the words right out.

By and by Lily gets to singing with me, and we sound very good together, especially when we sing the "Long, Long Trail," which Lily likes very much, and even old Doctor Armand joins in now and then, although his voice is very terrible. Anyway, Lily and me and Doctor Armand become very good pals indeed, and what is more I meet up with other citizens of St. Pierre and become friends with them, and they are by no means bad people to know, and it is certainly a nice thing to be able to walk up and down without being afraid every other guy you meet is going to chuck a slug at you, or a copper put the old sleeve on you and say that they wish to see you at headquarters.

Finally I get rid of this pneumonia and take the boat to Halifax, and I am greatly surprised to find that Doctor Armand and Lily are very sorry to see me go, because never before in my life do I leave a place where anybody is sorry to see me go.

But Doctor Armand seems very sad and shakes me by the hand over and over again, and what does Lily do but bust out crying, and the first thing I know I am feeling sad myself and wishing that I am not going. So I promise Doctor Armand I will come back some day to see him, and then Lily hauls off and gives me a big kiss right in the smush and this astonishes me so much that it is half an hour afterwards before I think to wipe it off.

Well, for the next few months I find myself pretty busy back in New York, what with one thing and another, and I do not have time to think much of Doctor Armand Dorval and Lily, and St. Pierre, but it comes along the summer of 1925, and I am all tired out from getting a slug in my chest in the run-in with Jerk Donovan's mob in Jersey, for I am now in beer and have no more truck with the boats.

But I get to thinking of St. Pierre and the quiet little house of Doctor Armand Dorval again, and how peaceful it is up there, and nothing will do but what I must pop off to Halifax, and pretty soon I am in St. Pierre once more. I take a raft of things for Lily with me, such as dolls, and handkerchiefs, and perfume, and a phonograph, and also a set of razors for Doctor Armand, although afterwards I am sorry I take these razors because I remember the old Doc does not shave and may take them as a hint I do not care for his whiskers. But as it turns out the Doc finds them very useful in operations, so the razors are a nice gift after all.

Well, I spend two peaceful weeks there again, walking up and down in the daytime and playing checkers and singing with Lily in the evening, and it is tough tearing myself away, especially as Doctor Armand Dorval looks very sad again and Lily bursts out crying, louder than before. So nearly every year after this I can hardly wait until I can get to St. Pierre for a vacation, and Doctor Armand Dorval's house is like my home, only more peaceful.

Now in the summer of 1928 I am in Halifax on my way to St. Pierre, when I run across Louie the Lug, and it seems Louie is a lammister out of Detroit on account of some job or other, and is broke, and does not know which way to turn. Personally, I always figure Louie a petty-larceny kind of guy, with no more moxie than a canary bird, but he always dresses well, and always has a fair line of guff, and some guys stand for him. Anyway, here he is in trouble, so what happens but I take him with me to St. Pierre, figuring he can lay dead there until things blow over.

Well, Lily and old Doctor Armand Dorval are certainly glad to see me, and I am just as glad to see them, especially Lily, for she is now maybe sixteen years old and as pretty a doll as ever steps in shoe leather, what with her long black hair, and her big black eyes, and a million dollars' worth of personality. Furthermore, by this time she swings a very mean skillet, indeed, and gets me up some very tasty fodder out of fish and one thing and another.

But somehow things are not like they used to be at St. Pierre with this guy Louie the Lug around, because he does not care for the place whatever, and goes roaming about very restless, and making cracks about the citizens, and especially the dolls, until one night I am compelled to tell him to keep his trap closed, although at that the dolls in St. Pierre, outside of Lily, are no such lookers as will get Ziegfeld heated up.

But even in the time when St. Pierre is headquarters for many citizens of the United States who are in the business of handling merchandise out of there, it is always sort of underhand that such citizens will never have any truck with the dolls at St. Pierre. This is partly because the dolls at St. Pierre never give the citizens of the United States a tumble, but more because we do not wish to get in any trouble around there, and if there is anything apt to cause trouble it is dolls.

Now I suppose if I have any brains I will see that Louie is playing the warm for Lily, but I never think of Lily as anything but a little doll with her hair in braids, and certainly not a doll such as a guy will start pitching to, especially a guy who calls himself one of the mob.

I notice Louie is always talking to Lily when he gets a chance, and sometimes he goes walking up and down with her, but I see nothing in this, because after all any guy is apt to get lonesome at St. Pierre and go walking up and down with anybody, even a little young doll. In fact, I never see Louie do anything that strikes me as out of line, except he tries to cut in on the singing between Lily and me, until I tell him one tenor at a time is enough in any singing combination. Personally, I consider Louie the Lug's tenor very flat, indeed.

Well, it comes time for me to go away, and I take Louie with me, because I do not wish him hanging around St. Pierre alone, especially as old Doctor Armand Dorval does not seem to care for him whatever, and while Lily seems as sad as ever to see me go I notice that for the first time she does not kiss me good-bye. But I figure this is fair enough, as she is now quite a young lady, and the chances are a little particular about who she kisses.

I leave Louie in Halifax and give him enough dough to go on to Denver, which is where he says he wishes to go, and I never see him again until the other night in Good Time Charley's. But almost a year later, when I happen to be in Montreal, I hear of him. I am standing in the lobby of the Mount Royal Hotel thinking of not much, when a guy by the name of Bob the Bookie, who is a hustler around the race tracks, gets to talking to me and mentions Louie's name. It brings back to me a memory of my last trip to St. Pierre, and I get to thinking that this is the longest stretch I ever go in several years without a visit there and of the different things that keep me from going.

I am not paying much attention to what Bob says because he is putting the blast on Louie for running away from an ever-loving wife and a couple of kids in Cleveland several years before, which is something I do not know about Louie, at that. Then I hear Bob saying like this:

"He is an awful rat any way you take him. Why, when he hops out of here two weeks ago, he leaves a little doll he brings with him from St. Pierre dying in a hospital without a nickel to her name. It is a sin and a shame."

"Wait a minute, Bob," I say, waking up all of a sudden. "Do you say a doll from St. Pierre? What-for looking kind of a doll, Bob?" I say.

"Why," Bob says, "she is black-haired, and very young, and he calls her Lily, or some such. He is knocking around Canada with her for quite a spell. She strikes me as a t.b., but Louie's dolls always look this way after he has them a while. I judge," Bob says, "that Louie does not feed them any too good."

Well, it is Lily Dorval, all right, but never do I see such a change in anybody as there is in the poor little doll I find lying on a bed in a charity ward in a Montreal hospital. She does not look to weigh more than fifty pounds, and her black eyes are sunk away back in her head, and she is in tough shape generally. But she knows me right off the bat and tries to smile at me.

I am in the money very good at this time, and I have Lily moved into a private room, and get her all the nurses the law allows, and the best croakers in Montreal, and flowers, and one thing and another, but one of the medicos tells me it is even money she will not last three weeks, and seven to five she does not go a month. Finally Lily tells me what happens, which is the same thing that happens to a million dolls before and will happen to a million dolls again. Louie never leaves Halifax, but cons her into coming over there to him, and she goes because she loves him, for this is the way dolls are, and personally I will never have them any other way.

"But," Lily whispers to me, "the bad, bad thing I do is to tell poor old Grandfather I am going to meet you, Jack O'Hearts, and marry you, because I know he does not like Louie and will never allow me to go to him. But he loves you, Jack O'Hearts, and he is so pleased in thinking you are to be his son. It is wrong to tell Grandfather this story, and wrong to use your name, and to keep writing him all this time making him think I am your wife, and with you, but I love Louie, and I wish Grandfather to be happy because he is very, very old. Do you understand, Jack O'Hearts?"

Now of course all this is very surprising news to me, indeed, and in fact I am quite flabbergasted, and as for understanding it, all I understand is she got a rotten deal from Louie the Lug and that old Doctor Armand Dorval is going to be all busted up if he hears what really happens. And thinking about this nice old man, and thinking of how the only place I ever know peace and quiet is now ruined, I am very angry with Louie the Lug.

But this is something to be taken up later, so I dismiss him from my mind, and go out and get me a marriage license and a priest, and have this priest marry me to Lily Dorval just two days before she looks up at me for the last time, and smiles a little smile, and then closes her eyes for good and all. I wish to say, however, that up to this time I have no more idea of getting myself a wife than I have of jumping out the window, which is practically no idea at all.

I take her body back to St. Pierre myself in person, and we bury her in a little cemetery there, with a big fog around and about, and the siren moaning away very sad, and old Doctor Armand Dorval whispers to me like this: "You will please to sing the song about the long trail, Jack O'Hearts."

So I stand there in the fog, the chances are looking like a big sap, and I sing as follows:

There's a long, long, trail a-winding
Into the land of my dreams,

Where the nightingale is singing,
And the white moon beams.

But I can get no farther than this, for something comes up in my throat, and I sit down by the grave of Mrs. Jack O'Hearts, who was Lily Dorval, and for the first time I remember I bust out crying.

So this is why I say Louie the Lug is no good.

Well, I am sitting there thinking that Jack O'Hearts is right about Louie, at that, when in comes Jack's chauffeur, a guy by the name of Fingers, and he steps up to Jack and says, very low: "Louie dies half an hour ago at the Polyclinic."

"What does he say before he goes?" Jack asks.

"Not a peep," Fingers says.

"Well," Jack O'Hearts says, "it is sloppy work, at that. I ought to get him the first crack. But maybe he has a chance to think a little of Lily Dorval."

Then he turns to me and says like this:

"You guys need not feel bad about losing your tenor, because," he says, "I will be glad to fill in for him at all times."

Personally I do not think Jack's tenor is as good as Louie the Lug's, especially when it comes to hitting the very high notes in such songs as "Sweet Adeline," because he does not hold them long enough to let Good Time Charley in with his bum-bum.

But of course this does not go if Jack O'Hearts hears it, as I am never sure he does not clip Louie the Lug just to get a place in our quartet, at that.

Hold 'Em Yale

What I am doing in New Haven on the day of a very large football game between the Harvards and the Yales is something which calls for quite a little explanation, because I am not such a guy as you will expect to find in New Haven at any time, and especially on the day of a large football game.

But there I am, and the reason I am there goes back to a Friday night when I am sitting in Mindy's restaurant on Broadway thinking of very little except how I can get hold of a few potatoes to take care of the old overhead. And while I am sitting there, who comes in but Sam the Gonoph, who is a ticket speculator by trade, and who seems to be looking all around and about.

Well, Sam the Gonoph gets to talking to me, and it turns out that he is looking for a guy by the name of Gigolo Georgie, who is called Gigolo Georgie because he is always hanging around night clubs wearing a little mustache and white spats, and dancing with old dolls. In fact, Gigolo Georgie is nothing but a gentleman bum, and I am surprised that Sam the Gonoph is looking for him.

But it seems that the reason Sam the Gonoph wishes to find Gigolo Georgie is to give him a good punch in the snoot, because it seems that Gigolo Georgie promotes

Sam for several duckets to the large football game between the Harvards and the Yales to sell on commission, and never kicks back anything whatever to Sam. Naturally Sam considers Gigolo Georgie nothing but a rascal for doing such a thing to him, and Sam says he will find Gigolo Georgie and give him a going-over if it is the last act of his life.

Well, then, Sam explains to me that he has quite a few nice duckets for the large football game between the Harvards and the Yales and that he is taking a crew of guys with him to New Haven the next day to hustle these duckets, and what about me going along and helping to hustle these duckets and making a few bobs for myself, which is an invitation that sounds very pleasant to me, indeed.

Now of course it is very difficult for anybody to get nice duckets to a large football game between the Harvards and the Yales unless they are personally college guys, and Sam the Gonoph is by no means a college guy. In fact, the nearest Sam ever comes to a college is once when he is passing through the yard belonging to the Princetons, but Sam is on the fly at the time as a gendarme is after him, so he does not really see much of the college.

But every college guy is entitled to duckets to a large football game with which his college is connected, and it is really surprising how many college guys do not care to see large football games even after they get their duckets are worth I suppose this is because a college oph comes along offering them a few bobs more than the duckets are worth. I suppose this is because a college guy figures he can see a large football game when he is old, while many things are taking place around and about that it is necessary for him to see while he is young enough to really enjoy them, such as the Follies.

Anyway, many college guys are always willing to listen to reason when Sam the Gonoph comes around offering to buy their duckets, and then Sam takes these duckets and sells them to customers for maybe ten times the price the duckets call for, and in this way Sam does very good for himself.

I know Sam the Gonoph for maybe twenty years, and always he is speculating in duckets of one kind and another. Sometimes it is duckets for the world's series, and sometimes for big fights, and sometimes it is duckets for nothing but lawn-tennis games, although why anybody wishes to see such a thing as lawn tennis is always a very great mystery to Sam the Gonoph and everybody else.

But in all those years I see Sam dodging around under the feet of the crowds of these large events, or running through the special trains offering to buy or sell duckets, I never hear of Sam personally attending any of these events except maybe a baseball game, or a fight, for Sam has practically no interest in anything but a little profit on his duckets.

He is a short, chunky, black-looking guy with a big beezer, and he is always sweating even on a cold day, and he comes from down around Essex Street, on the lower East Side. Moreover, Sam the Gonoph's crew generally comes from the lower East Side, too, for as Sam goes along he makes plenty of potatoes for himself and branches out quite some, and has a lot of assistants hustling duckets around these different events.

When Sam is younger the cops consider him hard to get along with, and in fact his monicker, the Gonoph, comes from his young days down on the lower East Side, and I hear it is Yiddish for thief, but of course as Sam gets older and starts gathering plenty of potatoes, he will not think of stealing anything. At least not much, and especially if it is anything that is nailed down.

Well, anyway, I meet Sam the Gonoph and his crew at the information desk in Grand Central the next morning, and this is how I come to be in New Haven on the day of the large football game between the Harvards and the Yales.

For such a game as this, Sam has all his best hustlers, including such as Jew Louie, Nubbsy Taylor, Benny South Street and old Liverlips, and to look at these parties you will never suspect that they are topnotch ducket hustlers. The best you will figure them is a lot of guys who are not to be met up with in a dark alley, but then ducket-hustling is a rough-and-tumble dodge and it will scarcely be good policy to hire female impersonators.

Now while we are hustling these duckets out around the main gates of the Yale Bowl I notice a very beautiful little doll of maybe sixteen or seventeen standing around watching the crowd, and I can see she is waiting for somebody, as many dolls often do at football games. But I can also see that this little doll is very much worried as the crowd keeps going in, and it is getting on toward game time. In fact, by and by I can see this little doll has tears in her eyes and if there is anything I hate to see it is tears in a doll's eyes.

So finally I go over to her, and I say as follows: "What is eating you, little miss?"

"Oh," she says, "I am waiting for Elliot. He is to come up from New York and meet me here to take me to the game, but he is not here yet, and I am afraid something happens to him. Furthermore," she says, the tears in her eyes getting very large, indeed, "I am afraid I will miss the game because he has my ticket."

"Why," I say, "this is a very simple proposition. I will sell you a choice ducket for only a sawbuck, which is ten dollars in your language, and you are getting such a bargain only because the game is about to begin, and the market is going down."

"But," she says, "I do not have ten dollars. In fact, I have only fifty cents left in my purse, and this is worrying me very much, for what will I do if Elliot does not meet me? You see," she says, "I come from Miss Peevy's school at Worcester, and I only have enough money to pay my railroad fare here, and of course I cannot ask Miss Peevy for any money as I do not wish her to know I am going away."

Well, naturally all this is commencing to sound to me like a hard-luck story such as any doll is apt to tell, so I go on about my business because I figure she will next be trying to put the lug on me for a ducket, or maybe for her railroad fare back to Worcester, although generally dolls with hard-luck stories live in San Francisco.

She keeps on standing there, and I notice she is now crying more than somewhat, and I get to thinking to myself that she is about as cute a little doll as ever I see, although too young for anybody to be bothering much about. Furthermore, I get to thinking that maybe she is on the level, at that, with her story.

Well, by this time the crowd is nearly all in the Bowl, and only a few parties such as coppers and hustlers of one kind and another are left standing outside, and there is much cheering going on inside, when Sam the Gonoph comes up looking very much disgusted, and speaks as follows:

"What do you think?" Sam says. "I am left with seven duckets on my hands, and these guys around here will not pay as much as face value for them, and they stand me better than three bucks over that. Well," Sam says, "I am certainly not going to let them go for less than they call for if I have to eat them. What do you guys say we use these duckets ourselves and go in and see the game? Personally," Sam says, "I often wish to see one of these large football games just to find out what makes suckers willing to pay so much for duckets."

Well, this seems to strike one and all, including myself, as a great idea, because none of the rest of us ever see a large football game either, so we start for the gate, and as we pass the little doll who is still crying, I say to Sam the Gonoph like this:

"Listen, Sam," I say, "you have seven duckets, and we are only six, and here is a little doll who is stood up by her guy, and has no ducket, and no potatoes to buy one with, so what about taking her with us?"

Well, this is all right with Sam the Gonoph, and none of the others object, so I step up to the little doll and invite her to go with us, and right away she stops crying and begins smiling, and saying we are very kind indeed.

She gives Sam the Gonoph an extra big smile, and right away Sam is saying she is very cute, indeed, and then she gives old Liverlips an even bigger smile, and what is more she takes old Liverlips by the arm and walks with him, and old Liverlips is not only very much astonished, but very much pleased. In fact, old Liverlips begins stepping out very spry, and Liverlips is not such a guy as cares to have any part of dolls, young or old.

But while walking with old Liverlips, the little doll talks very friendly to Jew Louie and to Nubbsy Taylor and Benny South Street, and even to me, and by and by you will think to see us that we are all her uncles, although of course if this little doll really knows who she is with, the chances are she will start chucking faints one after the other.

Anybody can see that she has very little experience in this wicked old world, and in fact is somewhat rattleheaded, because she gabs away very freely about her personal business. In fact, before we are in the Bowl she lets it out that she runs away from Miss Peevy's school to elope with this Elliot, and she says the idea is they are to be married in Hartford after the game. In fact, she says Elliot wishes to go to Hartford and be married before the game.

"But," she says, "my brother John is playing substitute with the Yales today, and I cannot think of getting married to anybody before I see him play, although I am much in love with Elliot. He is a wonderful dancer," she says, "and very romantic. I meet him in Atlantic City last summer. Now we are eloping," she says, "because my father does not care for Elliot whatever. In fact, my father hates Elliot, although he only sees him once, and it is because he hates Elliot so that my father sends me to Miss Peevy's school in Worcester. She is an old pill. Do you not think my father is unreasonable?" she says.

Well, of course none of us have any ideas on such propositions as this, although old Liverlips tells the little doll he is with her right or wrong, and pretty soon we are inside the Bowl and sitting in seats as good as any in the joint. It seems we are on the Harvards' side of the field, although of course I will never know this if the little doll does not mention it.

She seems to know everything about this football business, and as soon as we sit down she tries to point out her brother playing substitute for the Yales, saying he is the fifth guy from the end among a bunch of guys sitting on a bench on the other side of the field all wrapped in blankets. But we cannot make much of him from where we sit, and anyway it does not look to me as if he has much of a job.

It seems we are right in the middle of all the Harvards and they are making an awful racket, what with yelling, and singing, and one thing and another, because it seems the game is going on when we get in, and that the Harvards are shoving the Yales around more than somewhat. So our little doll lets everybody know she is in favor of the Yales by yelling, "Hold 'em, Yale!"

Personally, I cannot tell which are the Harvards and which are the Yales at first, and Sam the Gonoph and the others are as dumb as I am, but she explains the Harvards are wearing the red shirts and the Yales the blue shirts, and by and by we are yelling for the Yales to hold 'em, too, although of course it is only on account of our little doll wishing the Yales to hold 'em, and not because any of us care one way or the other.

Well, it seems that the idea of a lot of guys and a little doll getting right among them and yelling for the Yales to hold 'em is very repulsive to the Harvards around us, although any of them must admit it is very good advice to the Yales, at that, and some of them start making cracks of one kind and another, especially at our little doll. The chances are they are very jealous because she is outyelling them, because I will say one thing for our little doll, she can yell about as loud as anybody I ever hear, male or female.

A couple of Harvards sitting in front of old Liverlips are imitating our little doll's voice, and making guys around them laugh very heartily, but all of a sudden these parties leave their seats and go away in great haste, their faces very pale, indeed, and I figure maybe they are both taken sick the same moment, but afterwards I learn that Liverlips takes a big shiv out of his pocket and opens it and tells them very confidentially that he is going to carve their ears off.

Naturally, I do not blame the Harvards for going away in great haste, for Liverlips is such a looking guy as you will figure to take great delight in carving off ears. Furthermore, Nubbsy Taylor and Benny South Street and Jew Louie and even Sam the Gonoph commence exchanging such glances with other Harvards around us who are making cracks at our little doll that presently there is almost a dead silence in our neighborhood, except for our little doll yelling, "Hold 'em, Yale!" You see by this time we are all very fond of our little doll because she is so cute-looking and has so much zing in her, and we do not wish anybody making cracks at her or at us either, and especially at us.

In fact, we are so fond of her that when she happens to mention that she is a little chilly, Jew Louie and Nubbsy Taylor slip around among the Harvards and come back with four steamer rugs, six mufflers, two pairs of gloves, and a thermos bottle full of hot coffee for her, and Jew Louie says if she wishes a mink coat to just say the word. But she already has a mink coat. Furthermore, Jew Louie brings her a big bunch of red flowers that he finds on a doll with one of the Harvards, and he is much disappointed when she says it is the wrong color for her.

Well, finally the game is over, and I do not remember much about it, although afterwards I hear that our little doll's brother John plays substitute for the Yales very good. But it seems that the Harvards win, and our little doll is very sad indeed about this, and is sitting there looking out over the field, which is now covered with guys dancing around as if they all suddenly go daffy, and it seems they are all Harvards, because there is really no reason for the Yales to do any dancing.

All of a sudden our little doll looks toward one end of the field, and says as follows: "Oh, they are going to take our goal posts!"

Sure enough, a lot of the Harvards are gathering around the posts at this end of the field, and are pulling and hauling at the posts, which seem to be very stout posts, indeed. Personally, I will not give you eight cents for these posts, but afterwards one of the Yales tells me that when a football team wins a game it is considered the proper caper for this team's boosters to grab the other guy's goal posts. But he is not able to tell me what good the posts are after they get them, and this is one thing that will always be a mystery to me.

Anyway, while we are watching the goings-on around the goal posts, our little doll says come on and jumps up and runs down an aisle and out on to the field, and into the crowd around the goal posts, so naturally we follow her. Somehow she manages to wiggle through the crowd of Harvards around the posts, and the next thing anybody knows she shins up one of the posts faster than you can say scat, and pretty soon is roosting out on the cross-bar between the posts like a chipmunk.

Afterwards she explains that her idea is the Harvards will not be ungentlemanly enough to pull down the goal posts with a lady roosting on them, but it seems these Harvards are no gentlemen, and keep on pulling, and the posts commence to teeter, and our little doll is teetering with them, although of course she is in no danger if she falls because she is sure to fall on the Harvards' noggins, and the way I look at it, the noggin of anybody who will be found giving any time to pulling down goal posts is apt to be soft enough to break a very long fall.

Now Sam the Gonoph and old Liverlips and Nubbsy Taylor and Benny South Street and Jew Louie and I reach the crowd around the goal posts at about the same time, and our little doll sees us from her roost and yells to us as follows: "Do not let them take our posts!"

Well, about this time one of the Harvards who seems to be about nine feet high reaches over six other guys and hits me on the chin and knocks me so far that when I pick myself up I am pretty well out of the way of everybody and have a chance to see what is going on.

Afterwards somebody tells me that the guy probably thinks I am one of the Yales coming to the rescue of the goal posts, but I wish to say I will always have a very low opinion of college guys, because I remember two other guys punch me as I am going through the air, unable to defend myself.

Now Sam the Gonoph and Nubbsy Taylor and Jew Louie and Benny South Street and old Liverlips somehow manage to ease their way through the crowd until they are under the goal posts, and our little doll is much pleased to see them, because the Harvards are now making the posts teeter more than somewhat with their pulling, and it looks as if the posts will go any minute.

Of course Sam the Gonoph does not wish any trouble with these parties, and he tries to speak nicely to the guys who are pulling at the posts, saying as follows:

"Listen," Sam says, "the little doll up there does not wish you to take these posts."

Well, maybe they do not hear Sam's words in the confusion, or if they do hear them they do not wish to pay any attention to them, for one of the Harvards mashes Sam's derby hat down over his eyes, and another smacks old Liverlips on the left ear, while Jew Louie and Nubbsy Taylor and Benny South Street are shoved around quite some.

"All right," Sam the Gonoph says, as soon as he can

pull his hat off his eyes, "all right, gentlemen, if you wish to play this way. Now, boys, let them have it!"

So Sam the Gonoph and Nubbsy Taylor and Jew Louie and Benny South Street and old Liverlips begin letting them have it, and what they let them have it with is not only their dukes, but with the good old difference in their dukes, because these guys are by no means suckers when it comes to a battle, and they all carry something in their pockets to put in their dukes in case of a fight, such as a dollar's worth of nickels rolled up tight.

Furthermore, they are using the old leather, kicking guys in the stomach when they are not able to hit them on the chin, and Liverlips is also using his noodle to good advantage, grabbing guys by their coat lapels and yanking them into him so he can butt them between the eyes with his noggin, and I wish to say that old Liverlips' noggin is a very dangerous weapon at all times.

Well, the ground around them is soon covered with Harvards, and it seems that some Yales are also mixed up with them, being Yales who think Sam the Gonoph and his guys are other Yales defending the goal posts, and wishing to help out. But of course Sam the Gonoph and his guys cannot tell the Yales from the Harvards, and do not have time to ask which is which, so they are just letting everybody have it who comes along. And while all this is going on our little doll is sitting up on the cross-bar and yelling plenty of encouragement to Sam and his guys.

Now it turns out that these Harvards are by no means soft touches in a scrabble such as this, and as fast as they are flattened they get up and keep belting away, and while the old experience is running for Sam the Gonoph and Jew Louie and Nubbsy Taylor and Benny South Street and old Liverlips early in the fight, the Harvards have youth in their favor.

Pretty soon the Harvards are knocking down Sam the Gonoph, then they start knocking down Nubbsy Taylor, and by and by they are knocking down Benny South Street and Jew Louie and Liverlips, and it is so much fun that the Harvards forget all about the goal posts. Of course as fast as Sam the Gonoph and his guys are knocked down they also get up, but the Harvards are too many for them, and they are getting an awful shellacking when the nine-foot guy who flattens me, and who is knocking down Sam the Gonoph so often he is becoming a great nuisance to Sam, sings out:

"Listen," he says, "these are game guys, even if they do go to Yale. Let us cease knocking them down," he says, "and give them a cheer."

So the Harvards knock down Sam the Gonoph and Nubbsy Taylor and Jew Louie and Benny South Street and old Liverlips just once more and then all the Harvards put their heads together and say rah-rah-rah, very loud, and go away, leaving the goal posts still standing, with our little doll still roosting on the cross-bar, although afterwards I hear some Harvards who are not in the fight get the posts at the other end of the field and sneak away with them. But I always claim these posts do not count.

Well, sitting there on the ground because he is too tired to get up from the last knockdown, and holding one hand to his right eye, which is closed tight, Sam the

Gonoph is by no means a well guy, and all around and about him is much suffering among his crew. But our little doll is hopping up and down chattering like a jaybird and running between old Liverlips, who is stretched out against one goal post, and Nubbsy Taylor, who is leaning up against the other, and she is trying to mop the blood off their kissers with a handkerchief the size of a postage stamp.

Benny South Street is laying across Jew Louie and both are still snoring from the last knockdown, and the Bowl is now pretty much deserted except for the newspaper scribes away up in the press box, who do not seem to realize that the Battle of the Century just comes off in front of them. It is coming on dark, when all of a sudden a guy pops up out of the dusk wearing white spats and an overcoat with a fur collar, and he rushes up to our little doll.

"Clarice," he says, "I am looking for you high and low. My train is stalled for hours behind a wreck the other side of Bridgeport, and I get here just after the game is over. But," he says, "I figure you will be waiting somewhere for me. Let us hurry on to Hartford, darling," he says.

Well, when he hears this voice, Sam the Gonoph opens his good eye wide and takes a peek at the guy. Then all of a sudden Sam jumps up and wobbles over to the guy and hits him a smack between the eyes. Sam is wobbling because his legs are not so good from the shellacking he takes off the Harvards, and furthermore he is away off in his punching as the guy only goes to his knees and comes right up standing again as our little doll lets out a screech and speaks as follows:

"Oo-oo!" she says. "Do not hit Elliot! He is not after our goal posts!"

"Elliot?" Sam the Gonoph says. "This is no Elliot. This is nobody but Gigolo Georgie. I can tell him by his white spats," Sam says, "and I am now going to get even for the pasting I take from the Harvards."

Then he nails the guy again and this time he seems to have a little more on his punch, for the guy goes down and Sam the Gonoph gives him the leather very good, although our little doll is still screeching, and begging Sam not to hurt Elliot. But of course the rest of us know it is not Elliot, no matter what he may tell her, but only Gigolo Georgie.

Well, the rest of us figure we may as well take a little something out of Georgie's hide, too, but as we start for him he gives a quick wiggle and hops to his feet and tears across the field, and the last we see of him is his white spats flying through one of the portals.

Now a couple of other guys come up out of the dusk, and one of them is a tall, fine-looking guy with a white mustache and anybody can see that he is somebody, and what happens but our little doll runs right into his arms and kisses him on the white mustache and calls him daddy and starts to cry more than somewhat, so I can see we lose our little doll then and there. And now the guy with the white mustache walks up to Sam the Gonoph and sticks out his duke and says as follows:

"Sir," he says, "permit me the honor of shaking the hand which does me the very signal service of chastising the scoundrel who just escapes from the field. And," he says, "permit me to introduce myself to you. I am J. Hildreth Van Cleve, president of the Van Cleve Trust. I am notified early today by Miss Peevy of my daughter's sudden departure from school, and we learn she purchases a ticket for New Haven. I at once suspect this fellow has something to do with it. Fortunately," he says, "I have these private detectives here keeping tab on him for some time, knowing my child's schoolgirl infatuation for him, so we easily trail him here. We are on the train with him, and arrive in time for your last little scene with him. Sir," he says, "again I thank you."

"I know who you are, Mr. Van Cleve," Sam the Gonoph says. "You are the Van Cleve who is down to his last forty million. But," he says, "do not thank me for putting the slug on Gigolo Georgie. He is a bum in spades, and I am only sorry he fools your nice little kid even for a minute, although," Sam says, "I figure she must be dumber than she looks to be fooled by such a guy as Gigolo Georgie."

"I hate him," the little doll says. "I hate him because he is a coward. He does not stand up and fight when he is hit like you and Liverlips and the others. I never wish to see him again."

"Do not worry," Sam the Gonoph says. "I will be too close to Gigolo Georgie as soon as I recover from my wounds for him to stay in this part of the country."

Well, I do not see Sam the Gonoph or Nubbsy Taylor or Benny South Street or Jew Louie or Liverlips for nearly a year after this, and then it comes on fall again and one day I get to thinking that here it is Friday and the next day the Harvards are playing the Yales a large football game in Boston.

I figure it is a great chance for me to join up with Sam the Gonoph again to hustle duckets for him for this game, and I know Sam will be leaving along about midnight with his crew. So I go over to the Grand Central station at such a time, and sure enough he comes along by and by, busting through the crowd in the station with Nubbsy Taylor and Benny South Street and Jew Louie and old Liverlips at his heels, and they seem very much excited.

"Well, Sam," I say, as I hurry along with them, "here I am ready to hustle duckets for you again, and I hope and trust we do a nice business."

"Duckets!" Sam the Gonoph says. "We are not hustling duckets for this game, although you can go with us, and welcome. We are going to Boston," he says, "to root for the Yales to kick hell out of the Harvards and we are going as the personal guests of Miss Clarice Van Cleve and her old man."

"Hold 'em, Yale!" old Liverlips says, as he pushes me to one side and the whole bunch goes trotting through the gate to catch their train, and I then notice they are all wearing blue feathers in their hats with a little white Y on these feathers such as college guys always wear at football games, and that moreover Sam the Gonoph is carrying a Yale pennant.

A Piece of Pie

On Boylston Street in the city of Boston, Mass., there is a joint where you can get as nice a broiled lobster as anybody ever slaps a lip over, and who is in there one evening partaking of this tidbit but a character by the name of Horse Thief and me. This Horse Thief is called Horsey for short, and he is not called by this name because he ever steals a horse but because it is the consensus of public opinion from coast to coast that he may steal one if the opportunity presents. Personally, I consider Horsey a very fine character, because any time he is holding anything he is willing to share his good fortune with one and all, and at this time in Boston he is holding plenty. It is the time we make the race meeting at Suffolk Downs, and Horsey gets to going very good, and in fact he is now a character of means, and is my host against the broiled lobster.

Well, at a table next to us are four or five characters who all seem to be well-dressed, and stout-set, and red-faced, and prosperous-looking, and who all speak with the true Boston accent, which consists of many ah's and very few r's. Characters such as these are familiar to anybody who is ever in Boston very much, and they are bound to be politicians, retired cops, or contractors, because Boston is really quite infested with characters of this nature.

I am paying no attention to them, because they are drinking local ale, and talking loud, and long ago I learn that when a Boston character is engaged in aleing himself up, it is a good idea to let him alone, because the best you can get out of him is maybe a boff on the beezer. But Horsey is in there on the old Ear-ie, and very much interested in their conversation, and finally I listen myself just to hear what is attracting his attention, when one of the characters speaks as follows: "Well," he says, "I am willing to bet ten thousand dollars that he can outeat anybody in the United States any time."

Now at this, Horsey gets right up and steps over to the table and bows and smiles in a friendly way on one and all, and says: "Gentlemen," he says, "pardon the intrusion, and excuse me for billing in, but," he says, "do I understand you are speaking of a great eater who resides in your fair city?"

Well, these Boston characters all gaze at Horsey in such a hostile manner that I am expecting any one of them to get up and request him to let them miss him, but he keeps on bowing and smiling, and they can see that he is a gentleman, and finally one of them says: "Yes," he says, "we are speaking of a character by the name of Joel Duffle. He is without doubt the greatest eater alive. He just wins a unique wager. He bets a character from Bangor, Me., that he can eat a whole window display of oysters in this very restaurant, and he not only eats all the oysters but he then wishes to wager that he can also eat the shells, but," he says, "it seems that the character from Bangor, Me., unfortunately taps out on the first proposition and has nothing with which to bet on the second."

"Very interesting," Horsey says. "Very interesting, if true, but," he says, "unless my ears deceive me, I hear one of you state that he is willing to wager ten thousand dollars on this eater of yours against anybody in the United States."

"Your ears are perfect," another of the Boston characters says. "I state it, although," he says, "I admit it is a sort of figure of speech. But I state it all right," he says, "and never let it be said that a Conway ever pigs it on a betting proposition."

"Well," Horsey says, "I do not have a tenner on me at the moment, but," he says, "I have here a thousand dollars to put up as a forfeit that I can produce a character who will outeat your party for ten thousand, and as much more as you care to put up."

And with this, Horsey outs with a bundle of coarse notes and tosses it on the table, and right away one of the Boston characters, whose name turns out to be Carroll, slaps his hand on the money and says: "Bet."

Well, now this is prompt action to be sure, and if there is one thing I admire more than anything else, it is action, and I can see that these are characters of true sporting instincts and I commence wondering where I can raise a few dibs to take a piece of Horsey's proposition, because of course I know that he has nobody in mind to do the eating for his side but Nicely-Nicely Jones. And knowing Nicely-Nicely Jones, I am prepared to wager all the money I can possibly raise that he can outeat anything that walks on two legs. In fact, I will take a chance on Nicely-Nicely against anything on four legs, except maybe an elephant, and at that he may give the elephant a photo finish.

I do not say that Nicely-Nicely is the greatest eater in all history, but what I do say is he belongs up there as a contender. In fact, Professor D., who is a professor in a college out West before he turns to playing the horses for a livelihood, and who makes a study of history in his time, says he will not be surprised but what Nicely-Nicely figures one-two. Professor D. says we must always remember that Nicely-Nicely eats under the handicaps of modern civilization, which require that an eater use a knife and fork, or anyway a knife, while in the old days eating with the hands was a popular custom and much faster. Professor D. says he has no doubt that under the old rules Nicely-Nicely will hang up a record that will endure through the ages, but of course maybe Professor D. overlays Nicely-Nicely somewhat.

Well, now that the match is agreed upon, naturally Horsey and the Boston characters begin discussing where it is to take place, and one of the Boston characters suggests a neutral ground, such as New London, Conn., or Providence, R. I., but Horsey holds out for New York, and it seems that Boston characters are always ready to visit New York, so he does not meet with any great opposition on this point. They all agree on a date four weeks later so as to give the principals plenty of time to get ready, although Horsey and I know that this is really unnecessary as far as Nicely-Nicely is concerned, because one thing about him is he is always in condition to eat.

This Nicely-Nicely Jones is a character who is maybe five feet eight inches tall, and about five feet nine inches wide, and when he is in good shape he will weigh upward of 283 pounds. He is a horse player by trade, and eating is really just a hobby, but he is undoubtedly a wonderful eater even when he is not hungry. Well, as soon as Horsey and I return to New York, we hasten to Mindy's restaurant on Broadway and relate the bet Horsey makes in Boston, and right away so many citizens, including Mindy himself, wish to take a piece of the proposition that it is oversubscribed by a large sum in no time.

Then Mindy remarks that he does not see Nicely-Nicely Jones for a month of Sundays, and then everybody present remembers that they do not see Nicely-Nicely around lately, either, and this leads to a discussion of where Nicely-Nicely can be, although up to this moment if nobody sees Nicely-Nicely but once in the next ten years it will be considered sufficient. Well, Willie the Worrier, who is a bookmaker by trade, is among those present, and he remembers that the last time he looks for Nicely-Nicely hoping to collect a marker of some years standing, Nicely-Nicely is living at the Rest Hotel in West 49th Street, and nothing will do Horsey but I must go with him over to the Rest to make inquiry for Nicely-Nicely, and there we learn that he leaves a forwarding address away up on Morningside Heights in care of somebody by the name of Slocum.

So Horsey calls a short, and away we go to this address, which turns out to be a five-story walk-up apartment, and a card downstairs shows that Slocum lives on the top floor. It takes Horsey and me ten minutes to walk up the five flights as we are by no means accustomed to exercise of this nature, and when we finally reach a door marked Slocum, we are plumb tuckered out, and have to sit down on the top step and rest awhile. Then I ring the bell at this door marked Slocum, and who appears but a tall young Judy with black hair who is without doubt beautiful, but who is so skinny we have to look twice to see her, and when I ask her if she can give me any information about a party named Nicely-Nicely Jones, she says to me like this: "I guess you mean Quentin," she says. "Yes," she says, "Quentin is here. Come in, gentlemen."

So we step into an apartment, and as we do so a thin, sickly-looking character gets up out of a chair by the window, and in a weak voice says good evening. It is a good evening, at that, so Horsey and I say good evening right back at him, very polite, and then we stand there waiting for Nicely-Nicely to appear, when the beautiful skinny young Judy says: "Well," she says, "this is Mr. Quentin Jones."

Then Horsey and I take another swivel at the thin character, and we can see that it is nobody but Nicely-Nicely, at that, but the way he changes since we last observe him is practically shocking to us both, because he is undoubtedly all shrunk up. In fact, he looks as if he is about half what he is in his prime, and his face is pale and thin, and his eyes are away back in his head, and while we both shake hands with him it is some time before either of us is able to speak. Then Horsey finally says: "Nicely," he says, "can we have a few words with you in private on a very important proposition?"

Well, at this, and before Nicely-Nicely can answer aye, yes or no, the beautiful skinny young Judy goes out of the room and slams a door behind her, and Nicely-Nicely says: "My fiancée, Miss Hilda Slocum," he says. "She is a wonderful character. We are to be married as soon as I lose twenty pounds more. It will take a couple of weeks longer," he says.

"My goodness gracious, Nicely," Horsey says. "What do you mean lose twenty pounds more? You are practically emaciated now. Are you just out of a sick bed, or what?"

"Why," Nicely-Nicely says, "certainly I am not out of a sick bed. I am never healthier in my life. I am on a diet. I lose eighty-three pounds in two months, and am now down to 200. I feel great," he says. "It is all because of my fiancée, Miss Hilda Slocum. She rescues me from gluttony and obesity, or anyway," Nicely-Nicely says, "this is what Miss Hilda Slocum calls it. My, I feel good. I love Miss Hilda Slocum very much," Nicely-Nicely says. "It is a cose of love at first sight on both sides the day we meet in the subway. I am wedged in one of the turnstile gates, and she kindly pushes on me from behind until I wiggle through. I can see she has a kind heart, so I date her up for a movie that night and propose to her while the newsreel is on. But," Nicely-Nicely says. "It is a case of love at first sight on both marry a fat slob. She says I must put myself in her hands and she will reduce me by scientific methods and then she will become my ever-loving wife, but not before.

So," Nicely-Nicely says, "I come to live here with Miss Hilda Slocum and her mother, so she can supervise my diet. Her mother is thinner than Hilda. And I surely feel great," Nicely-Nicely says. "Look," he says. And with this, he pulls out the waistband of his pants, and shows enough spare space to hide War Admiral in, but the effort seems to be a strain on him, and he has to sit down in his chair again.

"My goodness gracious," Horsey says. "What do you eat, Nicely?"

"Well," Nicely-Nicely says, "I eat anything that does not contain starch, but," he says, "of course everything worth eating contains starch, so I really do not eat much of anything whatever. My fiancée, Miss Hilda Slocum, arranges my diet. She is an expert dietitian and runs a widely known department in a diet magazine by the name of *Let's Keep House.*"

Then Horsey tells Nicely-Nicely of how he is matched to eat against this Joel Duffle, of Boston, for a nice side bet, and how he has a forfeit of a thousand dollars already posted for appearance, and how many of Nicely-Nicely's admirers along Broadway are looking to win themselves out of all their troubles by betting on him, and at first Nicely-Nicely listens with great interest, and his eyes are shining like six bits, but then he becomes very sad, and says: "It is no use, gentlemen," he says. "My fiancée, Miss Hilda Slocum, will never hear of me going off my diet even for a little while. Only yesterday I try to talk her into letting me have a little pumpernickel instead of toasted whole wheat bread, and she says if I even think of such a thing again, she will break our engagement. Horsey," he says, "do you ever eat toasted whole wheat bread for a month hard running? Toasted?" he says.

"No," Horsey says. "What I eat is nice, white French bread, and corn muffins, and hot biscuits with gravy on them."

"Stop," Nicely-Nicely says. "You are eating yourself into an early grave, and, furthermore," he says, "you are breaking my heart. But," he says, "the more I think of my following depending on me in this emergency, the sadder it makes me feel to think I am unable to oblige them. However," he says, "let us call Miss Hilda Slocum in on an outside chance and see what her reactions to your proposition are." So we call Miss Hilda Slocum in, and Horsey explains our predicament in putting so much faith in Nicely-Nicely only to find him dieting, and Miss Hilda Slocum's reactions are to order Horsey and me out of the joint with instructions never to darken her door again, and when we are a block away we can still hear her voice speaking very firmly to Nicely-Nicely.

Well, personally, I figure this ends the matter, for I can see that Miss Hilda Slocum is a most determined character, indeed, and the chances are it does end it, at that, if Horsey does not happen to get a wonderful break. He is at Belmont Park one afternoon, and he has a real good thing in a jump race, and when a brisk young character in a hard straw hat and eyeglasses comes along and asks him what he likes, Horsey mentions this good thing, figuring he will move himself in for a few dibs if the good thing connects. Well, it connects all right, and the brisk young character is very grateful to Horsey for his information, and is giving him plenty of much-obliges, and nothing else, and Horsey is about to mention that they do not accept much-obliges at his hotel, when the brisk young character mentions that he is nobody but Mr. McBurgle and that he is the editor of the *Let's Keep House* magazine, and for Horsey to drop in and see him any time he is around his way.

Naturally, Horsey remembers what Nicely-Nicely says about Miss Hilda Slocum working for this *Let's Keep House* magazine, and he relates the story of the eating contest to Mr. McBurgle and asks him if he will kindly use his influence with Miss Hilda Slocum to get her to release Nicely-Nicely from his diet long enough for the contest. Then Horsey gives Mr. McBurgle a tip on another winner, and Mr. McBurgle must use plenty of influence on Miss Hilda Slocum at once, as the next day she calls Horsey up at his hotel before he is out of bed, and speaks to him as follows: "Of course," Miss Hilda Slocum says, "I will never change my attitude about Quentin, but," she says, "I can appreciate that he feels very bad about you gentlemen relying on him and having to disappoint you. He feels that he lets you down, which is by no means true, but it weighs upon his mind. It is interfering with his diet.

"Now," Miss Hilda Slocum says, "I do not approve of your contest, because," she says, "it is placing a premium on gluttony, but I have a friend by the name of Miss Violette Shumberger who may answer your purpose. She is my dearest friend from childhood, but it is only because I love her dearly that this friendship endures. She is extremely fond of eating," Miss Hilda Slocum says. "In spite of my pleadings, and my warnings, and my own example, she persists in food. It is disgusting to me but I finally learn that it is no use arguing with her. She remains my dearest friend," Miss Hilda Slocum says, "though she continues her practice of eating, and I am informed that she is phenomenal in this respect. In fact," she says, "Nicely-Nicely tells me to say to you that if Miss Violette Shumberger can perform the eating exploits I relate to him from hearsay she is a lily. Good-by," Miss Hilda Slocum says. "You cannot have Nicely-Nicely."

Well, nobody cares much about this idea of a stand-in for Nicely-Nicely in such a situation, and especially a Judy that no one ever hears of before, and many citizens are in favor of pulling out of the contest altogether. But Horsey has his thousand-dollar forfeit to think of, and as no one can suggest anyone else, he finally arranges a personal meet with the Judy suggested by Miss Hilda Slocum. He comes into Mindy's one evening with a female character who is so fat it is necessary to push three tables together to give her room for her lap, and it seems that this character is Miss Violette Shumberger. She weighs maybe 250 pounds, but she is by no means an old Judy, and by no means bad-looking. She has a face the size of a town clock and enough chins for a fire escape, but she has a nice smile, and pretty teeth, and a laugh that is so hearty it knocks the whipped cream off an order of strawberry shortcake on a table fifty feet away and arouses the indignation of a customer by the name of Goldstein who is about to consume same. Well,

Horsey's idea in bringing her into Mindy's is to get some kind of line on her eating form, and she is clocked by many experts when she starts putting on the hot meat, and it is agreed by one and all that she is by no means a selling-plater. In fact, by the time she gets through, even Mindy admits she has plenty of class, and the upshot of it all is Miss Violette Shumberger is chosen to eat against Joel Duffle.

Maybe you hear something of this great eating contest that comes off in New York one night in the early summer of 1937. Of course eating contests are by no means anything new, and in fact they are quite an old-fashioned pastime in some sections of this country, such as the South and East, but this is the first big public contest of the kind in years, and it creates no little comment along Broadway. In fact, there is some mention of it in the blats, and it is not a frivolous proposition in any respect, and more dough is wagered on it than any other eating contest in history, with Joel Duffle a 6 to 5 favorite over Miss Violette Shumberger all the way through.

This Joe Duffle comes to New York several days before the contest with the character by the name of Conway, and requests a meet with Miss Violette Shumberger to agree on the final details and who shows up with Miss Violette Shumberger as her coach and adviser but Nicely-Nicely Jones. He is even thinner and more peaked-looking than when Horsey and I see him last, but he says he feels great, and that he is within six pounds of his marriage to Miss Hilda Slocum. Well, it seems that his presence is really due to Miss Hilda Slocum herself, because she says that after getting her dearest friend Miss Violette Shumberger into this jack pot, it is only fair to do all she can to help her win it, and the only way she can think of is to let Nicely-Nicely give Violette the benefit of his experience and advice, of which he has a great deal.

But afterward we learn that what really happens is that this editor, Mr. McBurgle, gets greatly interested in the contest, and when he discovers that in spite of his influence, Miss Hilda Slocum declines to permit Nicely-Nicely to personally compete, but puts in a pinch eater, he is quite indignant and insists on her letting Nicely-Nicely school Violette. Furthermore we afterward learn that when Nicely-Nicely returns to the apartment on Morningside Heights after giving Violette a lesson, Miss Hilda Slocum always smells his breath to see if he indulges in any food during his absence.

Well, this Joel Duffle is a tall character with stooped shoulders, and a sad expression, and he does not look as if he can eat his way out of a tea shoppe, but as soon as he commences to discuss the details of the contest, anybody can see that he knows what time it is in situations such as this. In fact, Nicely-Nicely says he can tell at once from the way Joel Duffle talks that he is a dangerous opponent, and he says while Miss Violette Shumberger impresses him as an improving eater, he is only sorry she does not have more seasoning. This Joel Duffle suggests that the contest consist of twelve courses of strictly American food, each side to be allowed to pick six dishes, doing the picking in rotation, and specifying the weight and quantity of the course selected to any amount the contestant making the pick desires, and each course is to be divided for eating exactly in half, and after Miss Violette Shumberger and Nicely-Nicely whisper together for a while, they say the terms are quite satisfactory.

Then Horsey tosses a coin for the first pick, and Joel Duffle says heads, and it is heads, and he chooses, as the first course, two quarts of ripe olives, twelve bunches of celery, and four pounds of shelled nuts, all this to be split fifty-fifty between them. Miss Violette Shumberger names twelve dozen cherrystone clams as the second course, and Joel Duffle says two gallons of Philadelphia pepperpot soup as the third. Well, Miss Violette Shumberger and Nicely-Nicely whisper together again, and Violette puts in two five-pound striped bass, the heads and tails not to count in the eating, and Joel Duffle names a twenty-two-pound roast turkey. Each vegetable is rated as one course, and Miss Violette Shumberger asks for twelve pounds of mashed potatoes with brown gravy. Joel Duffle says two dozen ears of corn on the cob, and Violette replies with two quarts of lima beans. Joel Duffle calls for twelve bunches of asparagus cooked in butter, and Violette mentions ten pounds of stewed new peas. This gets them down to the salad, and it is Joel Duffle's play, so he says six pounds of mixed green salad with vinegar and oil dressing, and now Miss Violette Shumberger has the final selection, which is the dessert. She says it is a pumpkin pie, two feet across, and not less than three inches deep.

It is agreed that they must eat with knife, fork or spoon, but speed is not to count, and there is to be no time limit, except they cannot pause more than two consecutive minutes at any stage, except in case of hiccoughs. They can drink anything, and as much as they please, but liquids are not to count in the scoring. The decision is to be strictly on the amount of food consumed, and the judges are to take account of anything left on the plates after a course, but not of loose chewings on bosom or vest up to an ounce. The losing side is to pay for the food, and in case of a tie they are to eat it off immediately on ham and eggs only.

Well, the scene of this contest is the second-floor dining room of Mindy's restaurant which is closed to the general public for the occasion, and only parties immediately concerned in the contest are admitted. The contestants are seated on either side of a big table in the center of the room, and each contestant has three waiters. No talking, and no rooting from the spectators is permitted, but of course in any eating contest the principals may speak to each other if they wish, though smart eaters never wish to do this, as talking only wastes energy, and about all they ever say to each other is please pass the mustard.

About fifty characters from Boston are present to witness the contest, and the same number of citizens of New York are admitted, and among them is this editor, Mr. McBurgle, and he is around asking Horsey if he thinks Miss Violette Shumberger is as good a thing as the jumper at the race track.

Nicely-Nicely arrives on the scene quite early, and his appearance is really most distressing to his old friends and admirers, as by this time he is shy so much weight that he is a pitiful scene, to be sure, but he tells Horsey and me that he thinks Miss Violette Shumberger has a good chance.

"Of course," he says, "she is green. She does not know how to pace herself in competition. But," he says, "she has a wonderful style. I love to watch her eat. She likes the same things I do in the days when I am eating. She is a wonderful character, too. Do you ever notice her smile?" Nicely-Nicely says. "But," he says, "she is the dearest friend of my fiancée, Miss Hilda Slocum, so let us not speak of this. I try to get Hilda to come to see the contest, but she says it is repulsive. Well, anyway," Nicely-Nicely says, "I manage to borrow a few dibs, and am wagering on Miss Violette Shumberger. By the way," he says, "if you happen to think of it, notice her smile."

Well, Nicely-Nicely takes a chair about ten feet behind Miss Violette Shumberger, which is as close as the judges will allow him, and he is warned by them that no coaching from the corners will be permitted, but of course Nicely-Nicely knows this rule as well as they do, and furthermore by this time his exertions seem to have left him without any more energy. There are three judges, and they are all from neutral territory. One of these judges is a party from Baltimore, Md., by the name of Packard, who runs a restaurant, and another is a party from Providence, R. I., by the name of Croppers, who is a sausage manufacturer. The third judge is an old Judy by the name of Mrs. Rhubarb, who comes from Philadelphia, and once keeps an actors' boarding-house, and is considered an excellent judge of eaters.

Well, Mindy is the official starter, and at 8:30 P.M.

sharp, when there is still much betting among the spectators, he outs with his watch, and says like this: "Are you ready, Boston? Are you ready, New York?" Miss Violette Shumberger and Joel Duffle both nod their heads, and Mindy says commence, and the contest is on, with Joel Duffle getting the jump at once on the celery and olives and nuts.

It is apparent that this Joel Duffle is one of these rough-and-tumble eaters that you can hear quite a distance off, especially on clams and soups. He is also an eyebrow eater, an eater whose eyebrows go up as high as the part in his hair as he eats, and this type of eater is undoubtedly very efficient. In fact, the way Joel Duffle goes through the groceries down to the turkey causes the Broadway spectators some uneasiness, and they are whispering to each other that they only wish the old Nicely-Nicely is in there. But personally, I like the way Miss Violette Shumberger eats without undue excitement, and with great zest. She cannot keep close to Joel Duffle in the matter of speed in the early stages of the contest, as she seems to enjoy chewing her food, but I observe that as it goes along she pulls up on him, and I figure this is not because she is stepping up her pace, but because he is slowing down.

When the turkey finally comes on, and is split in two halves right down the middle, Miss Violette Shumberger looks greatly disappointed, and she speaks for the first time as follows: "Why," she says "where is the stuffing?" Well, it seems that nobody mentions any stuffing for the turkey to the chef, so he does not make any stuffing, and Miss Violette Shumberger's disappointment is so plain to be seen that the confidence of the Boston characters is somewhat shaken. They can see that a Judy who can pack away as much fodder as Miss Violette Shumberger has to date, and then beef for stuffing, is really quite an eater.

In fact, Joel Duffle looks quite startled when he observes Miss Violette Shumberger's disappointment, and he gazes at her with great respect as she disposes of her share of the turkey, and the mashed potatoes, and one thing and another in such a manner that she moves up on the pumpkin pie on dead even terms with him. In fact, there is little to choose between them at this point, although the judge from Baltimore is calling the attention of the other judges to a turkey leg that he claims Miss Violette Shumberger does not clean as neatly as Joel Duffle does his, but the other judges dismiss this as a technicality.

Then the waiters bring on the pumpkin pie, and it is without doubt quite a large pie, and in fact it is about the size of a manhole cover, and I can see that Joel Duffle is observing this pie with a strange expression on his face, although to tell the truth I do not care for the expression on Miss Violette Shumberger's face, either. Well, the pie is cut in two dead center, and one half is placed before Miss Violette Shumberger, and the other half before Joel Duffle, and he does not take more than two bites before I see him loosen his waistband and take a big swig of water, and thinks I to myself, he is now down to a slow walk, and the pie will decide the whole heat, and I am only wishing I am able to wager a little more dough on Miss Violette Shumberger. But about this moment, and before she as much as touches her pie, all of a sudden Violette turns her head and motions to Nicely-Nicely to approach her, and as he approaches, she whispers in his ear.

Now at this, the Boston character by the name of Conway jumps up and claims a foul, and several other Boston characters join him in this claim, and so does Joel Duffle, although afterwards even the Boston characters admit that Joel Duffle is no gentleman to make such a claim against a lady. Well, there is some confusion over this, and the judges hold a conference, and they rule that there is certainly no foul in the actual eating that they can see, because Miss Violette Shumberger does not touch her pie so far. But they say that whether it is a foul otherwise all depends on whether Miss Violette Shumberger is requesting advice on the contest from Nicely-Nicely and the judge from Providence, R. I., wishes to know if Nicely-Nicely will kindly relate what passes between him and Violette so they may make a decision.

"Why," Nicely-Nicely says, "all she asks me is can I get her another piece of pie when she finishes the one in front of her."

Now at this, Joel Duffle throws down his knife, and pushes back his plate with all but two bites of his pie left on it, and says to the Boston characters like this: "Gentlemen," he says, "I am licked. I cannot eat another mouthful. You must admit I put up a game battle, but," he says, "it is useless for me to go on against this Judy who is asking for more pie before she even starts on what is before her. I am almost dying as it is, and I do not wish to destroy myself in a hopeless effort. Gentlemen," he says, "she is not human."

Well, of course this amounts to throwing in the old napkin and Nicely-Nicely stands up on his chair, and says: "Three cheers for Miss Violette Shumberger!" Then Nicely-Nicely gives the first cheer in person, but the effort overtaxes his strength, and he falls off the chair in a faint just as Joel Duffle collapses under the table, and the doctors at the Clinic Hospital are greatly baffled to receive, from the same address at the same time, one patient suffering from undernourishment, and another who is unconscious from overeating.

Well, in the meantime, after the excitement subsides, and the wagers are settled, we take Miss Violette Shumberger to the main floor in Mindy's for a midnight snack, and when she speaks of her wonderful triumph, she is disposed to give much credit to Nicely-Nicely Jones. "You see," Violette says, "what I really whisper to him is that I am a goner. I whisper to him that I cannot possibly take one bite of the pie if my life depends on it, and if he has any bets down to try and hedge them off as quickly as possible. I fear," she says, "that Nicely-Nicely will be greatly disappointed in my showing, but I have a confession to make to him when he gets out of the hospital. I forget about the contest," Violette says, "and eat my regular dinner of pig's knuckles and sauerkraut an hour before the contest starts, and," she says, "I have no doubt this tends to affect my form somewhat. So," she says, "I owe everything to Nicely-Nicely's quick thinking."

It is several weeks after the great eating contest that

I run into Miss Hilda Slocum on Broadway, and it seems to me that she looks much better nourished than the last time I see her, and when I mention this she says: "Yes," she says, "I cease dieting. I learn my lesson," she says. "I learn that male characters do not appreciate anybody who tries to ward off surplus tissue. What male characters wish is substance. Why," she says, "only a week ago my editor, Mr. McBurgle, tells me he will love to take me dancing if only I get something on me for him to take hold of. I am very fond of dancing," she says.

"But," I say, "what of Nicely-Nicely Jones? I do not see him around lately."

"Why," Miss Hilda Slocum says, "do you not hear what this cad does? Why, as soon as he is strong enough to leave the hospital, he elopes with my dearest friend, Miss Violette Shumberger, leaving me a note saying something about two souls with but a single thought. They are down in Florida running a barbecue stand, and," she says, "the chances are, eating like seven mules."

A Very Honorable Guy

Off and on I know Feet Samuels a matter of eight or ten years, up and down Broadway, and in and out, but I never have much truck with him because he is a guy I consider no dice. In fact, he does not mean a thing.

In the first place, Feet Samuels is generally broke, and there is no percentage in hanging around brokers. The way I look at it, you are not going to get anything off a guy who has not got anything. So while I am very sorry for brokers, and am always willing to hope that they get hold of something, I do not like to be around them. Long ago an old-timer who knows what he is talking about says to me:

"My boy," he says, "always try to rub up against money, for if you rub up against money long enough, some of it may rub off on you."

So in all the years I am around this town, I always try to keep in with the high shots and guys who carry these large coarse bank notes around with them, and I stay away from small operators and chiselers and brokers. And Feet Samuels is one of the worst brokers in this town, and has been such as long as I know him.

He is a big heavy guy with several chins and very funny feet, which is why he is called Feet. These feet are extra large feet, even for a big guy, and Dave the Dude says

Feet wears violin cases for shoes. Of course this is not true, because Feet cannot get either of his feet in a violin case, unless it is a case for a very large violin, such as a cello.

I see Feet one night in the Hot Box, which is a night club, dancing with a doll by the name of Hortense Hathaway, who is in Georgie White's "Scandals," and what is she doing but standing on Feet's feet as if she is on sled runners, and Feet never knows it. He only thinks the old gondolas are a little extra heavy to shove around this night, because Hortense is no invalid. In fact, she is a good rangy welterweight.

She has blond hair and plenty to say, and her square monicker is Annie O'Brien, and not Hortense Hathaway at all. Furthermore, she comes from Newark, which is in New Jersey, and her papa is a taxi jockey by the name of Skush O'Brien, and a very rough guy, at that, if anybody asks you. But of course the daughter of a taxi jockey is as good as anybody else for Georgie White's "Scandals" as long as her shape is okay, and nobody ever hears any complaint from the customers about Hortense on this proposition.

She is what is called a show girl, and all she has to do is to walk around and about Georgie White's stage with only a few light bandages on and everybody considers her very beautiful, especially from the neck down, although personally I never care much for Hortense because she is very fresh to people. I often see her around the night clubs, and when she is in these deadfalls Hortense generally is wearing quite a number of diamond bracelets and fur wraps, and one thing and another, so I judge she is not doing bad for a doll from Newark, New Jersey.

Of course Feet Samuels never knows why so many other dolls besides Hortense are wishing to dance with him, but gets to thinking maybe it is because he has the old sex appeal and he is very sore indeed when Henri, the head waiter at the Hot Box, asks him to please stay off the floor except for every tenth dance, because Feet's feet take up so much room when he is on the floor that only two other dancers can work out at the same time, it being a small floor.

I must tell you more about Feet's feet, because they are very remarkable feet indeed. They go off at different directions under him, very sharp, so if you see Feet standing on a corner it is very difficult to tell which way he is going, because one foot will be headed one way, and the other foot the other way. In fact, guys around Mindy's restaurant often make bets on the proposition as to which way Feet is headed when he is standing still.

What Feet Samuels does for a living is the best he can, which is the same thing many other guys in this town do for a living. He hustles some around the race tracks and crap games and prize fights, picking up a few bucks here and there as a runner for the bookmakers, or scalping bets, or steering suckers, but he is never really in the money in his whole life. He is always owing and always paying off, and I never see him but what he is troubled with the shorts as regards to dough.

The only good thing you can say about Feet Samuels is he is very honorable about his debts, and what he owes he pays when he can. Anybody will tell you this about Feet Samuels, although of course it is only what any hustler such as Feet must do if he wishes to protect his credit and keep in action. Still, you will be surprised how many guys forget to pay.

It is because Feet's word is considered good at all times that he is nearly always able to raise a little dough, even off The Brain, and The Brain is not an easy guy for anybody to raise dough off of. In fact, The Brain is very tough about letting people raise dough off of him.

If anybody gets any dough off of The Brain he wishes to know right away what time they are going to pay it back, with certain interest, and if they say at five-thirty Tuesday morning, they better not make it five-thirty-one Tuesday morning, or The Brain will consider them very unreliable and never let them have any money again. And when a guy loses his credit with The Brain he is in a very tough spot indeed in this town, for The Brain is the only man who always has dough.

Furthermore, some very unusual things often happen to guys who get money off of The Brain and fail to kick it back just when they promise, such as broken noses and sprained ankles and other injuries, for The Brain has people around him who seem to resent guys getting dough off of him and not kicking it back. Still, I know of The Brain letting some very surprising guys have dough, because he has a bug that he is a wonderful judge of guys' characters, and that he is never wrong on them, although I must say that no guy who gets dough off of The Brain is more surprising than Feet Samuels.

The Brain's right name is Armand Rosenthal, and he is called The Brain because he is so smart. He is well known to one and all in this town as a very large operator in gambling, and one thing and another, and nobody knows how much dough The Brain has, except that he must have plenty, because no matter how much dough is around, The Brain sooner or later gets hold of all of it. Some day I will tell you more about The Brain, but right now I wish to tell you about Feet Samuels.

It comes on a tough winter in New York, what with nearly all hands who have the price going to Miami and Havana and New Orleans, leaving the brokers behind. There is very little action of any kind in town with the high shots gone, and one night I run into Feet Samuels in Mindy's, and he is very sad indeed. He asks me if I happen to have a finnif on me, but of course I am not giving finnifs to guys like Feet Samuels, and finally he offers to compromise with me for a deuce, so I can see things must be very bad with Feet for him to come down from five dollars to two.

"My rent is away overdue for the shovel and broom," Feet says, "and I have a hard-hearted landlady who will not listen to reason. She says she will give me the wind if I do not lay something on the line at once. Things are never so bad with me," Feet says, "and I am thinking of doing something very desperate."

I cannot think of anything very desperate for Feet Samuels to do, except maybe go to work, and I know he is not going to do such a thing no matter what happens. In fact, in all the years I am around Broadway I never know any broker to get desperate enough to go to work.

I once hear Dave the Dude offer Feet Samuels a job riding rum between here and Philly at good wages, but

Feet turns it down because he claims he cannot stand the open air, and anyway Feet says he hears riding rum is illegal and may land a guy in the pokey. So I know whatever Feet is going to do will be nothing difficult.

"The Brain is still in town," I say to Feet. "Why do you not put the lug on him? You stand okay with him."

"There is the big trouble," Feet says. "I owe The Brain a *C* note already, and I am supposed to pay him back by four o'clock Monday morning, and where I am going to get a hundred dollars I do not know, to say nothing of the other ten I must give him for interest."

"What are you figuring on doing?" I ask, for it is now a Thursday, and I can see Feet has very little time to get together such a sum.

"I am figuring on scragging myself," Feet says, very sad. "What good am I to anybody? I have no family and no friends, and the world is packing enough weight without me. Yes, I think I will scrag myself."

"It is against the law to commit suicide in this man's town," I say, "although what the law can do to a guy who commits suicide I am never able to figure out."

"I do not care," Feet says. "I am sick and tired of it all. I am especially sick and tired of being broke. I never have more than a few quarters to rub together in my pants pocket. Everything I try turns out wrong. The only thing that keeps me from scragging myself at once is the *C* note I owe The Brain, because I do not wish to have him going around after I am dead and gone saying I am no good. And the toughest thing of all," Feet says, "is I am in love. I am in love with Hortense."

"Hortense?" I say, very much astonished indeed. "Why,

Hortense is nothing but a big——"

"Stop!" Feet says. "Stop right here! I will not have her called a big boloney or whatever else big you are going to call her, because I love her. I cannot live without her. In fact," Feet says, 'I do not wish to live without her."

"Well," I say, "what does Hortense think about you loving her?"

"She does not know it," Feet says. "I am ashamed to tell her, because naturally if I tell her I love her, Hortense will expect me to buy her some diamond bracelets, and naturally I cannot do this. But I think she likes me more than somewhat, because she looks at me in a certain way. But," Feet says, "there is some other guy who likes her also, and who is buying her diamond bracelets and what goes with them, which makes it very tough on me. I do not know who the guy is, and I do not think Hortense cares for him so much, but naturally any doll must give serious consideration to a guy who can buy her diamond bracelets. So I guess there is nothing for me to do but scrag myself."

Naturally I do not take Feet Samuels serious, and I forget about his troubles at once, because I figure he will wiggle out some way, but the next night he comes into Mindy's all pleasured up, and I figure he must make a scratch somewhere, for he is walking like a man with about sixty-five dollars on him.

But it seems Feet only has an idea, and very few ideas are worth sixty-five dollars.

"I am laying in bed thinking this afternoon," Feet says, "and I get to thinking how I can raise enough dough to pay off The Brain, and maybe a few other guys, and my landlady, and leave a few bobs over to help bury me. I am going to sell my body."

Well, naturally I am somewhat bewildered by this statement, so I ask Feet to explain, and here is his idea: He is going to find some doctor who wishes a dead body and sell his body to this doctor for as much as he can get, the body to be delivered after Feet scrags himself, which is to be within a certain time.

"I understand," Feet says, "that these croakers are always looking for bodies to practice on, and that good bodies are not easy to get nowadays."

"How much do you figure your body is worth?" I ask.

"Well," Feet says, "a body as big as mine ought to be worth at least a *G*."

"Feet," I say, "this all sounds most gruesome to me. Personally I do not know much about such a proposition, but I do not believe if doctors buy bodies at all that they buy them by the pound. And I do not believe you can get a thousand dollars for your body, especially while you are still alive, because how does a doctor know if you will deliver your body to him?"

"Why," Feet says, very indignant, "everybody knows I pay what I owe. I can give The Brain for reference, and he will okay me with anybody for keeping my word."

Well, it seems to me that there is very little sense to what Feet Samuels is talking about, and anyway I figure that maybe he blows his topper, which is what often happens to brokers, so I pay no more attention to him. But on Monday morning, just before four o'clock, I am in Mindy's, and what happens but in walks Feet with a handful of money, looking much pleased.

The Brain is also there at the table where he always sits facing the door so nobody can pop in on him without him seeing them first, because there are many people in this town that The Brain likes to see first if they are coming in where he is. Feet steps up to the table and lays a *C* note in front of The Brain and also a sawbuck, and The Brain looks up at the clock and smiles and says:

"Okay, Feet, you are on time."

It is very unusual for The Brain to smile about anything, but afterwards I hear he wins two *C's* off of Manny Mandelbaum, who bets him Feet will not pay off on time, so The Brain has a smile coming.

"By the way, Feet," The Brain says, "some doctor calls me up today and asks me if your word is good and you may be glad to know I tell him you are one hundred percent. I put the okay on you because I know you never fail to deliver on a promise. Are you sick, or something?"

"No," Feet says, "I am not sick. I just have a little business deal on with the guy. Thanks for the okay."

Then he comes over to the table where I am sitting, and I can see he still has money left in his duke. Naturally I am anxious to know where he makes the scratch, and by and by he tells me.

"I put over the proposition I am telling you about," Feet says. "I sell my body to a doctor over on Park Avenue by the name of Bodeeker, but I do not get a *G* for it as I expect. It seems bodies are not worth much right now because there are so many on the market, but Doc Bodeeker gives me four *C's* on thirty days' delivery.

"I never know it is so much trouble selling a body before," Feet says. "Three doctors call the cops on me when I proposition them, thinking I am daffy, but Doc Bodeeker is a nice old guy and is glad to do business with me, especially when I give The Brain as reference. Doc Bodeeker says he is looking for a head shaped just like mine for years, because it seems he is a shark on heads. But," Feet says, "I got to figure out some way of scragging myself besides jumping out a window, like I plan, because Doc Bodeeker does not wish my head mussed up."

"Well," I say, "this is certainly most ghastly to me and does not sound legitimate. Does The Brain know you sell your body?"

"No," Feet says, "Doc Bodeeker only asks him over the phone if my word is good and does not tell him why he wishes to know, but he is satisfied with The Brain's okay. Now I am going to pay my landlady, and take up a few other markers here and there, and feed myself up good until it is time to leave this bad old world behind."

But it seems Feet Samuels does not go to pay his landlady right away. Where he goes is to Johnny Crackow's crap game downtown, which is a crap game with a $500 limit where the high shots seldom go, but where there is always some action for a small operator. And as Feet walks into the joint it seems that Big Nig is trying to make four with the dice, and everybody knows that four is a hard point for Big Nig, or anybody else, to make.

So Feet Samuels looks on awhile watching Big Nig trying to make four, and a guy by the name of Whitey offers to take two to one for a *C* note that Big Nig makes this four, which is certainly more confidence than I will ever have in Big Nig. Naturally Feet hauls out a couple of his *C* notes at once, as anybody must do who has a couple of *C* notes, and bets Whitey two hundred to a hundred that Big Nig does not make the four. And right away Big Nig outs with a seven, so Feet wins the bet.

Well, to make a long story short, Feet stands there for some time betting guys that other guys will not make four, or whatever it is they are trying to make with the dice, and the first thing anybody knows Feet Samuels is six *G's* winner, and has the crap game all crippled up. I see him the next night up in the Hot Box, and this big first baseman, Hortense, is with him, sliding around on Feet's feet, and a blind man can see that she has on at least three more diamond bracelets than ever before.

A night or two later I hear of Feet beating Long George McCormack, a high shot from Los Angeles, out of eighteen *G's* playing a card game that is called low ball, and Feet Samuels has no more license to beat a guy like Long George playing low ball than I have to lick Jack Dempsey. But when a guy finally gets his rushes in gambling nothing can stop him for a while, and this is the way it is with Feet. Every night you hear of him winning plenty of dough at this or that.

He comes into Mindy's one morning, and naturally I move over to his table at once, because Feet is now in the money and is a guy anybody can associate with freely. I am just about to ask him how things are going with him, although I know they are going pretty good, when in pops a fierce-looking old guy with his face all covered with gray whiskers that stick out every which way, and whose eyes peek out of these whiskers very wild indeed. Feet turns pale as he sees the guy, but nods at him, and the guy nods back and goes out.

"Who is the Whiskers?" I ask Feet. "He is in here the other morning looking around, and he makes people very nervous because nobody can figure who he is or what his dodge may be."

"It is old Doc Bodeeker," Feet says. "He is around checking up on me to make sure I am still in town. Say, I am in a very hot spot one way and another."

"What are you worrying about?" I ask. "You got plenty of dough and about two weeks left to enjoy yourself before this Doc Bodeeker forecloses on you."

"I know," Feet says, very sad. "But now I get this dough things do not look as tough to me as formerly, and I am very sorry I make the deal with the doctor. Especially," Feet says, "on account of Hortense."

"What about Hortense?" I ask.

"I think she is commencing to love me since I am able to buy her more diamond bracelets than the other guy," Feet says. "If it is not for this thing hanging over me, I will ask her to marry me, and maybe she will do it, at that."

"Well, then," I say, "why do you not go to old Whiskers and pay him his dough back, and tell him you change your mind about selling your body, although of course if it is not for Whiskers' buying your body you will not have all this dough."

"I do go to him," Feet says, and I can see there are big tears in his eyes. "But he says he will not cancel the deal. He says he will not take the money back; what he wants is my body, because I have such a funny-shaped head. I offer him four times what he pays me, but he will not take it. He says my body must be delivered to him promptly on March first."

"Does Hortense know about this deal?" I ask.

"Oh, no, no!" Feet says. "And I will never tell her, because she will think I am crazy, and Hortense does not care for crazy guys. In fact, she is always complaining about the other guy who buys her the diamond bracelets, claiming he is a little crazy, and if she thinks I am the same way the chances are she will give me the breeze."

Now this is a situation, indeed, but what to do about it I do not know. I put the proposition up to a lawyer friend of mine the next day, and he says he does not believe the deal will hold good in court, but of course I know Feet Samuels does not wish to go to court, because the last time Feet goes to court he is held as a material witness and is in the Tombs ten days.

The lawyer says Feet can run away, but personally I consider this a very dishonorable idea, after The Brain putting the okay on Feet with old Doc Bodeeker, and anyway I can see Feet is not going to do such a thing as long as Hortense is around. I can see that one hair of her head is stronger than the Atlantic cable with Feet Samuels.

A week slides by, and I do not see so much of Feet, but I hear of him murdering crap games and short card players, and winning plenty, and also going around the night clubs with Hortense who finally has so many bracelets there is no more room on her arms, and she puts a few of them on her ankles, which are not bad ankles to look at, at that, with or without bracelets.

Then goes another week, and it just happens I am standing in front of Mindy's about four-thirty one morning and thinking that Feet's time must be up and wondering how he makes out with old Doc Bodeeker, when all of a sudden I hear a ploppity-plop coming up Broadway, and who do I see but Feet Samuels running so fast he is passing taxis that are going thirty-five miles an hour like they are standing still. He is certainly stepping along.

There are no traffic lights and not much traffic at such an hour in the morning, and Feet passes me in a terrible hurry. And about twenty yards behind him comes an old guy with gray whiskers, and I can see it is nobody but Doc Bodeeker. What is more, he has a big long knife in one hand, and he seems to be reaching for Feet at every jump with the knife.

Well, this seems to me a most surprising spectacle, and I follow them to see what comes of it, because I can see at once that Doc Bodeeker is trying to collect Feet's body himself. But I am not much of a runner, and they are out of my sight in no time, and only that I am able to follow them by ear through Feet's feet going ploppity-plop I will never trail them.

They turn east into Fifty-fourth Street off Broadway, and when I finally reach the corner I see a crowd down the block in front of the Hot Box, and I know this crowd has something to do with Feet and Doc Bodeeker even before I get to the door to find that Feet goes on in while Doc Bodeeker is arguing with Soldier Sweeney, the door man, because as Feet passes the Soldier he tells the

Soldier not to let the guy who is chasing him in. And the Soldier, being a good friend of Feet's, is standing the doc off.

Well, it seems that Hortense is in the Hot Box waiting for Feet, and naturally she is much surprised to see him come in all out of breath, and so is everybody else in the joint, including Henri, the head waiter, who afterwards tells me what comes off there, because you see I am out in front.

"A crazy man is chasing me with a butcher knife," Feet says to Hortense. "If he gets inside I am a goner. He is down at the door trying to get in."

Now I will say one thing for Hortense, and this is she has plenty of nerve, but of course you will expect a daughter of Skush O'Brien to have plenty of nerve. Nobody ever has more moxie than Skush. Henri, the head waiter, tells me that Hortense does not get excited, but says she will just have a little peek at the guy who is chasing Feet.

The Hot Box is over a garage, and the kitchen windows look down into Fifty-fourth Street, and while Doc Bodeeker is arguing with Soldier Sweeney, I hear a window lift, and who looks out but Hortense. She takes one squint and yanks her head in quick, and Henri tells me afterwards she shrieks:

"My Lord, Feet! This is the same daffy old guy who sends me all the bracelets, and who wishes to marry me!"

"And he is the guy I sell my body to," Feet says, and then he tells Hortense the story of his deal with Doc Bodeeker.

"It is all for you, Horty," Feet says, although of course this is nothing but a big lie, because it is all for The Brain in the beginning. "I love you, and I only wish to get a little dough to show you a good time before I die. If it is not for this deal I will ask you to be my ever-loving wife."

Well, what happens but Hortense plunges right into Feet's arms, and gives him a big kiss on his ugly smush, and says to him like this:

"I love you too, Feet, because nobody ever makes such a sacrifice as to hock their body for me. Never mind the deal. I will marry you at once, only we must first get rid of this daffy old guy downstairs."

Then Hortense peeks out of the window again and hollers down at old Doc Bodeeker. "Go away," she says. "Go away, or I will chuck a moth in your whiskers, you old fool."

But the sight of her only seems to make old Doc Bodeeker a little wilder than somewhat, and he starts struggling with Soldier Sweeney very ferocious, so the Soldier takes the knife away from the doc and throws it away before somebody gets hurt with it.

Now it seems Hortense looks around the kitchen for something to chuck out the window at old Doc Bodeeker, and all she sees is a nice new ham which the chef just lays out on the table to slice up for ham sandwiches. This ham is a very large ham, such as will last the Hot Box a month, for they slice the ham in their ham sandwiches very, very thin up at the Hot Box. Anyway, Hortense grabs up the ham and runs to the window with it and gives it a heave without even stopping to take aim.

Well, this ham hits poor old Doc Bodeeker ker-bowie smack dab on the noggin. The doc does not fall down, but he commences staggering around with his legs bending under him like he is drunk.

I wish to help him because I feel sorry for a guy in such a spot as this, and what is more I consider it a dirty trick for a doll such as Hortense to slug anybody with a ham.

Well, I take charge of the old doc and lead him back down Broadway and into Mindy's, where I set him down and get him a cup of coffee and a Bismarck herring to revive him, while quite a number of citizens gather about him very sympathetic.

"My friends," the old doc says finally, looking around, "you see in me a broken-hearted man. I am not a crackpot, although of course my relatives may give you an argument on this proposition. I am in love with Hortense. I am in love with her from the night I first see her playing the part of a sunflower in 'Scandals.' I wish to marry her, as I am a widower of long standing, but somehow the idea of me marrying anybody never appeals to my sons and daughters.

"In fact," the doc says, dropping his voice to a whisper, "sometimes they even talk of locking me up when I wish to marry somebody. So naturally I never tell them about Hortense, because I fear they may try to discourage me. But I am deeply in love with her and send her many beautiful presents, although I am not able to see her often on account of my relatives. Then I find out Hortense is carrying on with this Feet Samuels.

"I am desperately jealous," the doc says, "but I do not know what to do. Finally Fate sends this Feet to me offering to sell his body. Of course I am not practicing for years, but I keep an office on Park Avenue just for old times' sake, and it is to this office he comes. At first I think he is crazy, but he refers me to Mr. Armand Rosenthal, the big sporting man, who assures me that Feet Samuels is all right.

"The idea strikes me that if I make a deal with Feet Samuels for his body as he proposes, he will wait until the time comes to pay his obligation and run away, and," the doc says, "I will never be troubled by his rivalry for the affections of Hortense again. But he does not depart. I do not reckon on the holding power of love.

"Finally in a jealous frenzy I take after him with a knife, figuring to scare him out of town. But it is too late. I can see now Hortense loves him in return, or she will not drop a scuttle of coal on me in his defense as she does.

"Yes, gentlemen," the old doc says, "I am broken-hearted. I also seem to have a large lump on my head. Besides, Hortense has all my presents, and Feet Samuels has my money, so I get the worst of it all around. I only hope and trust that my daughter Eloise, who is Mrs. Sidney Simmons Bragdon, does not hear of this or she may be as mad as she is the time I wish to marry the beautiful cigaret girl in Jimmy Kelley's."

Here Doc Bodeeker seems all busted up by his feelings and starts to shed tears, and everybody is feeling very sorry for him indeed, when up steps The Brain who is taking everything in.

"Do not worry about your presents and your dough," The Brain says. "I will make everything good, because I am the guy who okays Feet Samuels with you. I am wrong on a guy for the first time in my life, and I must pay, but Feet Samuels will be very, very sorry when I find him. Of course I do not figure on a doll in the case, and this always makes quite a difference, so I am really not a hundred percent wrong on the guy, at that.

"But," The Brain says, in a very loud voice so everybody can hear, "Feet Samuels is nothing but a dirty welsher for not turning in his body to you as per agreement, and as long as he lives he will never get another dollar or another okay off of me, or anybody I know. His credit is ruined forever on Broadway."

But I judge that Feet and Hortense do not care. The last time I hear of them they are away over in New Jersey where not even The Brain's guys dast to bother them on account of Skush O'Brien, and I understand they are raising chickens and children right and left, and that all of Hortense's bracelets are now in Newark municipal bonds, which I am told are not bad bonds, at that.

IF THIS BOOK INTERESTED

YOU, YOU MAY WANT TO READ

OTHER TITLES IN THIS SERIES.

MASTERPIECES OF SUSPENSE

Compiled by Rosamund Morris

Classic stories by such standout authors as Ben Hecht, John Russell, Anton Chekov, James M. Cain, and Robert S. Lemmon. Art vignettes enhance each chapter opening of the text.

Each story is preceded by a short biography of the author.

Detail: Size 4⅜" x 7⅛". 256 pages.

Paperback **$.75**

MASTERPIECES OF HUMOR

Compiled by Louis Morris

Classic stories by sluch standout authors as Max Shulman, O. Henry, James Thurber, Ludwig Bemelmans, Mark Twain, and Saki. Art vignettes enhance each chapter opening of the text.

Each story is preceded by a short biography of the author.

Detail: Size 4⅜" x 7⅛". 256 pages.

Paperback **$.75**

KILLERS IN PARADISE

By John Godwin

This is a collection of true crime stories about murders committed in the tropical zones in the world. These are very exciting stories which are guaranteed to hold interest. The range of locales is wide, and the people involved include a Maori tribesman who shoots up the whole countryside, and a sedate Brazilian businessman who hacks his wife to pieces.

Detail: Size 4⅜" x 7". 192 pages.

Paperback **$.75**

MASTERPIECES OF SUSPENSE

Compiled by [illegible]

Classic stories by such great authors as [illegible], Anton Chekhov, James M. Cain and Robert S. [illegible]. A [illegible] chapter opening of the text.

Each story is preceded by a short biography of the author.

[illegible] pages

Paperback [illegible]

MASTERPIECES OF HUMOUR

Compiled by [illegible]

Classic stories by such great comic authors as [illegible], O. Henry, James Thurber, Ludwig Bemelmans, Mark Twain, and [illegible] chapter opening of the text.

Each story is preceded by a short biography of the author.

[illegible] pages

Paperback [illegible]

KILLERS IN PARADISE

by John [illegible]

This is a collection of true crime stories about murders committed in the most peaceful places in the world. These are very exciting stories which are guaranteed to hold interest. The range of locales is wide, and the people involved [illegible] whole [illegible] who [illegible] his wife [illegible]

[illegible] pages

Paperback [illegible]